You Do

'Startlingly original, grabs from the very first
sentence, utterly compelling throughout.
A stunning idea superbly executed'
Daily Mail

'Searing and heart-breaking, genre-bending . . . triumphantly
reconfigures the traditional whodunnit
into something remarkable'
Ruth Ware

'*You Don't Know Me* is a brave debut by a barrister . . .
an impressively original courtroom drama'
The Times

'It's the voice that does it: edgy, conflicted, desperately
urgent. A startlingly confident and deft debut'
Tana French

'Exciting, highly original, cleverly plotted and
convincingly written'
Literary Review

'A dazzling debut – authentic, funny, sad,
sympathetic. I was utterly gripped. Rich in
understanding of human nature, acerbic on
the rights and wrongs of the justice system'
Gillian McAllister

'Timely, tense and original . . . Written with gritty
authenticity, this is compelling and important'
Heat

Also by Imran Mahmood

I Know What I Saw

You Don't Know Me

IMRAN MAHMOOD

PENGUIN·BOOKS

PENGUIN BOOKS

UK | USA | Canada | Ireland | Australia
India | New Zealand | South Africa

Penguin Books is part of the Penguin Random House group of companies
whose addresses can be found at global.penguinrandomhouse.com.

First published by Michael Joseph 2017
First published in Penguin Books 2018 .
This edition published 2021
001

Set in 13.02/15.43 pt Garamond MT Std
Typeset by Jouve (UK), Milton Keynes
Printed and bound in Great Britain by Clays Ltd, Elcograf S.p.A.

The authorized representative in the EEA is Penguin Random House Ireland,
Morrison Chambers, 32 Nassau Street, Dublin D02 YH68

A CIP catalogue record for this book is available from the British Library

PAPERBACK ISBN: 978-1-405-95264-4

www.greenpenguin.co.uk

MIX
Paper from
responsible sources
FSC® C018179

Penguin Random House is committed to a
sustainable future for our business, our readers
and our planet. This book is made from Forest
Stewardship Council® certified paper.

To Shahida who gave me life

To Sadia who changed my life

To Zoha who made my life

To all my brothers and sisters at the Criminal Bar,
who make the real speeches and fight the hard cases
every day, for such little recognition or reward

Before: HIS HONOUR JUDGE SALMON QC

Closing Speeches:

Trial: Day 29

Tuesday 4th July 2017

APPEARANCES

For the Prosecution: Mr C. Salfred QC

For the Defendant: In person

Transcribed from a digital audio recording by

T. J. Nazarene Limited

Official Court Reporters and Tape Transcribers

I

10:05

DEFENDANT:

"In 1850, Henry John Temple, Third Viscount Palmerston, made a speech to Parliament that lasted five hours. A Portuguese Jew called Don Pacifico who was living in Greece but who was born in Gibraltar had been attacked by a racist mob. He had been beaten. His home had been vandalized. His possessions had been stolen. The Greek police had watched all of this happen but had done nothing. Don Pacifico asked for compensation from the Greek government. The Greek government refused to give him anything. So he appealed to the British.

"What did Palmerston do? Palmerston considered this Gibraltan Jew to be a British subject. So he sent a whole squadron of Royal Navy ships to Athens to block its port. After eight weeks the Greek government paid up. It was when he was challenged by a hostile crowd in Parliament that Palmerston made his five-hour speech. In it he said, 'A British subject ought everywhere to be protected by the strong arm of the British government against injustice and wrong.'

3

"That is what it meant to be British then. In them days. Sorry, in those days, I'm a bit nervous. In those days if you were a British citizen, it did not matter if you were a Jew or Portuguese or a Gibraltan or whatever else. It was enough that you were a British subject. It was enough that wherever you were in the world, if harm came to you, you could count on the full might of all of England to come to your aid. This Palmerston, he sent a fleet of ships for one man!

"That is what England would do for just one of its men – even if he was a nobody Jew like Don Pacifico – the whole of England for one man. One hundred and sixty years later and this black Englishman can count on none of England. None of it. I can count on none of it except this tiny bit of it here in this room. For me, this is all of England right here. You are all of England and I need you now. I need the strong arm of your protection against injustice and wrong. I need you. I need you. I need you. And you need me. You need me so that you can be all of England."

Basically that is as far as I got up to. Then I thought to myself, 'What is the point?' I ain't no Lord Palmerston and no five-hour speech from me is going to start you cheering my corner. I ain't stupid. I know that no speech is going to get me out of this. But you know what? It was worth reading that bit out just to see your faces. I don't mean it as joke ting, but like as a thing to shake you up. You never knew that I could speak like a professor is it? But I just wanted you to know that there's more than just

4

that one side to me that you lot saw when I was giving evidence. I wanted to maybe, I don't know, surprise you. And let me tell you there's some surprises coming your way.

So maybe this is the first surprise. Why am I standing here doing this speech instead of my barrister? Why did I decide to stand before you all and tell it in my words? Don't get me wrong, I wasn't upset with him or nothing like that. It was more that we had a difference of opinions on certain subjects and I've got certain like extra information that he don't know.

Like I'll give you an example. You remember when I gave my evidence a couple of days back? Well that was one of them things we had opinions about. He wanted me to tell you what he called a 'plausible story'. 'Give them what they need to hear,' he goes to me. So I go to him, 'Nah bruv, I want to give them what they don't want to hear from me, the truth.' But he didn't like that too much. 'It's too rich for them,' he was saying, 'it's too rich for their blood.'

He was good, my QC, don't get me wrong. But I thought, he's not me. He don't know what I know. The problem for me was that although I know what I know, I don't know what he knows. Do I let him speak to you in your language but telling only half the story, or do I do it myself and tell the full story with the risk that you won't understand none of it? Can I even tell you the whole story? Would you believe it? I don't know man. I don't know. But what I do know is that I ain't going to be risking my life for this murder and not tell you what is true. Even if my barrister don't want me to do that.

So here's my confession. I gave you evidence on oath before. On the Holy Bible. But God knows what I told you in the witness box wasn't exactly the whole truth. It had some truths, don't get me wrong, a lot of truths, but it also had some maybe not truths. But that is the way he wanted it, my brief. 'It's not about the truth,' he says to me, 'it's about what they can believe.'

This upset me, I mean how can I swear to you to say the truth and then like tell you lies? So last night when I was trying to sleep I thought about it. A lot. And when I woke up I weren't happy, trust me. So this morning I said to him, 'Bruv, I need to start telling it like it is. This speech, my closing speech, it's my last chance.' And he goes, 'Well that's it.' He can't act for me no more for *ethical* reasons. Ethical reasons? I thought ethical was about truth, but apparently, it ain't. It's all about *impressions*. 'What impression do you think you are giving if you go into court now and tell them a different story? What do you think it's going to look like if you tell them *this new piece of information*?' 'Well maybe,' I says to him, 'I don't need to tell them *that thing*' – and truth be told I ain't even sure if I can tell you that thing. Coz if I do tell you that thing I'm not sure I would even survive it, you get me?

Don't get me wrong, I want to tell you but I'm just not sure if I can right now. I don't know what you'd think

6

about me if you heard that. Maybe you need to get to know me a bit first. The real me.

Right now you think, looking at me, that I'm just some foolish kid who go around shooting up people for no reason. I know you think that because I ain't stupid and you ain't stupid. I know my evidence, what I said to you from the witness box, weren't all that good. I know that. I know it was shady. So I know what you think is that I just shoot up that kid but that ain't it. That's just what they want you to believe. They want you to think that I'm a no-brain lazy kid who go into some random street and shoot a next man up for nothing. Don't be fooled though. They are good at that – fooling you. That's what this guy, Mr Prosecutor, does for a living. He does this day in, day out, and by the time he's finished with you, you're seeing white as black and black as white. I take my hat off to him. He is good. He's sneaky, but he is good. But you have to see past all this smoke he's been creating here and see what's behind it. Trust me you'll be surprised. You don't have to do it for me. Just do it as one of them things, just as an experiment. If I'm wrong, I'm wrong, and you do what you have to do. But if I'm right . . .

Start with the evidences. Okay the evidences don't look good for me but there aren't that many of them really. But before I go into all of that I just want to say this. Ignore what all I said or didn't say in my statement when I got up there in the box the other day. That don't matter really, does it, if there's no real evidence to tie to me to this murder? If the evidence is shit, what does it matter what I did or didn't tell you?

Okay so here it is. This is how I wrote them down:

1. A boy got shot who is from the same area I live in.
2. Three months before he got shot someone saw me apparently walking past him and saying to him, 'You're waste man.'
3. A couple of months before he was shot a witness saw Jamil, the dead boy, having an argument with a black boy about my age wearing a black hoodie with white Chinese-style writing on the back.
4. Cell-site evidence. The phone expert said that my phone was in the same cell-site as the deceased at the exact moment of the shooting. My phone was also in the same cell-site as his on the day that I was supposed to be arguing with the boy. And it was also in the same cell-site as his phone on the day that I was supposed to be saying, 'You're waste man.' All within one cell-site area. What did that expert say? Fifty or sixty metres?
5. The search of my flat. The police arrested me because they heard a rumour that I was involved in the shooting. They searched my flat and found a Baikal handgun. They found a black hoodie with white Chinese-style writing

on the back. They found my phone, which matched the cell-site evidences. They found my passport. They found an e-ticket for a flight to Spain. They found cash, thirty thousand pounds in my rucksack. They found the firearms discharge residue that the prosecution has been going on about, in my car and on the hoodie. They found me.

6. The police say that the bullet which killed the boy, Jamil, must have come from my gun. Ballistics. You remember the guy who came with all his charts and whatever. That bullet came from that gun he says.

7. They found a tiny particle of the dead boy's blood under my nails.

8. They found a few of my hairs in his car.

Open and shut innit? Enough said. You can go home now thank you very much for your attention. And if you did convict me on that you would probably go home and sleep all nice at night. I know that. But you have been sitting here for four weeks doing this case. What I was hoping was that you wanted to make them weeks count for something. But then I thought, I ain't so sure.

Maybe to you lot, this is just a thing to do innit? A nice break from your lives. You can get up every day and put on a clean shirt and come into this place and look at papers or whatever and nod or shake your heads. You can listen to him, the prosecution. You can listen to this

Judge here and feel like you are doing something. You can be all respectable. And when you leave here, after this case is done, you can go back to your lives to do whatever it is you do. But I don't disappear, you know, when you lot go home. I'm still here. I'm still a person innit? When your little boy who is maybe four or five years old right now and just starting school grows up, I'll still be in a prison cell. When he gets to like ten and starts his first day at big school, I'll still be doing my time. When he leaves and gets a job or goes to uni: I will still be here. Doing my life sentence. Because you didn't look hard enough. Because you didn't do your job. That's all I'm asking. Just listen to my story – I am innocent. I promise you, if you look hard enough you'll see it for yourself.

Just look at the evidence. That will tell you all you need to know. And trust me there is enough there to make you see what I am saying is real.

Break: 11:15

2

Before I was arrested for this murder I had a job. Well not a real job with pay as you earn and all that, but I had something that I did to bring in the dollars. I weren't no gangster either – what my thing was, was selling wheels. Cars. I love them. There's nothing you or anyone else can teach me about cars. I like the old ones. I like the new ones. I like the V8s, I like the naturally aspirated ones, I like the turbo-charged ones.

Anyway, what I realized was that most people don't always know what they got when they selling their cars. This one girl was selling what she thought was an old Vauxhall Carlton that used to belong to her boy-friend. But what she didn't know was that it wasn't just any old Carlton that was maybe worth about three hundred quid. This was a Lotus Carlton. A three point six litre twin-turbo three hundred and seventy-seven horse-power Carlton. Nought to sixty in five seconds. Top end, one hundred and seventy-six miles per hour. Twenty grand of anybody's money even though it's twenty years old. See I check my shit before I buy. And I tell you what else, most of the people when they buy from me, they check their shit too. You can't be selling no bangers to the people round where I live. They want to go over the thing with a magnifying glass. Every dent's a discount. Every bit of optional extra is extra, you get me?

So this has to be the same thing here innit? Are you just going to take what the prosecution say on their say-so or are you going to look at it carefully and check under the bonnet? Is it proper quality what the prosecution is selling you? Or is it just some made in Taiwan rubbish?

So look at the first piece of evidence. The dead boy was shot in the same area I live in. What I say about that is, so what? He was shot in the same area that all the people who live in that area live in. This is just a nothing argument and it's a nothing evidence. Do I even need to go on about this any more?

If he was shot in your areas would that mean that you shot him? No man. That is just stupidness. But Mr Prosecutor thinks it does and makes a big thing out of it. But that's just a thing he's got over me innit? He can say anything and it sounds proper bad. But when you look at it, it's just bollocks. Sorry Your Honour, it just slipped out. What I mean is if I could say it like the way he can say it, the prosecution, you would be saying 'this is just a rubbish evidence'. What, I was living there and so was the dead boy? Is that an actual evidence that means something? That don't mean shit. Come on, yeah?

Then look at the second evidence. I was seen walking

past the victim and that I said to him, 'You're waste man'. To the prosecution, and to everyone else that's been watching too many movies, that is supposed to be evidence. That is supposed to be me saying that the victim is a dead man. Like I'm some Mafia guy in an American film. Ha! Sorry, jury. Sorry if you knew what I knew and you grew up where I grew up you'd be laughing too. On the streets in London that means something else. Mr Prosecutor wouldn't know that because he's not from the streets. Not the real streets, the kind of streets I know, the kind of streets where people shoot each other. Actually maybe that's a bad example but you know what I mean. He's on a different level. I'm not saying that as a bad thing. It's just the truth. If I was going to one of his shooting parties or whatever, I wouldn't know what their words mean. When I hear the word 'estate' I think of a car with a long boot or maybe a council block. He probably thinks of a house in the country, you get me? We are from different worlds, me and him. I don't wish I lived in his world but I wish he spent a day in mine. Waste man!

Let me tell you about waste man. When I was about eleven I went to a new school. It wasn't the local state school, it was some next school a mile away because they didn't have room in my nearest one. It was one of them old seventies boxes that they must have thought looked cool at one time but by the time I got there it just looked like a falling-down block of flats. It had green panels, I remember that, with big square windows in between them. There was a yard that went all the way around where all us kids used to play at break time, with a railing round the outside to stop the kids spilling out into the road. That was it. Basically, it was like the most space they could make with the least money and wide open like a desert so there was nowhere anyone could hide.

There was this one place though. It was this fire escape kind of thing which ran down the side of the building in square spirals and under the last run of steps there was a like a well, you could call it. If you followed it all the way down it led to a locked metal door into some basement thing where the caretaker probably wanked himself off or whatever. That place, that was what we called 'the Spit'. It was one place you did not ever want to be.

Anyway you move ends and it's like moving into a different country. I moved and it was like I was in some war zone. In my first school it was maybe fifty per cent black. This place though, rah, it was like I had moved into BNP central. There was only like eight or nine non-whites in the whole school. It was like my eyes had suddenly gone from colour to black and white. And the kids, man! There was some proper racist shit going down there, trust me. Sorry Judge, I know what you said before about the swearing but it was, 'Nigger this, coon that, black bastard that.' Whatever though. That was just what it was. Some shit you got to just live with.

I learned to tune it out as much as I could. But I won't lie to you, there was times when I had to bust a few

14

faces. There's only a certain amount a person can take before he snaps. I didn't like to fight back all that much. Because apart from anything else it made me feel like every black dude who ever fought Rocky in them films. Everyone was always hoping that I would get my head kicked in. Mainly I just styled my way through as much of the shit as I could. If I could avoid a front-up, I would. You got to remember I was prettier than most of them boys so I had more to lose innit! Eventually though, after a few fights where I did a bit of damage, most people knew to leave me alone. People don't just want to pick fights that they can win. They want to pick fights that they can win easily. And if that's your thing then it ain't me you're looking for.

Anyway there was this one boy, Curt, one of the only other black boys at the school. He was this big fat dopey kind of kid. He was like a type of boy you could say anything to and he would just give you this drooly grin. Didn't matter what you said to him and it didn't matter that the boy even at that age was the size of a house, he would just smile straight at you. And I don't mean you could say just anything to him like call him a fat c—, sorry Judge.

I mean you could say that his mum did tricks for a quid and he would still just let it go. He was just one of them peaceful type of guys. But that was the problem. You let someone take the piss a bit then you may as well let him take a piss all over you.

Anyway these are just the lessons. It's kind of like

being in prison I guess. If you show even a bit of weakness, you will get taken apart. So you can imagine the shit Curt had to deal with.

To me it looked like bad luck was going to follow Curt round for life. He wasn't just over-sized and over-friendly, he was also a bit mixed up. His mum was a drug addict or an alcoholic or something and although we didn't know it at the time, she probably was hooking on the quiet. There were days when Curt would come into school with bruises on his face. You couldn't really see them that easy on him because he was so dark. But I could see them. I could always see them. On them days he wouldn't smile as much. He would just have this look like he was guilty of something. He wouldn't want to talk so much. He got a look on his face that even if you were a bit of an idiot you wouldn't want to take the piss out of him too much on them days – it was too harsh to dark him like that.

But those boys at our school didn't care about a kid's home life. I'm not saying they didn't have their own shit to deal with. No doubt they did. But that somehow didn't exactly make them go any easier on him. I used to watch them when they went for him. Some little stick-boy half his size would walk up to him and call him a nigger and Curt would just put his head down. Then the kid might jump up and slap him across the face. Still Curt would do nothing. There'd be all these kids laughing at him and jeering at him and I would be standing there thinking, 'C'mon man, you're twice the size of these

16

fools. Fuck them up proper.' But he never did. He just let it slide.

It seemed like to me they were just trying to get him to react. Like they knew deep down that he could kill them in a second if he was pushed hard enough but it was like they just couldn't help themselves. They wanted to see the Hulk breaking out of him. Anyway, they tried everything. They swore at him. They threw shit at him. They robbed him. Fucking whatever you could think of to do to a boy they did to him. Once they even chucked him into the Spit and tore all his clothes off him. Then when he was there crying in his pants, a hundred boys stood at the top of the well and spat fat green gobs down all over him. Some kid even tried pissing on him but couldn't get much on him. Eventually when the teachers came, Curt just wiped himself down, put his clothes back on and carried on like nothing had happened. Yeah, he was crying a bit and whatever but he basically did nothing.

I kind of liked Curt, man. In fact, he later became my best friend. You could even say my only real friend. But back then I didn't know him all that well. He didn't even stay in that school long because one day his mum was moved up to someplace out in North London and he had to go with her. But what I remembered of him from those days was how calm he tried to be and how no matter how much he tried to find peace, war just followed him. The boy was a magnet for trouble.

*

Yeah. I know this sounds like I'm on a bus route diversion. But I am getting there I swear down. So, Curt. One of these days he was just sitting by himself as he usually did on the step waiting for break to be over so he could get back to the safety of lessons. I went over and decided to just chill with him for a while. Because I was so feisty, usually when people would see me and him together they left him alone. So as far as I saw it I was doing him a favour. I can't remember what we were chatting about. We weren't exactly tight and he weren't exactly my boy then but we did have some shit in common.

At first I didn't notice that anything was wrong. I don't think anyone did really. There was noise, sure, but there was always people shouting at break like they was in a prison. What I do remember though is seeing Mark Warner. You know those thirteen-year-old boys who were thirteen in years but had faces like twenty-year-old men? He was one of them guys. He had a face that looked like it had never seen one happy day. Thing about him, though, was that he was one evil fighter. Yeah he was thin as a rope, but he was so fast that when he was fighting you didn't see the hands even move. They just blurred right in front of the other boy's face until that boy's face was on the ground. It was a weird thing to watch because you hated him up for it but at the same time there was something about it that had you glued to it. You couldn't take your eyes off him.

So Warner was there with his big fists and his busted face. He was just walking past with this wide 'I own the world' walk when he sees us and stops. 'Fucking black queers,' he goes or something. Now when shit like this happens to me these days, which if I am honest with you ain't too often, no one, I don't care who he is, gets away with it. You best be packing if you coming at me with that shit. Back then though, as I said, I only picked the fights I could win and trust me I weren't ever going to be in no mood to be dancing with Warner. So I look at the ground and just under my breath I goes, 'Fuck off,' and carry on talking to Curt.

I didn't even see it coming. All I know is that in the next second I'm on the deck and my face is beating like it's been hit by a baseball bat. I get up and my instincts take over. Before I have even had time to think about it I've taken a swing at Warner and then suddenly there is a crowd around us. I was like a hundred metres from connecting with my punch. My arm swings past his head and I almost go on the ground again. Warner though, he goes off like a machine. Punches coming at me like pistons. They are all so fast that it feels like I've just run into a brick wall. I go down immediately and then he is on me, his knees on my arms and his fists trying to ruin my face. I reckon another second or two and I would have been eating through a straw for life. I can't see nothing. All I can do is keep turning my head away and try and drown out the punches and the shouting crowd.

Anyway, just as I felt like I might go under, Warner just flies off me, backwards, his hands still moving but hitting nothing but air. It takes me a minute to work out what has happened. It's Curt. He just pulled him off me like he was picking up an angry cat. Warner struggles free and then when he sees it's only Curt, he turns on him. 'C'mon you fat nigger,' he goes and starts beating away at him. Curt does nothing at first. He just kind of ducks and takes the punches like he has been doing all his life. But then Warner shouts out, 'Fucking waste man!' and something just snaps.

Curt's eyes suddenly come to life like someone just turned on the ignition. He blocks Warner's punches with one arm and then with the other arm he swings straight at his head. He doesn't use his fist. He uses his whole arm. And that boy went down. I mean he crashed. You could even hear the crack as his head hit the pavement. The crowd starts going mental. People are shouting out Warner's name and saying things like, 'Are you going to let that jungle bunny show you up?' and all this. Warner staggers back to his feet and somehow, I don't know where he gets the strength from, he takes another go at Curt. Curt don't even think this time round. He catches Warner's fist with one hand then twists it round until the boy is screaming out. Then he puts the other hand on the back of his elbow. Then just like that he snaps it.

A few weeks after that Curt left the school. Like I said, I think his mum for some reason had to move and he went. But for years after that I used to think back to that day. What made him do it? We weren't mates then.

I didn't even really talk to him that much. If anything I felt sorry for him because he was weak. So why did he do it? I am pretty sure I wouldn't have stepped up for him. In fact I know I wouldn't have. I never did before. But I think I know now what it was. He could take all the shit, the coon, the nigger and whatever. He could even take the beatings and the humiliations. But what he couldn't take was being called that. 'Waste.'

To him, this went back to everything. It went back to his mum who was selling herself for a pipe. It went back to all the men that came and used her and left. It went back to his mum waking up with the shakes in her own sick and him having to clean her up and put her into bed. It went back to her telling him every fucking day that he was alive that she wished she had had him aborted. That he was a waste man. It went straight to his insides. I doubt even he knows why he reacted like that but I tell you something, if you called him 'waste' today he wouldn't stop at your arm.

I will say one thing though. That fucker deserved getting his arm broken. He had that shit coming to him and in my book it's not 'you get what you pay for', but 'you pay for what you do'. Every time.

Anyway when then this QC talks about 'You're waste man' as if it means you are about to be wasted, I have to laugh. It might be all just words to him but down on the ground this shit matters. It ain't just words, man.

I was going to start off by saying I never said those words to the dead boy anyway, but do you know what? I admit it. I did say that to him. That was me. But it did not and does not mean what he, Mr QC, wants it to mean. I called him a waste man. And he *was* a waste man, no matter whether he is dead or not. Where I come from, he was a waste man: an idiot, a waste of space, whatever. If I was a Mafia made guy or something, maybe I would have meant he was a dead man. But I ain't so I didn't. Mr Prosecutor needs to stop watching TV and get real for a few minutes.

This is what I mean about these evidences. You need to be looking at this shit properly. Because he ain't doing the job properly. He could be. But he ain't. He's trying to, what did he call it, *pull the wool over your eyes*. Shit yeah. That is exactly what he is doing right there. He is getting a big blanket and putting it over your heads. You don't think he could have found out what 'waste man' means before making a murder case on it? Course he could have. He probably even did. Nah. But he don't want you to know that.

Luncheon adjournment: 13:01

3

So where are we now with these evidences? Number three? This is easier than I thought.

A couple of months before he was shot a witness saw the dead boy having an argument with a black boy about my age and about my height wearing a black hoodie with white Chinese-style writing on the back. Actually there's a bit of number five evidence there too. A black hoodie with Chinese writing on the back was found in my flat by the police.

You know what I'm going to say because you heard me say it to the prosecutor in this room. A black boy my height and age could be any one of the black boys in that area alone. How many twenty-two-year-old, five foot eleven black boys are there who are living in Camberwell right now? Hundreds? Thousands? More than thousands? It is a black area. What is it that most white people say? 'I don't even see colour.' Ha! Well I tell you now, if you went down there tonight, you'd see a lot of colour on a lot of twenty-two-year-old, five foot eleven boys. Of course none of them would be as pretty as me, but you see what I am saying?

23

Then as well, how many black boys would there be who are from a different area but who are just visiting that area for one reason or another on a Saturday? So what I am saying is, is that a proper evidence or is it just one of them things? If that was the only evidence maybe I wouldn't even be here. Maybe you would say to yourselves, this is just a piece of rubbish that ain't worth nothing. And if you did say that I would agree with you. So can we throw that one away?

It's the hoodie though innit? That's what's getting you. A black hoodie would be one thing but one with white Chinese writing on it – that's too much of a coincidence, innit?

But is it though? If you look at it, you will see a label on that hoodie. When you go into your retiring room or whatever, take it out of the bag and have a look at the label on it. Do you want to know what it says? I will tell you what it says because I have had a look at it. It says 'XXL' and then in small writing it says this: 'Made in Taiwan'. Now that might not seem to be a big deal but if you think about it, it could be a big deal – or a medium deal at least. I ain't an expert or nothing but I am guessing that when the sweatshop that made this hoodie made this hoodie, they didn't make just one. They made ten thousand maybe. 'So what?' you might say. But ain't no Taiwanese people buying them hoodies. They're made for here. You can tell that because the washing label, or whatever you call it, is in English.

So, ten thousand hoodies maybe. One for every one

of them thousand twenty-two-year-old black males walking around that area on that day and nine thousand spare. And so what if one of these hoodies got found in my flat? If you went into the flats of all them people who bought one of these hoodies, do you know what you would find? You would find one of these hoodies. And you might find most of them or half of them or maybe even only a tenth of them would be black males my age. Why? Because it's people my age who wear hoodies. He, Mr Prosecutor, don't wear a hoodie on a Saturday night, I guarantee that. He's wearing some tweed suit or whatever. It's young people wearing them. People like me. So that's a thousand people it could have been apart from me. And you only have to look at me. Do I look like I am XXL to you? And this is me after a year of going to the gym every day, a straight-up-and-down medium all day long. So what you like about this number three evidence then?

Break: 14:30

4

So what I was trying to say was that this barrister for the prosecution, he likes to try and confuse you, but you can't let him do that. You have to clear away his smoke and look at the thing he's trying to say, properly. He likes smoke because when there's smoke your natural thing is to shut your eyes. Another thing he likes to do though is to add up all the tiny pieces of evidences and make a great big thing out of them. He takes a little piece here and another tiny piece here and says to you, 'Look at how big all these pieces are when you add them up.'

When I was a little kid we had this massive bucket at primary school with all these Lego pieces in it. This wasn't the racist school I was later put in. This was quite a nice place as I remember it. The walls were yellow. I remember that. And the chairs. I remember the little tiny chairs. Anyway Lego. I love Lego because, one, you can make anything out of it and two, it's indestructible. That's why all schools have them I reckon. That shit just doesn't break which means it's been there for ever. You probably all had a go at Lego. You probably all loved it.

You probably even wondering why you ever stopped playing with it. You probably can't even think of one bad thing to say about Lego. But I can.

The bad thing about maybe all Lego and definitely this Lego at my school was that there was never enough of the *right* Lego. There was never enough of the pieces you needed to make your thing, rocket-ship, house, car, whatever. You'd be making your house out of red Legos and then there'd be no red ones left because some snotty kid would have taken it. So then you'd move on to the blue pieces and when they ran out, the yellow ones. But even when you'd used all the normal Lego bricks there still wouldn't be enough. So then you'd have to use some next pieces, like those thin long pieces and even some of them flat grey triangle ones. Then finally when you were finished, your house or whatever would have all these crazy things on it like wheels instead of windows and random pointy bits in the walls. And you'd say, 'Miss, look at my house!' But it wasn't any house anybody had ever seen before. It was like some crazy nightmare house. And I knew, even then, when I was five or whatever, that when you put pieces together they have to be the *right* pieces. They have to fit or else it's not a real thing. It's an almost thing. Or a thing that nearly looks like the thing.

That's what he, this QC, likes to do. It's enough for him for the evidence to nearly look like a thing.

So anyway where was I? This is proper hard. It looks easy on the TV. You say a few words. You make the jury believe you, you cry, the jury cry, the jury say 'Not Guilty'. In my mind that was what it was going to be like. After I wrote out that bit at the beginning, Palmerston and all that shit and when I realized that I was in deeper than I thought, I wrote some ideas down of what I need to say. I reckoned I could just spit it out like some bad lyrics you get me? But this shit is hard. I got like fifty points I need to make but each one is taking long and I keep getting lost. So although it looks like I'm just chatting random shit but I'm not. It's *all* important. I'm just like finding it hard to keep tracks of all these little things I know I have to say but that I don't know how to say. And then there's also this other thing . . . And the more I think about it, the more I think I definitely need you to know it – laters though. It will make more sense, later.

Where was I? So yeah, this is what I wanted to say. The prosecutor is just doing all this mashing things together and making it into something that it ain't. So he is saying that one day I am having an argument with the boy and I say something to him, and next minute he winds up being shot in the head. He says that I must have shot him because I had some beef with him, or whatever, but that there is just another one of his sneaky things he likes to come out with. You have to look at it though. You have to use your senses. What is the motive? Why was I supposed to have shot him? What, because of the waste man thing? No one shoots no one because of some random argument he's had or there wouldn't be any kids left in London.

The prosecution is saying that they don't really have to prove motive. Maybe that is right what he is saying. He knows the law innit? What I say though is even if they don't have to prove a motive, you should look for a motive. Because he was shot. If you try and find what the reason for his shooting was you might end up with something. Maybe that's why Mr QC don't want to go there. But that don't mean you shouldn't go there. So what's it all about? Who would have a reason to shoot him if it wasn't me?

What he didn't mention in his speech was that the deceased, Jamil, was a gang member. Yes, he was nineteen. Yes, this gang he was in was just a nuisance nothing gang at first, dealing in a bit of weed and doing little robberies or what have you. It weren't no big man's gang. It was a gang though and to those kids in that gang or in any gang, it was life. This is real.

They join these gangs when they're just little kids and then the life gets them. They start with knives and at first the one with the biggest knife is the main man. Then it's the one who actually uses the knife, he's the main man. Then it's the boy who kills someone with a knife, he's the leader. And this is what their days become, grabbing for the top spot, who can outdo who, who can be the bigger man.

To you, it maybe sounds stupid. Little kids stabbing each other up over a bit of grass or whatever, but this is life for them. It gets in their heads and when it's in it's hard to get it out again. It's like a disease that makes you think that this thing is real, not that thing, and that killing a person is okay. It's not like they sit there thinking these things through. Nobody does. This is just their reality, like your reality is that it's okay to waste your life working till you're old and then to retire just in time to die. It's all stupidness. It's just that when you're in it, you can't see it.

What is real for these kids isn't ordinary day-to-day life, getting up, going to school, swearing at teachers. It's this fucked-up shit. This is what is real to them. I didn't really know that before. I mean I could see they were travelling down certain roads. But I didn't know why. I didn't know it weren't really a choice for a lot of them. These people you see on the news and politicians and what have you, they go on about this like it is a surprise to them that young boys in the life do this shit. But it ain't a surprise. If anything, it's a surprise anyone ever stops. These boys, their friends are like their brothers. They are the only ones they got, a lot of them, who even care they exist. Their mates are the people they go to when they're in the shit and it's their mates who get them out of it. And the gangs they're in are basically families to them. And that is obvious when you think about it. A boy will be ready to take a knife in the stomach if he has to for his gang bruv and what is that if it ain't family? I'm talking about a boy who's got no dad. Who's got a mum who can't control him but who thinks that all he needs is to go to church to fix him out. An actual family who don't give a shit about him. You take a boy like that, and trust me, they are all boys like that, then you shouldn't be surprised he's in a gang. The shit's inevitable. But people don't like to hear that. Because they want to make you pay for what you do. And don't get me wrong, I'm all about people paying for making choices. But these kids. They ain't choosing shit.

At the local school, I knew kids who were like eleven years old who would have bigger kids come up to them and be all like, 'You should join our gang'. And if you didn't, then someone would start some beef with you. Get you shook. And if you weren't like strong in your head, eventually you would just go, 'Yeah I'm in'. A lot of kids don't want to be dealing with some next beef as well as all the other shit going on in their lives. And then there's other kids. They ain't got no head for maths or history or whatever, so then older boys would target them. 'Yo blood, you ain't going to be no CEO. What you going to do for paper when you leave? Clean the streets? You should come work with us. We give you paper right now. Just go do this little pick up for me . . .' and rah rah rah. So if you got that going on in your school, what you going to do? If you have got some skills and you can handle yourself, like I could, you might be okay. But what if you ain't? You got no choices. It's either take a beating or you join a gang and get paid and get respect. And then it just becomes part of your life. It becomes a normal thing for a kid to sell drugs in his school. It becomes a normal thing for a kid to stab up some next kid for no reason. And once it is normal for

31

you, you don't have any reasons to change it. It just becomes life. Your life.

And I only realized this recently while I was in prison waiting for my trial. I been waiting a year for my case to get on. Remand they call it. And when you're on remand that long inside four walls with nothing to do, you will do two things you might never have done before in your life. No matter who you are. Think about shit. And read about shit.

The prison library is crap generally but occasionally you find something that is like finding a tenner on the street. It is like God just dropped something right in your hands for just you. There is this book I found called *The Hammerman*. I picked it up because I thought it was like a horror story or something. You know like a proper made-up story but it ain't. This is one of them true-to-life books. It's about South Africa in the olden days. I read it and I couldn't stop thinking about these kids in these gangs. It's the same thing, let me tell you.

So, all this apartheid shit was happening. Like a few white people in charge of all the blacks. If you were lucky and you were black you might be like a servant to a white guy. But if you were in bad luck, you might even be killed just for saying some next thing to a white person. Brutal. And if I was being tried out there back then this whole case would have been over in a day. One day. And only one verdict. Guilty. Sentenced to life. Game over. But if you were white and you killed a black person – nothing.

32

Anyway this one year, the white people in South Africa suddenly started getting all jumpy about their blacks. One day everything was cool and the next day they were locking themselves up behind these high, electrified gates at night shitting themselves about what was happening. See, some huge black man was breaking into their houses and smashing their heads open with a hammer. The shit was all over the papers for weeks and weeks. Everyone was hunting this guy. People were scared. And it didn't make them less scared when people started to calling him the Hammerman. For the whites it was like a name you might give to a monster. But for black people it was a superhero name. And he was like a superhero. He was mysterious. He was uncatchable. And the rumours were saying all kinds about him. He was seven feet tall. He was built like a fucking house. He could run faster than a cheetah. He was invisible. He could fly. The crazier the rumours got the easier people were finding to believe them. They turned him into a legend.

But you know what people were scared of the most? They didn't know why he was doing it. And those people needed to know why so that they could maybe understand it. Understand him. Understand the monster. And then maybe the monster can become a person, and anyone can kill a person, innit. Everyone was scared – except black people. They weren't scared.

Black people loved it. To them it was like at last someone was getting their own back for them. One man *could* change a whole country. It was amazing for them. If they could have sat down and dreamed up something they couldn't have dreamed up a better thing than this guy. Until Mandela got out, but this was ten years before that happened. This was in a time when there weren't even riots yet. A time before there was even the hope of a change.

It sounded like from what I was reading in that book that the whites were already a bit wary of black people. It sounded stupid to me at first. Why would they already be a bit scared of black people when most of them were like their slaves? But this is what the writer explains it like. They were scared of them because they couldn't read them. Their faces were blank to them. When a white man gave a servant a load of shit for dropping a glass and that man just stared back all blank, that fucked with them. They didn't know what they were thinking. And you can see it. You're there giving it rah rah to some servant and they just staring at you, saying nothing, not even with their faces. They must have been shit-scared about what they were thinking behind them blank faces. You want to know what your enemy is thinking.

Then here was this massive guy like a superhero calmly walking into white people's houses and smashing their faces in with a hammer. For no apparent reason. He weren't stealing any shit. He weren't raping no women. He was just smashing their skulls in with a hammer. They must have been like, 'What if the whole country starts doing the same thing?' The whites might have had all the money and power and what have you. But there were fucking millions of black Africans. Millions of them. All pissed off. All ready for a war. All ready for a bit of freedom and the chance to fight back. What if they rose up one day like the Hammerman and started some revolution shit?

Anyway, they caught him. They put him on trial. He didn't have no lawyers. He couldn't speak English but they didn't bother giving him no translator. Then they hanged him probably. End of that story. White people won. They could relax again and open their gates up and forget all about him. But then years down the road someone found a recording of this guy's speech that he made in court before they sentenced him to death. It was all in Zulu or whatever he spoke and he spoke all these words but no one knew what they were, whether he was chatting shit or poetry because nobody could be bothered to get a person into this court full of white people who could tell them what he was saying.

Well this reporter guy who had found it could tell you what he had been saying when he got it translated. This man, the Hammerman, had had one strange life, believe. He had been done for stealing a few years before and had been given a seven for it. Seven years for stealing! Trust, seven years in South Africa ain't no seven years in England. They made him break rocks for eighteen hours a day for five years. And this is what he told the judge just as he was about to be sentenced. He goes like, there were these rocks that he had to break all day in the heat with a small hammer. White rocks the size of a person's head. And after a time, when he looked at the rocks he didn't see no rocks any more. He saw heads. Big white heads that he saw himself breaking open for hours in the day. Then when he was let out he just flipped and did that one thing he knew how to do.

Now, I ain't sorry that they hanged the man. If you go round smashing people's heads in, people ain't going to be happy about it. As I said before, you pay for what you do. But I was sorry about that one thing. He was trying to say his piece, to explain what was going on in his head but nobody gave enough of a fuck about him even to want to hear him out. At least I got you lot. Anyway my point is that it didn't really make no sense that he was smashing people's heads in with a hammer. But that was what was in his head. It was his reality. Those rocks were the heads of the white people and everything they had done to him. Or maybe the white people's heads were just the rocks that he had been breaking for years. Whichever way it went down, it made sense to him because it got into his head and once it was there he couldn't get it out.

And that's the reason I'm telling you this. What happened there to that guy, it's the same as Jamil's gang, The Squad or whatever they called themselves. Something like breaking rocks is going on in their heads every day. Not real rocks obviously but other kinds of shit. If you're twelve and next boys come up to you and put a knife to your throat because you sold a bit of weed where that gang hangs out, then you get your boys and do the same back. And when you see one of them boys on the street by his own you make sure you put your knife in him, not just to him. And it sounds crazy and gangster but that is just what happens. What else they going to do? Not deal drugs? When you lot fill the TV with hundreds of gangster rappers drowning in money, what do you expect? Who is the role model for a young black kid on the street? Is it Barack Obama? Why do we have to look that far away to one man to find someone that these kids can be? Or should they be a boxer or a runner? We might as well tell them that they should want to be a lottery winner.

Fuck that shit. You know what the most saddest thing I ever saw was? Two schoolkid girls on the bus chatting about what they wanted to be. This one girl, fat like she had burgers for breakfast, was chatting to her skinny mate who looked like she never ate a breakfast in her life. This was like ten o'clock in the morning and although they should have been in school by then, they weren't. But it looked like they might have been on their way there, taking it casual. Anyway the fat kid in between mouthfuls of something leaned over to her mate and said this:

'What I'm going be, yeah, is, number one, astronaut, number two, a fashion designer and number three, a pilot.'

And the skinny kid went, 'Yeah my number one is astronaut. My number two is scientist and my three ain't pilot coz I'm scared of heights.'

'What about astronauts?' says fatty. 'They need heights too.'

'Nah,' says the other one, 'they don't.'

This is what they've done to these kids. They told them that they could be anything they wanted to but they lied to them. All they did was give them different dreams. But they're still only dreams.

So this is it. Kids are drug dealers, but they didn't make themselves drug dealers. And when you got drug dealers, you got drug dealers doing drug deal ting: shooting people. Even kids. Live with that. In fact you don't need to live with that. You already know this. You just don't care that much because it's not on your door. I don't blame you. If it wasn't on my door I wouldn't give a shit either. I'm the same as you. I don't give a shit about your shit and you don't give a shit about mine. That is fine. I'm not trying to make you give a shit about it. All I'm saying is that Jamil was shot because he was in a gang and he was dealing drugs and people that deal drugs get shot. That's it. And I'm sorry about that for his family. I'm sorry for his mum who is sitting in this court having to hear it all. But it is the truth.

Break: 15:30

5

So fourth evidence. The cell-site evidence. You lot know that the phone expert said that my phone was in the same, what did he call it, vector? Anyway like in the same fifty-metre area as the deceased at the exact moment of the shooting. And that it was in the same cell area as his a couple of months before that. You know, on the day that I was supposed to be arguing with the boy?

Look, I can know from your faces that you think that looks bad. And you know what? I ain't even going to lie to you. It does look bad. I give you that. I can't answer the full details of that one yet though. I got to come back to this one. It's like a thing of what I say about it right now won't make sense until I explain some other thing I need to tell you about.

So five. Erm, the police finding a Baikal handgun in my flat. And my passport. And that e-ticket for the flight to Spain with my name on it. Oh and the thirty grand. Sorry, I'm just trying to read the notes I made last night. Yeah and the firearms discharge residue on my clothes. Okay yeah sorry. Five. That one I got to get back to you on as well. Sorry, just a bit nervous.

39

Okay, so number six evidence. The police saying that the bullet which killed the boy must have come from my gun. Shit. Erm I can't do that one either at this time. Actually or number seven – the dead boy's blood under my nails. Or number eight, the hairs in his car.

No. Don't be doing that to me please. Don't be looking at the ceiling. I know how it looks. I know how it sounds. It is a lot but I do have explanations. It's just I can't really tell you it yet because it won't make no sense to you right now.

If I can just get a second? I just lost my thing of thought.

I got to put these papers down for a second.

You know, part of me thought if I told my speech myself then at least you get to feel a little bit of what it is like to be me. That if my QC did it then maybe you would all be thinking, 'Yeah it's all very well to put it over all shiny and slick but that fucker's still a murderer.' And I really did think that if I told my own story I could make you feel my life. But actually explaining the evidences out loud is proper hard. I know what I want to say to you in a ways but I can't get it out. And what makes it worse is that I know my brief would have been all over it. You heard him in this trial. He's an operator. You got to give him that. No wonder they call them QCs 'silks'. Because he is smooth, you get me. But then he wouldn't say what I need to say, what you have to hear, and that stuff I can't even work out how to say to you.

But maybe it don't matter who tells the story because

there's no way of making a person understand what it is to be you. What your thoughts are when you wake up. Why the first thing you remember is some random thing about your dad or whatever. How that random thought makes you do one thing and not the next thing. No one can explain those things. But it is those little things that answer the questions.

All the number five, number six, all that evidence, it's not one of them things that you can just talk your way through like logically point by point. You need to like get under my bonnet and see what it is that is making my cylinders go. You have to do what they didn't do for that hammer guy in South Africa. You got to be in my head. See what I been seeing. Hear what I been hearing. Because unless you do that, you won't really be able to understand what I'm trying to say. It's like, say it was a car accident you were dealing with. And someone died. All you would be able to do is to say that that car killed that man. You wouldn't know whether it was because it was driven at him on purpose. Or whether it was because the brake fluid was drained. Or if it was one of the tyres had a blow-out. You would only be able to see the ending. That is what the prosecution is counting on. He don't want you to look at the causes because that fucks him up innit? Whereas I am all about the causes. If I'm looking at an engine that won't start, if I don't know the causes how do I know if I can fix it?

It's that kind of thing that answers why the Baikal was in my flat. 'The gun of choice for gangsters', as he puts it. I'll be honest with you. The gun is mine. I went out and I bought it, but it ain't like one of them things. I didn't buy it to shoot no boy. It was because of my family.

In my life, apart from a few mates, there is my mum, my girlfriend and my little sister. They are the main people in my life.

My sister is called Blessing which is strange because really she is a curse. I'm joking man! She is a blessing for real. She is like every bad thing you can put on me, you can put ten good ones on her. We are just two years difference in age. But those two years is the only time we really ever been apart. For more than twenty years, whatever I've been through she's been through and she has brought me through. That's her sitting there with my mum. That's who she is: my little sister. That's who it is, if you've been looking, that has been crying all the way through this thing. That is just her. If anyone hurts me, it hurts her. She can't help it. That's just how she is made up.

I didn't want her to be here for this, for any of it. But she is her own woman and no amount of me telling her is going to stop her doing what she needs to do. If you look in them eyes you'll know what I mean. You can see the steel in them. But where you can see only steel, I can see something else. I can see Mum in her. Mum who can get a shoe and be beating you with it but love you at the same time. That's maybe every mum, but it ain't every sister.

So that is me, nearly all surrounded by women. Mum and Bless was who I grew up with. Dad came and went. That is the best thing you could say about him. When he wasn't tripping he was okay. Sometimes he would stay for a day or maybe a week or whatever but he'd always go again. 'I a rolling stone, son. If I don't keep movin' something a-happen to me.'

When he was using though, boy, that was another thing. If Mum was in, maybe we had a chance. But usually he'd come when she was out working. He would come in looking like all kinds of shit. And he would have this face, like a pleading begging face. Just give him something to tide him over. Just a lickle something to medicine him. Even when I was ten and Bless was like eight, he would be banging on the door asking for money. What kind of fucked up shit is that – we were kids – what money did we have? Other times if he was high on some other thing it was like a fire would come out of him.

This one day in the school holidays when I was about fifteen, me and Bless were hoovering up and tidying up or whatever before Mum came back from work. Trust me if my mum came back having told you to clean and you never cleaned, she would have made you pay for it later. So we were kind of arguing about who got the shit job of hoovering with this old 1920s or something hoover and who just got the dusting to do when the bell goes.

43

It's Dad. His eyes are all red like he's been to hell and just got kicked out. His patchy old beard is looking the same colour as his dirty hat and both are looking like they have been rolling around in the dirt for a few days. He is mumbling about some 'urgent urgent' thing and even though we know he is tripping we let him in anyway. That is the only thing to do or else he won't go and the last thing we want is for Mum to come home and find him lying in our doorway, high.

So he comes crashing in through the door hardly able to keep upright. He is knocking over everything he comes near. There is shit smashing left right and centre. I had never seen him like this. 'What the fuck do you want Dad?' Nothing, no answer. Or at least nothing I can make head or tails of. Then he starts proper rooting around like he is looking for something. The leather settee goes upside down. The fat-arsed TV goes on the floor. Drawers are coming out of the kitchen cupboards. All the while he is mumbling some shit or other. 'Where is dis ting?' or whatever in his mind he thinks he has lost in our flat, 'Tell me where tis.'

We are just trying to calm him down. Bless is telling him she is going to make him a coffee but he isn't listening to anything. I am following him around either picking up some shit he has just knocked over or picking him up when he knocks himself over. If there had been a camera you could have sold this clip to the TV. It was like comedy if you could have just muted the sound off.

Next minute the front door rattles and opens. It's

44

Mum. Now with Mum, it's one of them things. She is a proper Nigerian lady and anyone who knows a Nigerian mum knows that you don't want to mess with an angry one. So she sees red and starts yelling at him, 'Get out of the house, get out get out. Useless man. Get out!' But she ain't like read the situation. He isn't just his usual floaty high. This was some next thing he is on. Then he looks at her like he has seen her for the first time. He is just staring for like two minutes. Then he stumbles forward until he's in her face and she can probably smell the drink on him.

'You jus' a woman,' he says and then bam, next thing he's got his hands round her neck and has pushed her to the floor. I'm like what the fuck? And I jump on his back punching and kicking him but he whips me off like I'm some kind of little toy and throws me far off. Bless is screaming and Mum is flat on the floor. Dad is on her and then he starts punching her face like he's hammering nails in with his fist. Again and again he is beating her with proper man punches. Mum's face is just a bloody pulpy mess. I am just paralysed sitting there. I don't know what to do. It's like my mind has stopped working and my body's broken down.

Then this next thing happens. Bless has picked up the iron and she starts to hit him with it. But she is only thirteen years old and she don't have enough past in her to do anything serious to him. If it happened now, no doubt she would finish the job for real, but back then there just weren't enough fight in her. She didn't have the anger that only a lot of life can give you, you get me? So anyway she starts to hit him with the iron but it's just bouncing off his shoulder. Dad gets hold of her. Pulls the iron from her hand and then – and then it happens. He smacks Bless in the face with it. Immediately there is blood everywhere. Bless drops to the ground like she is dead. I thought she *was* dead. Then he stops. It's like he's just woken up. He drops the iron. Walks to Mum. Picks up her handbag. Empties her purse. Leaves.

Nah. Don't be looking at her face. Look at me. Keep your eyes on me. It was my fault. I was the man. I should have been the one to pick up the iron or a knife or something. I wanted to. Afterwards, when we were in the hospital it was all I could think about. I could have done this. I could have done that.

They were in beds next to each other. Weeks they were there. Mum had a fractured eye socket. Bless had a broken jaw and lost half a tooth. But I lost too. I lost my sister in a way. Yeah it had been shitty in that house for enough time. But it had never been like this. This time when he did what he did, he took her voice with him. She didn't speak for years. Part of it was the injuries but mostly it was that she had run out of words. Nothing could explain it, nothing could make it right, nothing could say what she was feeling. But I could. I could feel it. It was like a feeling of someone standing on your heart and pressing down until it was just meat.

In those weeks while they were recovering something was happening to me too. I can't explain it exactly, it was just one of them things like there was only one thing on my mind. Focus. That is what it was. I knew there was no way I was letting anything like that happen a second time. So I went out, spoke to some people, and got a gun. That Baikal. Yes, gun of choice for gangsters. But not because it's like a special amazing cool gun. It's because it's cheap. They are just converted Russian or Czech or something starting pistols. They don't make them with serial numbers. They can fit in your pocket. They take virtually any ammo. It's a gun for a kid with no money.

So when he says, 'Oh look at this, we have found a gun in his flat, and it's the same type of gun that killed Jamil and it's a gangster gun, and he must have had it for a reason,' he is right. It is a gangster gun. But that also means that every kid in London in a gang has one or can get one. And if, as I believe, Jamil was shot because of all this gang shit he was involved with, then no wonder he was shot by one of them guns. And he is also right that I had it for a reason, 'a deadly reason' or whatever he said. I was going to kill my dad if he ever came near my sister or my mum again. I swear down. I would have killed him in a second.

He can do what he did, that is just a choice. He can choose to break my sister's jaw and mess up my mum's face. That is his choice. It is his freedom. But freedom isn't free. In my eyes if you going to make a choice, you better start saving up for the price of it. Lucky for him he didn't come bothering us again. But I waited for

47

seven years with that gun in my kitchen drawer. He didn't come. Good luck for him. Bad luck for me that the police found it in my drawer.

But here's the thing of it, yeah, why would I have kept it if I had just shot someone with it? That is just stupidness. That is probably the thing that annoys me the most. He, Mr QC, thinks I am stupid. To him I am dumb, with no thoughts going on in my head. Shoot up some next kid and keep a fifty quid gun on me in case I want to use it again? Come on man.

In fact he is the one who isn't thinking. Why did I walk past Jamil and tell him he was a waste man? Has he thought about that? Like I keep saying, look for the reasons. The reasons will show you the way. What he says, I've written it down, '. . . is all the worse for this fact. It was an apparently chance encounter with a stranger that led to this callous act.' Chance encounter with a stranger, is that what he thinks? I will let you and him into a little secret. It wasn't no chance encounter and it wasn't no stranger. I knew him. I knew Jamil. I don't mean I knew him like maybe his family did. I mean I knew him. I think it's time I told you some shit.

I don't know.

Look I'm tired and I'm not thinking straight. I know you lot think it's my own fault. I should have kept my barrister for the speech. Maybe you're right. But the fact is that when it is your life on trial you will do everything you can to save it. I'm fighting for my life right now. Yeah I can go through all the evidences like I been

48

doing. In just a little bit of time I been through like four of them. Four rubbish points the prosecution is convicting me on. And I still want to say what I got to say about the other four. But that ain't enough really and truly. You need to know like a fuller story of what shit went down. What was going on in my life. How can you understand it otherwise? How can you understand me if you don't know about me? How can you judge me?

Throughout this trial, I been listening and you been listening. And you been looking at evidence and I been looking at you. I see your faces when you see a bit of evidence. You got this look like, 'You are fucked mate.' And I agree with you in a ways. Some of the next evidences do fuck me a bit. But it ain't about whether I was wearing some next hoodie or using my phone near a boy. It's about did I commit a murder. And I did not do this murder. It weren't me. It was someone else.

Long adjournment: 16:45

IN THE CENTRAL CRIMINAL COURT   T2017229

Before: HIS HONOUR JUDGE SALMON QC

Closing Speeches:

Trial: Day 30

Wednesday 5th July 2017

APPEARANCES

For the Prosecution: Mr C. Salfred QC

For the Defendant: In person

Transcribed from a digital audio recording by

T. J. Nazarene Limited

Official Court Reporters and Tape Transcribers

6

Okay, so do I just carry on from yesterday then?

As I was saying yesterday. I knew the dead boy, Jamil. But on the street people never called him Jamil, they called him JC. Maybe because he was thin or maybe it was his Jesus beard. But JC is what I knew him as. He was one of them plastic gangsters. He was skinny as a twelve-year-old girl but he was always acting like he was a big man. I knew him from around the area and that but I also knew him for another thing. He knew Kira, my girl. You could say that everything that happened to me – this case, the murder – it all goes back to Ki.

What can explain to you lot about Kira? Kira is like the most beautiful thing you ever saw. She is the sort of person who if she walks down the road ten boys will be staring at her like Rihanna just walked past them. She has these grey eyes that lock on to you when she looks at you. And if she is looking at you, doesn't matter that she has these long legs and a walk that makes you think she is swaying in the wind, you be looking her right in those eyes. Locked in. Wide grey eyes that reach all the way to the edges of her face. Grey eyes are quite unusual anyway but on a black girl, doesn't matter that she's mixed race, they stand out like cat's eyes. On her though, they don't jump out like that, they just kind of fit. They match her wide mouth and her high cheeks. They match her skin. The eyes belong to the face and the face could have no other eyes but those.

I saw her for the first time eight years ago during the time that Bless and Mum were in hospital recovering after Dad. I had just been in for visiting time and I was feeling proper low. The specialist had just been and said that Bless would always have that thing where the side of her face drops. Don't look at her man, please!

They said maybe it would get better all on its own but probability was that it would always be more or less like that. But he said at the end with a half-smile like he was offering up hope, 'There's nothing to stop her from talking. Nothing physical that is. Just see if you can get her to come out of herself.'

He says it like that. Like it's the easiest thing in the world. Like there is some door that she can open in herself that can let her leave and speak again.

I had just got on the bus from the hospital and was still probably thinking about some nasty shit that needed to be done to Dad. Bless was still locked up in her own world. She still hadn't said a word. She had been there in the hospital for a few weeks by then but still not a sound out of her. She just shut out the world and shut herself down. I didn't know what was going to happen to her

54

and so I was just as you would expect. Face down; lost in my own head.

The back of the bus, upper deck is my spot, or as near as I can get to the back. But because of all this, all that old shit didn't seem to matter to me any more and I just chucked myself down stairs at the back and stared out the window. It was maybe fifteen twenty minutes later that I looked up and saw her sitting opposite me. She had her earphones in and was nodding quietly to the music that was buzzing out of them. She was just wearing this white vest and jeans but I couldn't stop staring at her. Her eyes were closed and made it seem like she was dreaming. She was just there, eyes closed, a slight smile on her face and just, nodding to a beat in her ears.

I stared at her for maybe ten minutes. It felt kind of weird like I was looking through a keyhole at her. But I carried on looking. I couldn't help it. I remember thinking that I would be okay as long as her eyes stayed shut. But just as I was finishing that thought her eyes snapped open and locked me down. Shit. Busted! Them eyes. Dazzling grey. Almost silver. When they on you. You can't do nothing.

I couldn't look away. I couldn't say anything because them earphones was doing all the chatting. So in the end I just laughed. She raised her eyebrow and hooked a finger through the leads and released the buds.

'What you laughing at?' she goes. She definitely wasn't impressed.

'Nuffing man,' I say, still laughing. 'You proper caught me though innit?'

'Ain't you got nothing better to do than eyeing up girls?' she goes and sticks her earbuds back in and snaps her eyes shut until it's time for me to get off.

Ten minutes more she keeps them closed. There is no expression on her face at all. It's just a blank. I almost nudge her to say goodbye to her when I finally had to get off, but I didn't have the balls at that time.

On the walk home I couldn't stop thinking about her though. She was hot but that wasn't it. I just felt like I recognized her, or something like that. And that was how it was for the next few days. My mind was somewhere else. Even when I was in hospital I was thinking about her most of the time. Every time I got on the bus home, I sat on the lower deck, hoping maybe I would see her. I did that for ages without a single sighting even. I can't tell you how depressing it was. One day though, my luck changed.

I was already sitting at the back of the bus when she gets on like the wind carried her. It was sunny and she was wearing the summer like it was clothes. Her skin was glowing, she had on this little checked shirt. She was fit no doubt. And, no lie, she kind of smelled like chocolate. This time I was ready for her though. I stuck out my hand and said hi. She looked at it like I'd just offered her a fish. 'I don't shake hands with strangers,' she says, and put her buds in and shut her eyes.

I got off before she opened them again. I was proper

gutted. She had been on my mind for days, then when I saw her I blew it. Shit. So I'm not like a kind of guy who just gives up so I spent a lot of time thinking about a plan so that if I saw her again I wouldn't mess it up this time.

What I did was I kept this bit of paper on me in case I saw her. Truth be told I had this paper on me for ages on the off-chance. Then one day finally I saw her again when she got on my bus. This time I knew what to do. Only thing was that she was sitting two seats away from me and some great big fat thing was sitting next to her and I couldn't get near her. I waited and waited though and when the other one gets off I make my move and rush in next to her on her two-seater. She didn't even seem to see me but I turn towards her and give her the paper. She takes it, opens it and looks at me at last. Trapped in again. Them eyes.

'What do I want to know your name for?' she says.

'So you can shake my hand innit coz you don't shake hands with strangers. And you got my digits there in case you want to call me,' I say and laugh. 'See I got you. Little smile but still a smile,' I add.

'Whatever,' she says and rolls her eyes. But she kept the paper though and even an idiot knows that that was a good sign.

It was a full two months though before she agreed to let me take her out. And even then she made it sound like she was doing it out of pity. 'You look like you need a good meal in you,' she had said. 'Be round at mine at seven sharp. If you're late, you will be.' Ha. Still remember them exact words.

She happened to live not that far from me and so I walked it. Although it was already well into October, it was still warm enough for people to be in the streets drinking and hanging out. I had just bought these new trainers so I was giving them a spin and truth be told I was looking alright. I walked past a group of kids by the stairs at the main door to the block where she lived. This kid Jamil was there even though at that time I didn't know that's what his name was. To me he was just some kid hanging with his boys. I did know one of them though and I checked him. He nodded back at me and turned back to his boys so I slipped past them all and bounced up the concrete steps to her door.

She opened it looking like a Hollywood movie star, long dress, bare shoulders and still smelling of chocolate. 'Come in,' she goes and turns into the hallway. I follow her in.

I didn't really know what to expect. Sometimes you go round a mate's flat and it could be the exact same everything as your own flat, same windows, same doors, same rooms, same layout but at the same time it could feel like you had just stepped into another world. Someone would have like everything modern in their yards, all the gadgets, flat-screen whatever. Someone else would have like the same shit that they had in the eighties, you get me, with all like nest of tables and big soppy posters on the walls in black plastic frames. So I had no idea what I was about to step into, but I thought I would be prepared for whatever and take it in like it was just normal.

Kira lived by herself since she was like fifteen. She had no mum, the dad was wherever and the one brother she had, Spooks, was always in and out of jail, so it was just one of them things. Her place though was a complete surprise to me. It was the same shit, as I say, square rooms, low ceilings, iron-framed windows, old radiators. Just your standard council thing. But the thing that made her place different was the books. Every surface had a pile of books on it stacked as neatly as they could be and as high as they could get without toppling down. I don't mean just the tables and chairs and what have you, but the floor too. Except for a space that made a path from the doors, it was basically books all the way round. They went round the sofa, the table legs, round the TV, everywhere you could see. It was like she'd robbed a library.

'This place is alright, you know,' I say because I really couldn't think of anything else to say. My heart was going a bit if I'm honest with you. She didn't say anything but shrugged her shoulders a little as if to say 'whatever' and sat down on the leather sofa. There was a space for her legs but nothing more than that.

'You got enough books innit?' I say. She reaches over to what was probably once a small table but what was now just a high pile of books and hands me a beer.

'You got one chance to impress me,' she says flashing them grey eyes at me.

I took that as my cue to start babbling and I do just that for the next four hours. To this day I am not sure what I said to her, but something I said seemed to do the trick because after that night as far as anyone was concerned she was my girl.

Break: 10:55

7

When Mum and Bless met her for the first time, they both loved her. Kira loved them too. Sometimes a good thing can happen to a person for no reason. She was the good thing that happened to all of us. Don't get me wrong, she was no angel by any means. She could have these dark moods that would stretch out for weeks. She could snap at you for the tiniest thing and she could rage at you like it was the end of days and she was there to judge you. But underneath all that and underneath all the pretty features and the wide eyes, she was a good person. When she came round to the flat she would always make some food up for Mum and Bless and clean up the place a little before she left. And even though Bless was more or less silent, when Kira was around, she picked up a lot and sometimes you even got the feeling that she was on the verge of coming back to us.

Over the seven years we been together Bless and Kira became more like sisters than anything else. Bless liked being round her. She liked the quiet that she came with.

They would sit together sometimes. Ki would read her books and Bless would just be Bless. She could just 'be', you get me. And sometimes you got the feeling that they didn't need words to say what they were saying. But as for me and Kira, in my mind, we were Romeo and Juliet, well maybe Romeo and some girl who was like Juliet but could be a bitch and if she wanted to could probably knock you out, especially if you called her a bitch, which I only did very rarely. Seriously, though, we were tight.

We clicked but it's hard to see why we did. We weren't exactly similar. In fact you could say that we were like chalk and cheesestring. I was sixteen and I left school. She went to college. I was eighteen and was just starting with the whole buying and selling cars thing. She got her A levels and signed up to one of them Open University things. I loved cars. She loved books. I hated books then. She hated cars. You couldn't even say that we looked at things the same way.

This will give you an idea of what she was like. About a year and a half ago, she was still living in her flat with the books but she came round my yard every now and then to stay over but mainly I stayed at hers. She didn't really feel my place if you get me, but I always made a point of 'How comes it's always me round at yours and you never like to come to mine?' so from time to time she came. Anyway this one Saturday afternoon she comes round to mine and starts to make herself a cup of tea. I'm playing on my PS3 or whatever and she comes and sits next to me drinking her tea. Anyway, maybe fifteen minutes go by and eventually I get the hint and feel like I should close down the game. I'm like, 'Just let me finish this level off and save it' but she ain't really that bothered. She just seems to be chilling.

So when I finally switch off the game she goes, 'You know that boy who's so and so's little brother?' and I go, 'Yeah, I know.'

'He's just broken into your car.'

'What?'

'The red one. The convertible.'

'What the fuck you talking about? He's just broken into my Z3?' I get up and start looking for the keys.

'I don't know. It's the red one.'

'What and you saw him doing it?'

'Yes.'

'Why the fuck didn't you say something?'

'I did. I'm saying now.'

'Fuck Kira. Didn't you stop him? Did you call the police?'

'No! Why would I call the police?'

'Ki he's just jacked my car and you don't do nothing? What is wrong with you man?' I say and run out of the door to my car.

Fucking thing has a smashed window and the glove compartment has been cleaned out and even the little coins or whatever I had in the ashtray are all gone. But it's the window man. Fucking window's smashed. And you might think I'm overreacting and that but windows

63

on a car, they are almost impossible to replace properly. You can never get that factory finish thing right. The seals ain't ever the same again and in the morning the fucking thing will steam up every time. And all the little fucking shitty pieces of glass everywhere that you keep finding for the next ten years. Shit. Sorry, just thinking about it rages me.

So Kira has followed me into the street and I'm all vex still and I'm shouting at her. What the fuck is she thinking of, you know what I mean?

'Where you going?' she says when she sees me get in the car.

'I'm going to murder him,' I go.

'You ain't going nowhere,' she says and gets in the other door and leaves it open so I can't drive away.

'Give me one fucking reason why not?' I say looking at her.

'You don't know what's going on with him,' she says. 'There could be a hundred reasons he had to jack your car.'

'I don't give a fuck Ki,' I say, shouting. 'That boy has to pay one way or another.'

'You go round there and we are over.'

'What? What the fuck you talking about? Why do you care about that little shit?'

'Do you even know that boy?' she asks. 'He could be starving. He could be on drugs. There could be anything going on with him.'

'So fucking what?'

'So people don't do shit for no reason,' she says and gets out of the car.

I didn't speak to her for a week after that but I didn't go round and sort out that boy. I never really understood what the hell she cared about him for, she didn't even know him. But she didn't want to talk any more about it. All she said was, 'You don't know what you would do if you were in his shoes.' And that was good enough for her. Although I never said it to her, I think I worked out later what it was all about. At the bottom of it, it was all about her brother Spooks I reckon. He was inside on a long stretch for some drug shit and the way she saw it, was the way only family would see it. He was in the wrong place at the wrong time. As far as she saw it this kid was just the same as Spooks. Victim of circumstances. I didn't see the shit the same way. You don't go past jail and straight to Go or whatever. If you do your crime and you get caught. You pay up. Simple as that.

I let it go though, for her sake. I really didn't want to and I really wasn't taken in by how she laid it down. Her brother was a waste man too as far as I could tell but she loved him and I loved her. So it was what it was. And I tell you this, I wouldn't have let this go for anyone but her. I needed her in my life. I had no doubt that she would have left me if I had gone that day and given the boy a taste of something. Whether it was because she believed in what she believed or whether it was because she was born stubborn, she would have walked out. I didn't exactly respect that, it was more that I couldn't do without her in my life. She was like the roof over my head. I needed her to keep me dry. It seemed like she had been around since for ever and I couldn't even begin to imagine what it would have been like if she hadn't been there.

So when she went then, that first time, it proper knocked me out.

Break: 11:50

8

12:00

I know to you guys, this seems like another one of them bus replacements. Proper long. But if you just stay with me you will see why you need to hear all this.

See, Kira, she literally just disappeared. It was only a week after this whole car thing so at first I thought she was still pissed off about it. She had no reason to be pissed off though because I had dropped it, like I said I would. But you know how it is with some women, they can be pissed off at you even when you do exactly what they want you to do. No offence to the jury ladies you get me. And the worst thing is that they expect you to know why you pissed them off even when as far as you are concerned, it's you that should be pissed off at them.

I had been expecting her to drop into my place that Saturday and help me with picking out some paint and stuff. It was kind of a surprise for her. I had just sold a car and I was a bit flush and I thought if I maybe did the place up more in like a ways that she would, she might be happier to stay round more. She didn't turn up though. Which was weird because this girl was never late. I mean never.

I waited for an hour maybe before trying her mobile but it rang dead. But then she was always changing her digits as we all were. You'd get a sim with a deal on it, use it and then move on to the next sim with the next deal. That was standard. So when I couldn't get her on her phone to me it was just one of them things. Nothing to stress about. She was pissed off for no reason but as I knew, she didn't always need a reason. She sometimes did that. She would get on one about something that I never even knew I had done and then the next day I would hear all about it. So even though I was worried I wasn't really. I was more angry by then. I was doing my usual thing, racking my brains trying to work out what shit I might have done wrong. I checked my texts – did I say something wrong in one of them? I checked her birthday and other days for if I had missed any 'special' ones. I couldn't work it out.

I didn't hear from her all that day. The whole day was wasted. I didn't get no paints. I didn't get anything done in fact because I was stressing about why she was mad at me. By the time I went to bed, truth be told I was angry. In my head I was wishing all kinds of shit on her. I was screaming at her, I was having these imaginary conversations with her, everything. I'd be doing her voice in my head and then I'd come back at her with my own voice. Like a proper row. It was fucked up.

The next morning I woke up and checked my phone. Nothing. I called Mum and Bless who were still living together then, but they hadn't heard from her either.

68

Then I thought about trying her friend, Maria. She had this one friend who, to tell you the truth, I didn't like all that much. Whenever I saw her she always gave me this look like I weren't good enough for her friend. She might have been right about that but I didn't think she really needed to make it that obvious. Ki was like, 'Leave her alone, she's just looking out for me', but I reckoned maybe she was into her herself. But the problem was I didn't have her number. I mean, why did I need her mate's number? Except I did need her number at that moment. Then I remembered that she worked in some women's clothes shop in Elephant and decided I would just have to go there and speak to her face to face.

It was one of them shops that had a name like Uniqueé and which only someone like my mum might go into. I jumped on the bus down there thinking that if I didn't get no joy from Maria, I could go back via Kira's flat and see if she was maybe there. I pushed open the door and it made this kind of clanging sound to tell the till people that someone had come in. The place was darker than it should have been because some of the ceiling lights had gone and it smelled like those rolls of cloth my mum bought to make clothes out of. There were these round rails full of patterned blouses or whatever and I squeezed past to get to the counter. No one was there so I waited until eventually some old lady shows up and makes a face at me.

'Is Maria here?' I go trying to act like I don't feel too awkward in this place. She shouts out at the back and then Maria comes through, stone by stone. I don't mean to be you know, fattist, but she was so fat that it was like she came through in instalments. She looked at me and crossed her arms in front of her.

'You seen Ki?' I say as cool as I can.

'Why what you done to her?' she says, because she was always suspicious of me for some reason.

'Nothing man! Just wondered if you'd seen her?'

'I haven't seen her or heard from her. But tell her why she not replying to my texts when you see her,' she says and turns back to where she came from.

'Yeah,' I say to her back and then duck back out the shop, worried that Ki hadn't even contacted her friend. Maria didn't look like she was covering for her. She didn't even seem that bothered. But why would she? To her, she wasn't even missing.

So I jumped back on the bus to get to her yard. I walked the short distance from the bus stop and straight away started having that row with her in my head again. By the time I knocked on her door, the argument was in full flow. I was still expecting her to be there, you see. I waited. I swear I could almost see her walking to the door, her face pale from no sleep. Her eyes maybe fat from crying. But she wasn't there. So I sat on the floor outside her door for maybe half an hour not knowing what to do next. I needed to call somebody who knew her, knew where she might be.

Spooks as I said was in prison so I couldn't ask him where she was, not that I would even know how to get hold of him. I didn't even know his real name because even Kira called him Spooks. There was no other family so that was a dead end. And Ki wasn't really a person for loads of friends so there was nothing to check there after I had tried Maria.

On the second day when she weren't there I started worrying properly. No texts or calls on my phone. I tried her yard again but there was no answer. I went to the phone shop where she was temping, but they hadn't heard from her even though she was supposed to be there that day. By then I was getting so para I even considered going to the Feds. But that would have made it into something else I wasn't ready for so I didn't. I tried Mum and Bless again but they hadn't heard anything either. What had happened? I checked my phone every two minutes hoping for something. By then I wasn't even angry any more, I just wanted to know she was somewhere and alive. Then, when I had basically run out of hope, I tried all the hospitals in the area. Nothing. Thank God though, you get me?

That night I put away my pride and went to the Feds. They did their thing and took a few details but as far as they was concerned I wasn't really anybody who could be asking them sort of questions. A parent, maybe a brother even, but some next boy like me? Nah they weren't interested but at least they did tell me that as far as they knew she weren't dead. I swear down, I was besides myself and baffled at the same time. Where the fuck, sorry Judge but I need to say it, where the fuck was

71

she and how was I going to find her? It was like she'd just gone up in smoke.

I had basically run out of ideas so on the third day I broke into her yard. She had been wanting me to have a key anyway but I had been all weird about it because then she would want a key to my place and well, at the end of the day I am a guy innit? Anyway I went round there at night, quite late, and basically just pushed the door in. All it had was a Yale lock and the door was just plywood really so it didn't fight back all that much. The door splintered at the lock and swung open. I went in. It was dark and smelled kind of musty but not really anything unexpected. I turned on the light and the place jumped into view. It was just the same as the last time I had been there. The books had grown in number but now they were mainly on the shelves that I had put up for her in every room. Part of me still had a hope she would be there. Maybe lying in bed or something. Even lying in bed with another guy would have been better than what I saw, which was basically no Kira. Just a space without her in it.

I spent the night at the flat rooting around seeing if there was something somewhere that might explain where she was. Her clothes were all still in her wardrobe. All her stuff was untouched. There was a half-drunk cup of tea in the sink. A couple of unopened letters on the doormat. Nothing at all though to tell what might have happened. I stayed till the morning because I didn't want to leave the place with a broken lock and then as soon as it was light I called Bless round to babysit the place while I got some tools and fixed the door. She stayed while I mended the door and then we left together. As we were walking down the concrete steps, Bless turned to me squinting one eye against the daylight. Something about her expression at that moment or the way the light touched her skin, suddenly reminded me of the Bless I knew from years ago. From the days when I could look at her without sinking. She looked at me hard and took a breath as if she was going to speak. And right then she did. For the first time in nearly seven years. 'Y-you have to find her. You h-have to.'

'I know Bless,' I said, 'but how?'

Luncheon adjournment: 12:55

9

The streets are a strange place. Always someone somewhere got a rumour to tell or sell. When Jamil was shot, the police said that they came looking for me because of a rumour. Well that ain't a surprising thing in itself. It's a lie, but that's another story. But rumours are definitely everywhere, that is true. Eventually one of these rumours came my way. It was telling me that someone had spotted Kira in North London. 'My Kira?' I said. 'North London? Don't be fucking stupid.' But Kira, as I said earlier, wasn't a girl that you could easily mistake.

To you maybe north and south ain't nothing but a line on a map. But to me and the people I grew up with it's like a different country. You can go up to Camden Town with your girl or what have you for a day out but you better not be going up there with your boys unless you are fully prepared to get into something. You don't even have to be ganged up to cause a beef. You could just be a normal guy out with your mates and people will assume you are in a gang. It's just an age thing. I heard loads of stories of young guys being knifed up just for straying into the wrong ends. Even when they were on their own.

74

People look out for you. And if they don't know you and you're on their patch, they will come after you. For no reason other than you walking on their ground, you get me. So for her to be up in North was definitely a worry, even though she was a girl. Why she was up in North was a whole different question.

It wasn't long before everyone round my ends knew that I was looking hard for Kira and it wasn't long before mans were coming to me with bits and pieces of information. Most of it was shit. I even went up there, Camden, Chalk Farm and them kind of places a couple of times to see what I could see, but what I saw was nothing.

Then this one guy I knew who had just come out of Belmarsh Prison told me something that sounded legit. He weren't like a mate of mine, more just someone I knew from the area. He was like a face. People knew him. Anyway I saw him one day on the street and he stopped me to ask me if I could get him some wheels. And I was like, 'Course fam.' And then he starts telling me he's heard about my Ki and I might be interested to hear what he's heard. And I was like, 'Shit bruv. Tell me what you know.' Turns out this guy had shared a landing with Kira's brother who was on the same wing doing a ten for some fucked up shit he had gotten involved in. I knew a bit about Spooks from his sister but I didn't know the details till then.

What I heard was that Spooks had been a crack and meth dealer. He weren't nothing high up, just a soldier.

But a drug soldier is like a real soldier in one way and that is that he is usually the first one to get popped. When Spooks got caught though, it turned out he was looking at a fifteen guaranteed. Fifteen years! The Feds had gone to his yard and found the whole fucking circus there. There were scales, cutting agents, a bag of pills and a kilo of coke. They even found a nine mil. It was the shooter that was going to bury him. Five years for that and probably another ten on top for the drugs.

Now there are two kinds of people in the world. There are those who can do a fifteen-year sentence standing on their heads and there are those who can't. The ones who can ain't usually drug addicts. Spooks was a crack addict and like crack addicts everywhere he would have sold his mum for a draw if she'd been alive. When he found out he was looking at a fifteen, Spooks apparently collapsed on the spot. When he came round again, he did the only thing he could. He went Queen's Evidence on his supplier. For that he got a text from the police and a discount of five years on his time. It also got him a death sentence from the supplier. Nobody likes a grass innit?

This shit is all supposed to be secret. The police tell you that they will keep your name out of it. They don't even mention in court that a person has helped the police. The judge don't even mention it in court. The judge just gets the 'text', which is basically a note, from the police and then gives a low sentence. That is what is supposed to happen. Word is what actually happened was that after the sentence the police went to see the dealer and told him that Spooks had grassed him up. Just so that they could try and get the dealer to give a confession. They basically didn't give a shit what happened to Spooks. Far as they were concerned, he was just a low life. Which, to be fair, he was. Still is.

That first night on the wing must have been a nightmare for Spooks. It would have been bad enough that he was clucking, you know like cold turkey, but on top of that he was a grass. And you know what happens to a grass in jail or if you don't you probably can guess. Four separate people tried to shank him that night and three of them didn't even have nothing to do with it. They just didn't like informers. So after that they put him on the numbers, which is like segregation, and he spent the next two years on twenty-three-hours bang-up. Twenty-three hours in a cell is some hard time, I tell you. I don't even think they lock up zoo animals that long. But as far as Spooks was concerned he was better off there than in general population. In general pop, he knew he wouldn't even last as long as it took for him to shit himself.

He was safe for a while but he was still waiting for what he knew was inevitable. One way or another they would get to him. He knew that.

They got to him eventually through the screws. And I know about screws, the prison guards. I been on remand for the last year waiting for my trial. I'm not supposed to tell you that I am currently in prison in case it prejudices my case. It's like if I'm in prison waiting for my trial I must have done the crime. But I don't mind telling you. I'm up on a murder, that's prejudice enough. Besides, I'm bound to be on remand – it is murder, innit? Where else they going to put me? You ain't stupid. You know that they put murderers in prison while they wait for their trial. Even if they are innocent. Like me.

When I started I thought prison was like them and us. Us, being the inmates and them being the screws. It's not like that. What it is, is them and them and you. In fact screws and other prisoners got more in common with each other than they got with you. That sounds weird but it's true. Because no inmate and no screw gives a fuck about you unless there's something in it for them. And a screw will do what he wants and if what he wants is to give you up to some next villain, he will. Some do it for a few dollars on the side. Others will do it just for kicks. Anyways it was the screws that got to him. They let a boy on to the wing pushing a library trolley and just as Spooks came to pick up a magazine or something, he wet him up. It wasn't pretty.

Maybe I should tell you lot about that. Stuff you learn in prison, man. 'Wet-up'. What it is, yeah, is you get a cup of boiling water. Dissolve a load of sugar in it to make it stick. Then you throw it in the guy's face. Brutal. I know. But it turns out that he deserved every second of agony he got.

Once he knew they could get to him even on the numbers, he had no choice but to make another deal.

This time though he had to deal with his dealers and not Five-O. He didn't have that much he could bargain with though. The money was all gone – what there had been of it. He didn't have any power and he didn't have any drugs. All he had was himself, which was basically a broke crack-addict dealer with nothing but his stones in his pockets. But these boys have a ways of getting blood from stones. And that is what they got from him. His blood. His sister. My Kira.

Okay, so I have forgotten what I am telling you all this for. This must be the reason these QCs write everything down. Well what it is yeah, is that I can write but my writing ain't like exact for one thing and for another thing I write quite slow. For you, hearing that must be like, 'Oh yeah he must be thick' or whatever. Maybe I am a bit in terms of writing but not in terms of talking. Virtually no one in my school was good at writing, but most of them could chat shit for England. Then again you get what you pay for and what we paid for in that school was fuck all. I wonder what he paid for his schooling though? This prosecutor? Thousands I bet. So he can fuck off.

I mean if he went to my school and ended up where he is I'll give him enough respect, I swear down, blood. Did he though? Or did he go to some thousands of pounds a year private school in a bow tie?

So this pisses me off, since we're talking about him. He goes on about it was a tragedy that JC or Jamil, whatever you want to call him, was shot dead at the age of nineteen. That ain't no tragedy, believe. You think even Mr Prosecutor believes JC's death is a tragedy? Please . . . A tragedy is what happened to Kira. That girl had nothing. Nothing, you get me. She had a crack-dealer brother and that is it. She was living on her own when she was fifteen. Working in Tesco for whatever night hours she could – always with a book in her hand while other people had theirs hands in the till. And then this shit comes along and makes it worse. You show me a tragedy and I will show you her.

So yeah, I am sorry in a ways. But in another ways I can't help feeling angry about it.

So where was I? I remember – Spooks. Spooks, sold his sister to save his own sorry-arse life. He should have rather killed himself than did anything to that girl. But that is it. You can't change what happened. The boys he had been running with was some serious boys. They weren't no plastic gangsters like JC and those kids. These boys were men. And they were proper hard mans. To give you an idea let me tell you what happened to some boy last year who didn't know who he was playing with. And I know the Judge is looking at me like how many times are we going on diversion. But you need to know about this.

These guys that Spooks sold out to, ran all of North London. They sold heroin and crack on almost every corner of every estate from Camden to Seven Sisters and Tottenham. Yeah you can't see it where you go because you don't know your way round. If you go to Seven

Sisters or wherever, you probably go on the main road and you will see the usual shit. McDonald's, the shitty menswear shops full of some fucked up African clothing and big pointed crocodile skin shoes and you will think, 'Oh poor fuckers, that is so deprived.'

But you need to get off the main roads to see what it is really like. Go around the back, where the roads run out and you will see these massive estates you hear about whenever they talk about gun crime on the news. They are hidden, which is a surprise considering how huge these places are, but they are only hidden from you. They ain't hidden from us who live there.

Anyway all these estates in the North are run by this crew called Glockz. Kira's brother Spooks was a member of this gang as it happens. Anyway Glockz don't like strange faces on their patch. So this one guy pulls up in his Range Rover one day and starts selling draws out of his car window to anyone who wants some. It's not five minutes before word gets round that some Pagan is on their turf.

You guys are looking at me with them blank faces again. So I'm guessing it's something I said. Is it 'pagan'? Okay, okay. So 'pagan' is like what you would call a rival gang member if you was in a gang. Which I ain't. Obviously.

So Glockz hear about this guy and send some soldiers round to see what's gwanning with this joker in his Range Rover on their patch.

Three guys tap on the window and the driver gets out

smiling. He points a fucking MAC-10 at them and these boys run off, terrified. Big man thinks that's the end of it. But that is not how this shit works round those ends. In another five minutes six cars pulled round and blocked off the Range Rover. Four men from each car came out and surrounded it. Then all the tyres are stabbed out and when the Range Rover drops six inches like it's just had enough and collapsed, the guy gets back out of his car.

He holds his MAC-10 in the air like in a surrender and pulls out this cheesy grin over his face. 'Hey,' he says. 'This ain't even got no bullets man. We can share up the action bredders. Plenty to go round yeah?'

Sixteen men with wheel braces, baseball bats, big long fuck-off knives, one even had a Samurai sword, spend five minutes going to work on this guy. By the time they finished, this guy had to be scraped off the ground with a shovel.

These were the guys that Spooks had supposedly sold his sister to. My Kira! When I found out, I went white. Well you know what I mean. You might as well find out that your girl's dead. I spent weeks feeling as if she had died. I couldn't even begin to imagine what sort of shit they had lined up for her. But all I had was my imagination and in it, they spent a few weeks breaking her down and then when she finally got a taste for the needle she did whatever.

Sorry. Just give me a minute yeah?

*

82

In my head they got her and they drugging her
and – sorry.

I can't even believe I'm crying after everything else that
happened with her later. But just thinking about it here
and now brings it back. I feel like I'm back there. Living
it and —

Is it okay to have a break, Judge, for like five minutes?

Break: 15:15

IO

What I was trying to say before I got all messed up before the break was that you can't really understand what drugs will do to a person. Yeah you have heard about it but you probably haven't ever seen it, first-hand, up close. When a person gets addicted, and believe, it don't take long, it's like nothing else. I can't even describe it. How do I explain to you what it does to a person? Actually it does about five different things at once.

First it takes your mind. It takes everything that drives a human being out and throws them all away. Crack or heroin ain't got no room for anything else in a person's life. Not family, not work, not clothes, not washing, not even food. Think about it for a second, what it must be like to be like that. You wake up in the morning or afternoon or whatever and you have only one thing on your mind. You want nothing else, just that hit. You don't want food or drink, you don't want to get dressed, you don't want to speak to anyone, you don't even want to take a shit. So you hunt high and low for a hit. And then another one. Until eventually it takes your body and bit by bit destroys it.

Then it takes your conscience. You would jack your own mum on her own doorstep for some money for a hit. There is nothing you won't do for your fix. Then when everything else is gone or ruined, crack will take your soul. When that happens, you ain't even a person any more. You're just some breathing meat and bones.

It makes me laugh. I heard some people on the tube once talking about prostitution, just chatting shit and that. This one woman she goes, 'Eugh, disgusting. Why would you do that to yourself?' when some woman I'm guessing she thought was a prostitute walked on. 'Just think of all those horrible men you would have to have sex with,' blah blah blah. This is why you would do that to yourselves. For a hit, a person will do much worse than that. A man would cut off his own dick for it. Trust. It is not a game. The only thing that keeps you going is the promise of another hit. Weird thing is that the only reason any of them is still alive is because they are keeping themselves alive for the next high.

That is what they were doing to Kira. I felt helpless just thinking about her. She was gone. Untold horrible shit was happening to her. And to make matters worse there was nothing I could do about it. What could I do? I am many things but I ain't Sam L. What you would do is probably phone the police. What the police would do though as I found out is pretty much nothing.

She wasn't missing. She was an adult. If she wanted to go hang out in the North with some bad boys and smoke a bag of crack that was up to her. Why the fuck should they do anything about it? I got nothing against Five-O for what it's worth. Yeah some of them are low-lifes but they basically no different from like a bin man or whatever. They do what they have to do and no more. If someone empties a bin all over the street on your road, they might pick it up. If you empty one all over your own front yard, they leave it the fuck alone. If you want to live in a pigsty what business is it of anyone else's?

That was that then. She was gone and my head had gone into some dark places. I started to think about her in like the past tense even though it had only been a couple of weeks. How she used to sit when she was reading her book. What she used to wear when she went to work. What the last thing she said to me was. What the last thing I said to her was. And that, that is what woke me up in the end. I had said some shit to her after the argument we had had about how I would allow the boy who smashed my Z3 for her.

'I'll let it go but only because I ain't ready to let you go.'

Or if it wasn't exactly them words it was something like that. Or maybe I didn't even say it out loud, I had just thought it. Anyway the point I am making is that here I was already letting her go after just a couple of weeks. What kind of a man did that make me?

I thought about it for a long time. Of course I couldn't just go into those estates and start shooting the place up. I didn't even know where she was. But, I knew that if I asked around enough of the people who hung around that area I might at least find out where she was. My plan

86

was then to hang around and wait until I saw her and then to take her.

It wasn't a great plan. But it worked and I did find out where she was in the end. How I found her though, for that I have to tell you about Curt. He was the key to finding Kira. And the key to a lot of other shit too.

After Curt got moved schools back in the day, I didn't see him for a while. He just kind of disappeared and I didn't really think too much about it. Shit like that happened to kids like that. One day they were there and the next day – gone. A week or a month passed and truth be told I forgot all about him. Like I said before, we weren't really tight. To me he was just that big kid who broke that idiot's arm. Then one day, I must have been about sixteen then, on my way to the shops or something, I see this huge boy blocking my way on the pavement. Now this kind of shit is always a bit tense you get me. It's basically one person's way of fronting up the next person. Who has got the biggest balls and who is going to pussy out? I was never really the pussying-out kind you get me. Most people round my ends already knew that and after a few scrapes people knew who I was and they let me just get on my way. Even though I was never in no gang shit, people knew better than to mess me up. See, my thing was if you stayed out of my way I would stay out of your way. But if you put your face in my face, chances are I would rip yours off. Don't get me wrong though. I hated all that. I didn't like to have to go to war

87

over some bit of macho bullshit but the fact was I would if I had to.

So here was this same kind of shit happening all over again. This is me, more or less the same height when I was sixteen as I am now. Here was this boy, more or less the size of a house. Shit. So my tactic with these big fuckers is to stamp on the kneecaps and then just unleash till boy's kissing tarmac. If they are tooled up then usually I bounce. As fast as I can. Virtually nothing worth getting sliced up for man. And if there is a chance that some boy is in a gang, I swallow my pride and jet. So him and me get closer to each other. I am looking at the ground but I know we getting closer because this big lump is blocking out the light he is that big. I don't recognize him from around these ends so I figure that he ain't in no gang or no gang from around here. And he is alone. We get closer until there is almost no light between us. And I swear just as I am about to jump on the boy's knees, I hear, 'Yo blood.' I look up and this face has cracked open and is feeding me this bright-lights smile. 'Fuck,' I goes, 'Curt? Boy what they feeding you, ha ha?'

Since that day we was tight, he was a proper friend, and he was there with me from then on. As I said, I have to tell you about him because he's important, to everything that happened. He's part of this story.

When I first saw him again, Curt, he hadn't changed all that much but he was definitely different. He was more serious. And these days he weren't taking no shit

88

from no one. At that time he weren't in a gang either. We both had managed to sidestep that whole thing which was no small thing round our way. Usually every other week, if you were a known name, some next man from a gang would come knocking on your door trying to recruit you. There weren't a thing they wouldn't promise you and there weren't a thing they wouldn't threaten you with if they wanted you. They weren't really that bothered about me even though a member is still a member and numbers are always important. But Curt they wanted. They were desperate for that boy and if you saw the size of him you could see why.

But the thing about Curt I soon found out was that he wasn't really cut out for that shit. For one he weren't really interested in money all that much. For two he hated being told what to do. Normally those two things alone would have ruled him out. A gang don't want a person who they can't control. Most people like to think that they won't be controlled but then most people are liars. Most people will do any shit if the price is right and that basically means that they are controllable. Curt was different though.

I was with him one day a couple of years ago when three local boys stopped him in the street.

'You Curt innit?' one of them goes and when Curt nods he carries on talking, 'I want to give you the chance of a lifetime blood.'

Curt tries to walk away because he knows what they are after but they block his path making a wall. Then the leader of these three goes, 'I could give you a grand right now or I could shank you. Up to you blood.'

'Shank me,' he goes.

The three look at each other like, *what the fuck is going on?* If it was me I'd be maybe trying to fast-talk my way out of it, but this is some new shit to these boys. The leader, a little guy with one of them five panel caps pulls a shank out of his pocket and shows it to Curt. Curt takes a long look at the blade and then says, 'What about you two?' he says looking at the other two. Curt is standing there like he has been cemented into place. I, though, am on my toes, getting ready to jump in if the shit gets feisty.

The others show their weapons, grinning, but Curt doesn't move.

'Shank me,' he goes. His fists are still in his pockets.

The leader comes nearer and holds his blade low. 'We ain't even fucking wid you blood,' he says.

Suddenly Curt whips his hand out of his pocket and grabs the knife by the blade.

'Shank me,' he says, his face flat like a plate.

The boy's eyes all panic and he's trying to pull the knife back but he can't release it from Curt's grip. There is blood coming from Curt's hand but you wouldn't know it from looking at his face.

One of the others steps forward with his own knife and takes a swing at Curt. But this is a boy who's never used a knife before. I can tell that because of the way it's in his hand. He's holding it like he's holding a phone. I know that if you want to use a knife you hold it in your

fist with the blade down, sharp edge out. This gives me enough chill to step into him and give him a couple of quick punches to the face. He drops down and I jack his knife while he's still dazed.

Curt is still holding the blade. The boy at the other end of it is still ashy from fear. He looks at me with his boy's knife in my hand and then runs. 'You fuckers are dead. Dead!' he goes as he's running. I look around for the third boy but it seems like he went a while back. They came with three blades and left with one.

'Fuck man,' I say to Curt, looking at his hand.

'It's nothing,' he says and clenches it shut again, blood spilling out the sides.

'Nah man, it ain't.' I go and take my bandana off and tie it round. I pull it tight until the blood soaks through the cloth and then tie a double knot. Curt doesn't flinch the whole time. I look at him for a reaction but I can't find one.

'That don't make me gay,' I say and we both start creasing.

We got to be good friends while he was in the ends. Curt would come round my yard and Mum would cook him dinner. She liked him even though he usually ate twice what she had in the house. In fact I reckon deep down she wouldn't have liked him half as much if he didn't eat so much. It was just one of them things. When he sat there eating, he looked like a child. There was nothing in the world at that moment. Just him and his plate.

She would pretend to moan about it afterwards. 'The boy's father must be a horse. Next time he comes I will give him a bag of oats.' But there was also the mum thing that kicked in. As far as any mum is concerned when she's feeding her kid's friend, she's really just feeding her own kid. And then, she also knew that Curt didn't have a mum like I did. I mean he had a mum, but she weren't no real mum. I think at the end of it that is the reason he kept asking if he could come round. Just so that he could get the feeling of what it might have been like to have a normal mum. And even though sometimes she would say, 'So the horse is coming to dinner again?' I knew that secretly Mum liked him.

In fact when he came round one day two years ago to tell us that he was moving back up to North London I remember seeing the look on Mum's face. She had the same look in her eyes that she had when I told her I was moving out. She was trying not to cry and to style it out but a tear sneaked out of the corner of her eye anyway.

'I hope you will still be coming back to see your friend, eh?'

Curt just looks at the floor, saying nothing.

'I will make you dumplings if you like them,' she says and turns back to her cooking.

Every now and then Mum would mention him. 'Have you seen your horse friend?' or 'Instead of sitting in front of games all day long you should call up your horse friend and speak to a person.' So I would call him from

time to time and see how he was getting on. Anyway once I heard the rumour that Ki might be somewhere up in North London, Curt was the natural person to call. In fact he was probably the only person I even knew from North London.

Break: 15:50

II

I met him up just after ten o'clock in the McDonald's on Seven Sisters Road. I had forgotten how big the boy was. That or he had grown since I last saw him. He was sitting at one of the tables and I walked over and checked him. He stood up while I sat and then sat again and put his huge hands on the table in front of me.

'Man you look old,' he goes and laughs this great big bear laugh that he has and which would have shook the table over if it hadn't been bolted to the floor.

'Listen blood, I need your help on something innit,' I said and told him about Kira.

'It's fucked up man. I liked that girl,' he says and looks down at his two burgers.

'Bro I been turning London inside out looking for her.'

'You need to forget about her man,' he says after taking a giant bite out of his burger. 'I hear she been caught up.'

'Glockz?' I say.

Curt takes a second bite of his burger and it's gone. He chews slowly and just after he swallows he picks out another from a box on the table. Even a Big Mac looks tiny in his hand.

94

'It's what I hear,' he says.

'I just need to know where she is Curt.'

'That I can help you with blood,' he says and demolishes the second burger.

From what I gathered, Curt wasn't exactly hooked up to Glockz but he had certain privileges. He knew the General for one and so had a way of finding shit out if he needed to.

'Man I thought you were against all that gang shit,' I said to him, 'How the fuck you all Glockz?'

'Long story,' he says. 'Long. But if you want to know where she is at, link me in a couple of days. I give you whatever I got.'

'Safe bruv. I'll check you in a couple of days' I say, and leave.

When I link up with him two days later all the smiles was gone from his face.

'You'll find her working King's Cross, Camden, them kind of streets,' he says looking at the ground.

'Shit,' I say, because that is all I can think. Curt looks down as if he wants to be somewhere else. 'I owe you,' I say at last and touch his shoulder with my fist as I get up to go.

'Nah man,' he says.

'Is she okay?'

'I doubt it.'

'Fuck.'

'You know who her brother is?' he says raising an eyebrow at me.

'Yeah.'

'Proper freak innit.'

'Yeah blood. Proper.'

As I turn to walk away something doesn't feel right in what he's telling me. She was working the streets already? Normally it took more than a couple of weeks to get them crazy for crack before they walked the streets. It just didn't really make sense to me. I look across at him.

'One thing though bro. They broke her down quick innit?'

'Nah. That's the weird thing man. She just agreed from what I hear.'

'What?'

'She's clean. She just made them promise that they had Spooks' back.'

I didn't even bother going home after seeing Curt. I just wanted to find her and if there was a chance she could be there on a street right at that minute, I didn't want to waste it. I jumped on the bus to Camden and got off near the tube. Camden on a Saturday night is pretty much heaving to look at it from the outside. But only parts of it are, really and truly. The Lock. Stables Market. The Canal. All them areas where the tourists go, they are rammed. But I knew that she weren't going to be in no tourist places. That's not what Curt meant when he said Camden. He meant the kind of places where a pimp could let a girl loose and catch hold of her if she got up to any shit, without anyone trying to step up. Deserted places. Back alley places. A place where if you went there, you went there for a specific reason.

I decided to walk down Camden High Street and head towards like where the canal is. Just behind the hospital and round the back of King's Cross Station. It was pretty wild there still, even though there was all these new buildings coming up everywhere you looked. But these new places were just where people could see. There was still hidden places. Secret places no one wanted to see. I carried on to the towpath where a lot of the prostitutes had been forced to move. Cleaning the place up, is what they called it but in truth it was just brushing up dirt and moving it someplace else. I didn't see her and to be honest with you I was relieved. I didn't want to see her in them kind of places. Then just before I called it a night I decided to head up nearer to York Way. More dead space. Or nearly dead.

I found her under a bridge.

I can't even tell you what it was like to see her again. This was a girl I had been stretching my eyes to see for the last couple of weeks. I would look at crowds of people, scanning thousands of faces like the Terminator, looking for her. If someone had her hair or was wearing something that looked like what she might wear I would run across to them and tap them on the shoulder. I didn't mind looking like a weirdo, I just needed to find her. So when I saw her standing there in a doorway near that bridge I was so surprised that I looked straight past her. I mean, I saw her. I thought it was a face I recognized from somewhere but it wasn't her I was seeing. Then I looked again. And it was her. She was like her own ghost. Her face which had been a face that could stop cars had lost all its light. It was just like she had gone and left her body behind on autopilot.

I was all set to just walk over and get her when I saw a car pull up and wind its window down. Some next man was talking at her but she was looking straight into the distance. Then a guy comes over, one of these Glockz boys probably, and takes some money off of the driver and then pushes her in the back seat. And just like that she was gone. Again.

I waited all night for her to come back but she never came back. I didn't know where she'd gone or whether she was alive even. By the time I went home it was light and I felt worse than I did before I saw her. I went back the next day and then the next day after that but nothing. One time there was a different girl there but not Kira. I even spoke to her but she didn't know who Kira was and then I ran as a Glockz boy had come running over. He was shouting that he'd shoot me and whatever for wasting his time but I didn't care about that.

After that I linked up Curt again and asked him to find out what the score was. They moved these girls around a bit, he told me. You couldn't leave a girl in one place. It was bad for business. Punters wanted new faces and if they saw the same old face day after day they would go elsewhere. And then some of the others would grow too attached and that also caused problems of a different kind.

Curt gave me a list of other places to try so I tried

them but I didn't find her again. I had some wheels that I was finding it difficult to sell on and started driving round to look for her. You could only cover so many miles on foot and bus so I knew I needed to drive. The wheels made it easier even though these weren't my ends and I didn't want to be tagged for my car. Boys recognize your ride and the kind of ride I was rocking weren't no Ford Fiesta that you could be invisible in. This one was an Audi A3 with some bad alloys on it and for the first time in my life I wished I was driving some old man's car that wouldn't attract any attention. It might sound stupid to you but there are kids out there who know who owns every car in their area and who will ring out the bells if some phat car turns up scouting the estate.

Even so, I went from place to place, looking and looking. In one night sometimes I went to six or seven different spots in King's Cross, Swiss Cottage, Angel, Tottenham, everywhere on my list. Then about five days after I first saw her, just as I was losing hope, I saw her again. The same place I saw her the first time. Just by a small doorway under the steel bridge at King's Cross. Though it was her if you looked hard enough, it still wasn't really her. It was just a shadow.

I told myself that next time I saw her I'd be ready for whatever. I didn't want to see her and then have to run off when some Glockz gang-banger came bouncing up. So I took along a gun, the same gun that I kept for seven years waiting for dad to turn up. I had it with me now in my waistband even though I thought it was unlikely that I would actually need it. I pulled up to near where she was standing to think about how I was going to play it.

I still couldn't believe it was her. You don't know what it's like to look for a person you love for so many hours in so many days and nights and not find her. And then suddenly she is there. It proper made my heart go.

Just then though, some other car pulled up in front of me and parked next to her. The driver had wound his window down and was talking to Kira's ghost. *Please don't get in*, I was saying to myself, *just don't get in*. It looked as though she was about to though so I started up my car and pulled up immediately behind and started beeping my horn. I was hoping that the noise might spook the other driver or something but it didn't. All it did was make him get out of his car and shout over at me to fuck off.

I get out and walk over to where they are both standing. I've got my hand over the gun which is covered still by the bottom of my hoodie and as I get closer I start to check out this guy's face. Is he a hero type or is he a see-a-black-man-and-run type? I can't tell exactly but I need to test this one out before I do anything. I get to about three feet away and Kira sees me for the first time. She almost smiles as if she has forgotten where she is and has seen someone she recognizes but then just as quickly a look of panic fills her face.

'She's coming with me bruv,' I say and go to take Kira by the arm. The guy looks like he is going to back off but he is still thinking about it you can tell. No guy likes to be fronted out by another guy especially when there's a girl around – even if that girl is a prostitute. I turn my back to him to give him a chance of leaving without having to get into a row. Kira is still holding on to me. She is shaking a bit but I don't know whether it's the cold or whether it's me trembling that's making her shake. For sure my heart is going bam bam bam.

We are at the car door when the pimp guy or whatever comes pelting across the road with his arms out. 'What the fuck you doing with my girl?' he shouts as he's running. I can't run off now without causing a massive beef so I stop. I want to just take her away like a normal punter or whatever, peaceful, just another paying customer. I do not want to start something in the middle of North London with some Glockz soldier. My heart is getting loud in my chest. Boom boom boom now. It is so loud I swear he can hear it.

'What's up blood?' I say. 'Just looking for a bit innit?'

'He was here first,' he says and points his face at the other guy who is now trying to get back in his car.

'Yeah but he's going innit.'

'He ain't fucking going anywhere. Oi bruv. You was here first,' he says to him holding his arm. The guy was already white but now he has turned into a sheet. No doubt this wasn't any kind of shit he'd planned for either.

'Yeah, well I'm here now though. What's wrong with me?' I say quickly adding a bit of volume to put the first punter off.

'She don't like you though pussy boy. So, you best fuck off.'

'She wants to come with me,' I say and by now I am shitting myself. This guy is a big guy. Not muscles or nothing just big and solid like a punchbag. If it hadn't been for Kira, I would have fucked off a long time ago.

'What this clapped-up bitch wants is what I tell her she wants,' he says coming right into my face. He is so close some of his spit lands on my lip. It is disgusting but I can't wipe it off.

'I got enough dollars man,' I say and take a wad of cash out my pocket to show him.

He snatches the money straight out of my hand and says, 'I said fuck off. I ain't going to tell you again, blood.'

I let go of Kira. The gun is still there in my waistband. It feels heavy. It's too heavy for these bottoms I got on and it feels like any minute it's going to drop down my leg. He turns to leave with Ki and all I can think is that I need to keep him here somehow. I need to do something. The punter guy runs off. He's left his car there and just run off. Now there's just the three of us. It feels like we are nowhere.

'If you ain't giving me the bitch,' I say as cold as I can, but the word bitch sticks in my throat, 'then you giving me back my paper, blood.'

The guy spins around with his eyes on fire and arms out wide. 'You think you can fuck wid me bruv?' he says

and steps right into my face. 'Fuck wid dis, yeah bruv.
Fuck wid dis.'

I suddenly feel a hard object up against my stomach
and I look down.

It's a gun.

Long adjournment: 16:45

IN THE CENTRAL CRIMINAL COURT   T2017229

Before: HIS HONOUR JUDGE SALMON QC

―――――――――――――――――――

Closing Speeches:

―――――――――――――――――――

Trial: Day 31

Thursday 6th July 2017

APPEARANCES

For the Prosecution: Mr C. Salfred QC
For the Defendant: In person

Transcribed from a digital audio recording by

T. J. Nazarene Limited

Official Court Reporters and Tape Transcribers

I2

Have any of you lot ever held a gun in your hands? It's not like you see in the films where you can put one in the inside pocket of your jacket or stick it in your jeans and forget you got it on you. A gun is a heavy thing. It weighs you down. When you pick one up it's like you can feel the seriousness of it. You can sense the life it can take and the damage it can make. A gun is a living breathing thing in a ways. And it's even got a voice. As soon as you pick one up it starts whispering shit to you. It's whispering all in your ears. All the time you have it on you it's whispering. *Wsss wsss wsss wsss.* And it's saying just one thing to you over and over. It's saying, 'Let me out.' It wants you to shoot it.

I can tell by his face he's feeling it now. His gun wants to shoot me. Kira senses something too and starts to scream. The guy steps back but keeps the gun aimed at me. He whips round with his other arm and grabs Kira by the hair and pulls down hard. She lets out this noise like a kicked dog.

I step forward and then stop quickly and hold my

hands out. 'Blood, it's cool. It's cool. I'm going,' I say and start stepping back slowly.

'It's too long for that shit bruv,' he says and pulls Kira's head down by his knees, so she can only see the ground. 'You don't want to see this, baby,' he goes, and straightens out his gun arm.

I'm suddenly aware that my own gun is heavy in my waistband. As soon as I get it out, everything happens at once. The Glockz boy's eyes go big and he takes a step back. Kira struggles free from the guy's grip and freezes. Then a second later she starts to shout 'Oh my days oh my days oh my days' over and over. I point the gun at the Glockz and tell him to fuck off. But there is something in my voice that cracks just as I'm saying it that makes me sound like a kid. His face changes. He smiles like an evil smile and takes a step towards me, gun leading the way. 'I'm going to shove this up your hole innit,' he says and takes another step towards me. My mind is all syrupy as he comes closer. I want it to start working again. It feels like there's a dead battery in there and I just need something, some spark to get it going. Then out of nowhere Kira screams and my head comes alive. The motor starts working again. Smooth like a straight-six engine.

I shoot. It hits him somewhere in the shoulder and he spins round and hits the deck screaming out. There's splatters of blood in my eyes. I can barely see what's going on till I wipe them clean with my sleeve. I look down to where he was but he has gone. Just disappeared.

There is like a small puddle of blood on the ground but no person there. I look around wildly but can't see him. I panic, expecting any moment that he's going to jump me from behind. Round and round I go searching. Then finally I catch sight of him and see him staggering off to where he came from behind the bridge.

I take Kira's arm and push her into my car. I start it up. My hands are shaking. My heart is slamming so hard against my ribs I believe that it's going to burst into pieces. It is so loud now it is frightening me. Somehow though I manage to get past it, put the car into gear and drive off.

I'm all over the road. The blood is pumping through me. Banging in my ears. I look over at Ki and see that her mouth is opening and shutting but I can't hear a thing with all this noise in my head. It must be the gunshot. I'm still deaf from it. But I keep driving. Revving hard from what I can see of the rev counter, but still hearing nothing.

I keep going, swerving at first, but after a minute or two the driving gets more level. I turn the corner but I'm in a dead end. I spin the car around one eighty and drive back past the puddle of blood. Where the hell did I come from? I drive a bit further but I can't seem to find a way out of this maze. Suddenly every turn leads me to a road that has been blocked off with iron bollards or has been pedestrianized. Fuck. Eventually I make a turn and find the road that brought me here and before I know it I am heading home, with my girl in the car.

Just saying it now brings it back. My heart is going right now here in this court. Fuck! I know, language, but serious, that was some scary shit. You don't know until you in one of them situations how you going to react. You might be okay but you might choke you get me? That could have been me on that day. I could have choked and if I had maybe that would have been the end of days. But life hadn't finished with me. There was still chapters to go. More story to tell. That's how I look at it anyway.

I'll let you guys into a little something. My QC, before I sacked him, told me under no circumstances to tell that story. 'Why?' I goes. 'Why not?' He says it's just going to prove you are guilty. It proves, one, you have a gun. It proves two, you are willing to carry it. It proves three, that you are willing to shoot someone with it. It proves four, that you are clever enough to get away with it.

I take his point and that but bottom line is I think that's rubbish. It don't prove nothing. You lot already know I had a gun in my flat. And everyone knows that people don't have guns unless there are circumstances under which they will use it, otherwise no point in having one in the first place. But this was self-defence. That boy was going to kill me for sure. I saw it in his eyes. I was there, you weren't. He had a gun in my face. I can still see it. This was a real thing. He would have killed me and there would have been no one to tell you about it. Do or die. I did what I had to do. But I didn't kill him though. At least no one has come forward and said I killed him. If I killed him, charge me with that. I will fight that one too. And I tell you now, I can bust that case. Self-defence all day long. But don't be charging me with no bullshit next shooting of some kid I didn't shoot. Fuck that shit.

Anyway you got it all now. Sorry my QC wherever you are. I had to tell it though. That was the only way to explain how the police found that firearm discharge residue in my car. It was from that shooting, members of the jury. It was from shooting that Glockz prick not from shooting Jamil. That explains most of evidence number five.

Anyway, Kira was home but she wasn't by no means safe. Actually she was safer than we thought at that time, but we didn't know it then. At that time, the way we saw it, the biggest danger to her was herself. The drive back home was a long one. Although she started off dazed and spaced out it wasn't long before she turned into a maniac. She started banging on the windows and screaming to be let out. I didn't get it at first. What the fuck was the problem? I wasn't expecting no hero's welcome or nothing, but I definitely wasn't expecting the abuse that came out of her mouth right then. But the truth is that was my own fault. I hadn't thought the shit through at all.

When I found her, I was so like consumed by how to get her out I hadn't thought about what to do with her once I had her. I was making this shit up as I went along.

Find her. Oh, I found her – what now? Get her out. Oh, I got her out – what now? Take her home. No, don't fucking take her home that is the first place they will come looking. That is how my mind works. In a straight line.

Kira thought differently. If my mind was a pencil drawing of a stick-man, hers was a Michael Angelo. She had what you call it, perspective. And all that other stuff, colour, 3D, the lot. I had a big head and stick arms. Eventually after the screaming had died down and I managed to persuade her not to open the car door and try and run off every time I stopped at a light, she told me what was on her mind. If she wasn't there when they came looking for her, they would off her brother, she says. Simple as that.

I hadn't even thought about that for a second. In my head as long as she was gone from that place, from them, she was safe. Tell the truth I didn't really give a shit about Spooks. He was a nobody crack addict. If I had thought about it beforehand though I would still have done it but I would at least have been prepared for how Kira reacted.

I managed to calm her down after a while and get her to my yard without her jumping out. 'I've got a plan,' I kept telling her, 'I've got a plan', even though I didn't. Big head and stick arms remember. On the way though, I thought of something that might become a plan, even if it wasn't an actual plan yet.

'Nobody knows you've been taken by me innit? As far as any of them Glockz is concerned, some next man, a gang member maybe, took you at gunpoint for no better reason than to fuck with them.'

She stared ahead at the windscreen and I knew I was in for one of them long silent treatments.

'And I shot one of them innit so they have to be thinking that it's some gang thing. No boyfriend would have pulled anything like that. As far as that guy knew I was a customer and I shot him up because he was giving it rah rah rah.'

She looked at me and said nothing.

When she do that silent thing anything could be going on in her head, so believe me when I say I was relieved when she finally said, 'Okay maybe you're right.'

When we got to my flat I put her straight into a hot bath. Even poured in a load of shampoo to make bubbles for her. She didn't want to get in but after a bit of persuasion she finally did. It was like she didn't have the energy to argue with me, which if you know Kira was something serious. I knew it was serious anyway. She made me wait outside while she changed. I went back a few minutes later and knocked on the door with a cup of tea.

'Put it outside,' she goes. 'I'll get it later.'

I stood outside the door listening. See maybe if I could hear her crying. 'Can I come in Ki?' I say at last.

'No,' she says so I went back into the living room and waited. TV off.

By the time she came out in my dressing gown she seemed a bit better. Her cheeks were still red from the heat of the bath and her hair was wrapped in a towel. She looked more Ki and less ghost. I got up to try and hold her but she shrugged me off and sat down with her knees to her chest and her eyes to the floor.

'Ki,' I goes.

'Just give me some time,' she says. So I did.

The next few days were really strange and a bit dream-like. On the one hand she was back and every time I remembered it, when it crept up on me, I felt like this wave of relief wash over me. But then when I looked at her, if she was sitting reading a book or just watching TV, she had this look that made me realize that maybe she wasn't really back after all. Not in the sense that it was the same Kira who'd come back to me. She wasn't the same. She was a different Kira come back to me.

I tried to speak to her every now and then, when I made her a cup of tea or brought her some soup, but she weren't really interested. I knew I needed to give her some time but all I could see was this girl that I loved just slipping away from me and the harder that I tried to hold on to her the thinner she became until I had almost no grip left on her. I was desperate. I didn't know what to do. It wasn't like I needed to know what happened to her in that time she was with Glockz. But I did need to know whether what they did to her was something that could be fixed. Even if not straight away, just one day, you get me?

The one thing she could bring herself to talk about

was Spooks. She was still terrified that someone some-where was going to maybe stick a shank in him for her disappearing.

'What you care about him for anyway?' I said to her once and she just says, 'Don't.' Her eyes flashed me one of them looks and I knew that I couldn't even go near that right then.

Later that same day she made me promise to see if I could find out if her brother was still alive.

'I will. Don't worry about him. Worry about you,' I said.

'Just do it.'

'I'll get a message through don't worry,' I said.

She looked at me and flared her nostrils.

'Fine,' I said, 'I'll go and see him. In prison.'

'And you'll make sure that nobody comes looking to him?' she said, eyes wide open.

'I'll put a few rumours in the right places about some new gang causing a problem in those ends. I'll say some gangster's been causing trouble in North. Throwing his weight around. Fucking up people's patches. Nicking their whores. Don't worry. Spooks, that piece of shit, will be clear.'

And that is what I did. And at the same time I made sure that nobody knew Kira was with me.

Now that probably doesn't sound all that difficult to you lot. She's not famous. How hard can it be to keep her on the low? Well even though she's not famous a person

can still have a rep. In fact everyone has a rep. Some
people have good reps. Some people have shit ones. But
people round my ends know all the people round my
ends. It's like it's their business to know. They know who
is going out with who. They know whether this man has
got a baby for this next girl and how many babies he's
got for how many girls. And trust me a girl like Ki is a
girl that gets noticed by everyone. And not just men. In
fact it's the girls that are most likely to mark her. They
want to know what all the other girls are doing because
if any of them is doing it near their own mans, they will
have something to say about that. And Kira, like I said,
was a type of a girl who could worry a lot of other girls
just by turning up.

In the end, though, it wasn't really that hard to keep
her low profile at the beginning. She basically had no
desire to go out anyway. She would just sit in my room
staring into space. Occasionally she would pick up a
book but her eyes would glaze as if all she could read
was her own thoughts.

After a few weeks had passed things were no better
as far as Ki was concerned. She was still locked in her
own head. I tried every known thing then to get her
out of herself but nothing really had any effect. In desperation I told Mum about it. I didn't tell her all details,
just that some men had put her in a car. Mum started
to freak out at first but then I managed to calm her
down some. 'You can't tell no one about it Mum. I mean
it,' I goes. I really didn't want to have to tell Mum but I

didn't have any other ideas and she sometimes had some good ones. In the end the best she could do was tell me not to worry and that Ki just needed some time to heal.

A day after I told Mum about her, she called me and told me that she had made Ki a doctor's appointment.

'You did what? I told you didn't I? No one. You can't tell no one about it Mum. It's serious Mum.'

'I did not tell anybody about it. Just I said to Blessing to make an appointment with the doctor for Kira. Just depression. Not to say about kidnapping and all of these matters.'

'You told Bless? Mum!' I say. I definitely didn't want her talking to Bless about it.

'Of course I tell your sister. You want me to have a mental breakdown all on my own, foolish boy?'

'Alright alright. No one else Mum. I mean it. No doctors. No friends. No church people. No one,' I said and hung up. I called up the surgery straight away and told them that it was a mistake. Fuck knows who would have seen her if she wandered over there. Plus I wasn't sure I wanted no doctor to be finding out that her problem was that she had been kidnapped by a gang and pimped out. It was too dangerous to do that. Most likely the doctor would have called the Feds and I didn't want no police turning up and putting blue lights over her head, you get me. So I thought of other ways.

One of the first things I did was to go round to her flat to pick up some things for her. Some clothes, yes, but mainly something for her to read. She needed her books round her. To her they were like her friends. Or family even. It's weird I know, but book people are weird, trust me.

I waited till it was dark and drove up in the A3 and parked somewhere out of the way but close enough to load it without making too many trips. As I walked up to the door I suddenly had a flashback to that day when I came round looking for her. The door was still splintered at the frame from when I broke in that time and the new lock I had fitted was still there like a surprise I had forgotten about. It was out of place though. It was too new and didn't fit in with the peeling paint on the door. The key went in smoothly and turned. At first I was half wondering if someone might have already been round there looking for her but the door was still locked. It all looked fine to me. I went in and turned on the light and it flooded the room.

I took a look around and everything was like I remembered it. Maybe something seemed off but I wasn't sure what exactly. The books all looked like they did when I had left it. Nothing seemed like obviously wrong. I decided it was probably my mind playing me and went into the bedroom and started piling clothes into the bin liners I had brought with me. I had just got two bags full and was moving them into the living room when I saw it. Just out of the corner of my eye. By the window. The net curtain there was like fluttering but I knew no window were open when I left it. I walked over and pulled the curtain back and saw the bottom of it had been smashed in. I looked down at my feet. Glass everywhere. Shit.

I quickly threw some books into a carrier bag and left, locking the door behind me. Then I ran. If someone saw me then someone saw me. It didn't matter. I could be anyone. A family member. Someone just checking in, taking some stuff. Whatever. What I knew though, was that dem man were looking for her. This weren't good. I jumped in the car and drove off quickly.

When I got back that night, Kira's face lit up a little when she saw her books. Then they dimmed right back down again. Wrong books apparently. I told her I would go back and get more for her, but truth was I knew I weren't going back there again. I didn't tell her about the break-in. No need to worry her any more than she was already.

I tried other things I thought might help too. Some herbal stuff, St John's something and some Chinese medicine shit too but it was no good. This wasn't one of them things that could be medicined. This was one of them things that just had to be mourned over time. She was never going to get over it, just like you never really get over a death. All that happens is that the sorrow gets older. It's like a light that gets fader and fader. One day after years and years have passed maybe the sorrow is too covered in dust to properly see what it is but it is still there. It's just harder to see.

I knew that the only thing anybody could do for her

was to let her heal as Mum had said. In the first few weeks, believe, I thought it was too late for her. She didn't eat. She didn't sleep and she looked grey. When she made any sound at all it was usually to cry or occasionally to scream out. In them moments I felt like my heart had caved in. I can't even explain it, blood. It was like a deep, deep pain that felt like all my insides were collapsing in on itself. I felt like a demolition building falling to the ground, where it did that collapsing thing. It was like my heart had collapsed from the inside.

In desperation I decided to speak to Bless about it. She already knew something was up after speaking to Mum so I figured it wouldn't be the end of the world if I spoke to Bless. I picked up the phone and called her. I didn't have no time for small talk so I got straight to it.

'She's in a bad way, sis. I don't know what to do to bring her out of her head.'

'J-just give her time. She will get there on her own. She just needs a bit of t-time,' Bless says quietly.

'I don't think time is going to do it Bless. If anything, time is making the shit worse,' I say, cupping the phone in case Kira can hear me from the next room.

'Maybe right now it is. But in a few days, or a few w-weeks, she will get better. It's like being in a tunnel. You don't know how long it will stay d-dark but if you walk long enough, the light will come. Eventually.'

I didn't know at that time that Bless was right, but I did know that she knew something about being in tunnels so it gave me hope.

But what I hadn't counted on was how long them tunnels could be.

Those were days when she wanted to kill herself.

She asked me to do it for her once and I tell you I would have. She was hurting so badly that I would have done anything to free her from it. If you would have seen her then yourselves, with your own eyes; if you would have heard her crying in her sleep, I guarantee you would have thought about it too. It would have broken me to do it but I would have done it for her. I would have murdered her just to help her to leave the world behind. You don't understand, man, I loved her. I loved her with every cell in my body. I would have done it in a heartbeat.

What saved her, what saved me, in a funny way, was seeing Jamil, the deceased, on the road one day.

Break: 11:30

13

11:45

I know that sounds weird what I said before the break, that seeing Jamil that day saved us. But it's true. This was the day we've all heard about when I called him a waste man. I had been on my way to pick up a few bits of food and stuff for Mum and for me and Kira, when I saw him.

He was just chatting to a couple of girls when he clocked me. As I said, I knew Jamil from just being in the area and shit. We weren't mates or nothing but I knew him to nod at or whatever. So I was going to the shops and he was there on the street just doing his thing. I ignored him as I usually did but this time instead of ignoring me as he usually did, he held out his arm to stop me. He pulled me to one side, away from the girls, like he was about to share me a secret. To begin with he was just whassup and whatever, chit-chat, and then right out of the blue he just comes out with it. 'I hear Kira's back in town. Where you hiding her blood?' he says and grins at me out of the side of his mouth.

My face turns from friendly to something else. I give him this look like I don't even know him and go, 'What you chatting about man? Don't be chatting shit like that at me.' I stand face to face with him just to make him know that I ain't even messing with him.

'Nah blood,' he says, backing away a bit, 'I'm just saying that's all. It's nuffing man. Don't worry about it.'

I am panicking because I don't know what he knows, if he knows anything. Or maybe he's just bluffing.

'Why you saying shit though?' I say to him. 'You know where she is? You even seen her?' I say with anger in me.

He looks at me and moves like he's about to walk away. I can feel he doesn't want to start a thing over nothing without his mans with him for back-up.

'Nah bruv. Relax. I was just you know testing out some rumours. That's all. But it's all cool bruv. If you saying you ain't got her, then you ain't got her, innit?' he says and starts off in the other direction.

'Nah, blood,' I say. 'It ain't cool. Don't be chatting shit about my girl when you know I'm looking for her.'

Truth be told I was panicking, properly panicking. I didn't know how the fuck he had found out but I was scared. As he leaves he turns to give me a I-know-what-you-been-up-to smile. Before he gets too far I call out to his back, 'Waste man.' And then I leave too. As much as he doesn't want to be starting something here in the street, neither do I. But I had no idea that those words that I said just like that would be bouncing back at me over a year later. And causing all this.

*

I don't know how he knew Kira was back, if he even did know. She hadn't even been out of the flat since that day under the bridge. Then suddenly I realized what it was. Since she had been back I had stopped looking for her. That's what he must have been thinking. That the only reason I stopped looking for her was because I had found her. I felt sick about how stupid I had been.

I had to deal with this quickly. I did the shopping and ran back home in a sweat. My mind was going crazy like a hundred miles an hour. I knew that if anyone else believed what he was saying, or even heard what he was saying, that somebody would be knocking my door down any day. I decided that somehow I needed to spread the rumours that I promised to spread; that Kira was taken by some gang-banger. That she was kidnapped by them for whatever purposes. Whatever, just as long as nothing pointed her back to me. I also decided I needed to act like I was still looking for her.

So who knows how Jamil knew Kira was back, like I say, if he even knew at all. Jamil was tied up in all that gang shit himself so it's possible that he heard through the vine that she was missing but I never really got to the bottom of it. I knew he was in a little gang that they called The Squad. I remember they went through a load of names, like Money Squad and SouthEast Squad and whatever, even Flying Squad at one point, like it was just jokes. But as I knew it, it wasn't proper big man gang like Glockz. It was just kids.

I found out later, too late, that The Squad had changed

in the previous few months. It had grown. The shit had started getting serious. Truth be, it might have changed anyway. They probably would eventually have grown up into a full working man gang given enough time. But the thing that catapulted them into the big leagues was just something you could call luck. Bad luck or good luck, it's up to you how you see it. Whichever way you call it though, that luck was all linked in with these guys we came to know as the Olders.

Look this is a lot for anyone to get just looking from the outside. Gangs and shit aren't like in the movies. They're complicated and have rules that don't make no sense to other people from other places. They have history. They don't just come out of nowhere. Before a big gangster was a big gangster he was a baby gangster. And before he was that he was the next thing. It sounds obvious maybe to a person like me but maybe not to you. I grew up hearing about all this shit. It's part of like my local knowledge. Everyone round my ends knows about this. But you probably ain't from my yard so I need to try be clear about this because it matters, for later.

The Olders was like these old-time big drug dealers who got sent down in the eighties and nineties for ten, fifteen, even twenty years at a time. Proper big names who had been into all kinds of shit including guns and armed robberies.

Anyway these Olders started leaving jail at about this time. It was weird but they were like all coming out at about the same time or that's how it seemed to us. Every day an old name would turn up on the vine. 'Oh you heard about Caesar – he out now and looking for a crew.' That kind of thing. And the one thing they all had in common apart from being Olders was that they wanted to get out there and start making some P. You know, 'paper'. Money. But this time they didn't want no risk if they could help it. But they were happy to pay some kids to take the risk for them and sell their drugs for them. On commission. This was where Jamil and his boys came in. This is how they begin to link in.

It became kind of a well-known thing that JC had hooked up with some of these Olders. It wasn't just that his crew became known for it. Really and truly it was *him* that was known for it. People began to know *him*. He became like a, not exactly famous, but just like a known name round our ends. And for why? Because he became about the most highest volume salesman those streets had ever known. I don't mean like those Olders who bring in twenty keys. That's different. But on the street, as a street merch, he was like superstar. But I didn't know that then. Because like I told you, I ain't no gang-banger.

So once he'd got in with one of these Olders, JC turned from a kid who was just interested in pushing other kids around to something like a businessman. Before you knew it he was everywhere. He pushed the stuff wherever he could and nothing and no one was off-limits, not even school kids.

But it was more than that. JC, Jamil, was dangerous, anybody with a mind could see that. Because he was organized. His best idea, and the idea that earned him big money and big respect, was that he was modern and systematic. If there was a lull in one area, he would take his rocks and sell them in some other area. He would go online, find all the schools and colleges in a five-mile radius and hit them all one by one. He would do the schools first for new customers, then the colleges, then a bit later on in the day he would knock on the pubs and late, late at night he would do the clubs. When it was quieter, like early and mid-week when the clubbing crowd was light, he got himself known amongst the crack houses and started dealing there. He had crack dens on his books all over town, you know, places where people could do their drugs without being bothered by no one; places where there was a load of customers all together all wanting the same thing. A crack den is some nasty shit you get me. But it meant that before long he got to know the small-time dealers and the prostitutes who hung out there.

The whores were excellent business for him. He used the same tactics that the Olders used with him. He gave the girls a free rock for every twenty they took and they loved it. The girls sometimes had punters who wanted action and wanted it while they were getting high. The girls got to double their profits and he got to shift even more gear. The boy was methodical I give him that. There was even a rumour that he had a spreadsheet on

127

his phone. His dealer list was electronic. That was a first for street dealers. Most of them just had scraps of paper with numbers on. Jamil had encrypted lists. The boy was new generation, you get me?

Around about this time Jamil started to get proper brazen and was moving gear all over London. Don't get me wrong, he was still small-time, dealing to users mainly, but he was rolling over a lot of rocks. The Olders were amazed by the kid. In the May they had started him off on ten rocks, by August he was taking two hundred rocks a week and driving a new whip. They told him to be careful not to get pinched, because kids with fifty grand rides tended to get pinched a lot. But he didn't care about none of that. As far as he was concerned he had his own crew to watch his back and now it was a crew he could arm.

When he went off to do a trade, he kept a couple of goons with him and there was always a few extra nearby on the end of a phone just waiting for him to say the word. His two main guys though was Shilo, who was just a hench, and Binks who was a shooter. They went where Jamil went and they were pretty effective. Shilo was one busted motherfucker. He was the size of a bus and had a face like it was made of smashed glass – all glued back but it didn't quite fit if you know what I mean. He didn't say much but he wasn't one of them types of people who needed words to get his point over. The other guy, Binks, was the complete opposite but if anything he could have been worse. This boy couldn't keep his mouth shut. He was thin to look at but if you mistook that for weak you'd have been wrong. Seemed like he shoot up people for fun sometimes. If anyone looked at him the wrong way, there was as good a chance that the gun would come out. Probably a Baikal innit?

Sorry. I know. Bad joke. It's proper tense doing this, with you all looking at me.

Anyway, although I didn't know it at the time, round about when Kira was taken up northside, Jamil and his boys started to hit North for serious. It was just a co-incidence. If it had been a month before, then it's possible that none of this would have happened. I mean he might even still be alive today. And that's the thing my brief didn't want me chatting about, coz yeah I know what happened to Jamil, but I didn't kill him. My brief goes to me, it don't work like that, even if that is the truth you shouldn't say this. But I have to, don't I? To make you all see what I seen and feel what I'm feeling innit?

Anyway, Jamil moved into the northern territories and started to shift gear like it was on sale. That was some bold move though, because North didn't like people walking on their grass any more than South did. And it wasn't long before Glockz started to notice him.

They had heard stories of some dudes pushing in on their patch or whatever, but they hadn't yet got a proper look at any of them. Usually when a Pagan – a rival gang member as I told you before – hits another crew's yard, they shout out about it wherever they can. They make a big noise. They tag the street up – graffiti everywhere.

They make their names known. They want to be noticed. For them kind of gangs it's all about reputation. Jamil was different though. As I said he was smart. When he went into new ends, he didn't tell no one who he was or where he was from. If someone he was dealing rocks to thought he was just another Glockz soldier, he just went along with it. Mostly though, no one asked and no one got told; they just wanted a hit. In fact, half the people that dealt with him, if you asked them, would have sworn down that Jamil was Glockz. Just ask them if you like or the police can. Jamil didn't give a fuck either way. He would have told them he was Bloods or Crips if it sold him more rock.

So far he hadn't been cornered by Glockz because he was working some proper hideaway places. He was going to them out of the way crack dens that other people didn't go to. Like he did in the South, he went to schools. He went to colleges. And then just when it was starting to get on top, he'd go back to his ends in South and start trading there again until the heat was off. So it shouldn't really have surprised me that when I saw him that day, he knew about Kira. That fucker had ears everywhere.

After I saw him I went home and sat on my bed for time and just mulled this shit over. It was quite serious. The way I thought of it was this. If one day Jamil gets trapped by Glockz and they started threatening him, all he had to do was start chatting about Kira. 'I know where that Kira bitch is who shamed you innit. I'll give

her up. You let me go rah rah rah'. It would be no time
then before they sent a fucking army to kick our doors
down. They wouldn't need no definite reasons even.
They probably would have done it just on his say-so, just
to make things even after Jamil had pissed on their
patch. You come to North, we'll come to South. All it
needed was the smallest push.

Then, after hours of turning it round and round in my
head, I found the beginnings of a plan. And no, in case
you're wondering, my plan was not to shoot him in the
head.

Luncheon adjournment: 13:05

14

14:15

I needed to go and see Kira's brother Spooks anyway
because I had promised Kira I would see if he was okay.
I knew I could get to see him quite quickly because he
never had any visitors really. Kira loved him but she
would never have gone into a prison just to see her
brother and know that he was there for years more. Nah,
she loved him maybe too much to see him like that. Why
she loved him is anyone's fucking guess.

Spooks though, it turned out, wasn't really in no mood
to give me a V.O., a visiting order from the jail, but he
still had the dregs of a conscience and as he was getting
cleaner, it was getting stronger. He knew his sister was
out there and he knew that someone had taken her right
after he had sold her out. This was causing him untold
grief inside, but so far he had managed to persuade anyone who asked that he had no idea where she was. Glockz
had no interest in her for any like personal reason. They
just couldn't look like they lost her to anyone else and
plus there was always the possibility that she might
inform on them so they were desperate to find her.

As the time had gone by though, these boys were

getting more and more feisty. They were sure that Kira would have contacted him and they were starting to get proper agitated with him. Then when I wrote to him and told him that I had something to tell him about Kira, he agreed to send me the V.O. He couldn't get it to me fast enough.

So there I was, days later, opposite him in a jail. All these hard boys everywhere. Some of them were famous, kind of. Not in the sense that you would know them but I would and the people I grew up with would. There was one guy who had burned his own mum. There was a whole family of cousins and what have you who were all inside for a murder each. Then there was Spooks and people like him. Just junkies that people knew but didn't give a fuck about.

He was already sitting at this table by the time I got through all the searching and stuff. He was wearing like an orange vest thing and was all hunched over. I walked over and nodded at him and he nodded back. I tell you one thing though, given that he was a junkie and given that he was six feet tall and lanky and smelled like an old man, he weirdly looked like Kira. I couldn't put my finger on it exactly. Maybe it was in the eyes or something in the face but whatever it was I wasn't expecting it and it put me off a bit.

'I'll come to the point bruv, it's about Kira,' I goes, looking straight at him.

'What you know about her?' he says, lifting his head at me.

'What do you know?' I ask.

'I don't know nuffing man.' He starts shifting in his seat and is all scratching his arms and shit in a way that makes me itch.

'Well I do know something,' I says. He looks at me and is suddenly all awake.

'What do you know? Blood if you know where she is you better tell me.'

'I know you sold her to a fucking gang. And I know that next man got hold of her. What I want to know is where I can find this boy.'

And he goes rah rah rah, I didn't sell my sister man, it weren't even like that blah blah blah. Then something clicks in his drug-wrecked mind and he realizes what I have said.

'Wait you said you wanna know how to find "this" boy. You mean you know who's got her?' he says all wide-eyed.

'Yeah,' I say. 'I just don't know where the dumb fuck is.'

'Who's got her, blood? This is important,' he goes leaning in at me so I can smell his breath.

'What?' I go leaning away from him. 'You mean you don't know who's even got her? The fuck am I talking to you for then?'

'Bruv you got to tell me. I mean it bruv,' he says and now his eyes are shooting all around the room.

'Why the fuck should I tell you anything?' I say and then I make as if to leave. He holds my arm and pins it to the table. He's got some scared eyes in that head and you can see him now thinking. The wheels are going slowly but they are turning.

'Listen bruv I admit it yeah, I did a wrong thing innit. But I can get her away, you just got to tell me who has her. Who's got her?'

'Fuck man,' I say and pull my arm free. He is beginning to shake from the tension and all I have to do is to let it build up some more. Finally I slap the table with one hand as if I'm fed up with the whole thing.

'You probably find this out anyway,' I say. 'I'm surprised you don't know already. Some Somali boy,' I say. 'This prick called Jamil.'

'Jamil? I ain't never heard of no Jamil. Who the fuck is he?'

I look at him for a long time and make out like I am not about to tell him anything. Then I rub my eyes and say, 'If you can get her back, Spooks, get her.'

'I will I will,' he goes, all desperate, 'but you got to give me details. Who is this fool?'

'Just some boy innit who is running his own squad. He's started dealing over North London. They call him JC. You fucking get him Spooks. Or this is on you bruv,' I goes. And then I actually go.

On my way home I give Bless a quick call.

'Hi, sis. Just me. How's mum?'

'Y-you know, usual. Crazy. How's Kira?'

'Missing you I think. Hard to say. She's a bit better. Worried. I don't know,' I say, not sure what I am trying to say.

'Y-you should all come round to Mum's. Just pop in for a few minutes.'

'Yeah, I can't really do that right now. Maybe in a couple of weeks when things are a bit more chill,' I say. Bless says nothing and I feel like I need to fill in the spaces. 'So what's going on with you?'

'Nothing. Got f-fired from work,' she says eventually in a quiet voice.

'Shit Bless. What the fuck happened?'

'Y-you know Malaika, the one with all them little sisters? I saw her p-putting some lipstick in her bag.'

'And?' I say intrigued.

'And the manager noticed that there were a few missing when she did a stock take.'

'Yeah, and?'

'And I t-told her I had taken it.'

'What do you do that for, Bless?' I say shocked.

'Didn't want her to lose her job.'

'Shit Bless,' I say. But I ain't surprised. No really. This is the kind of thing that she does. Once when we were kids, I remember my mum was proper having a go at her because she hadn't tidied her room. Mum had a high anger in them days. Now, if you look at Mum you would not see it, she has proper chilled with age. But back then she was like an old bomb. She'd go off without warning you get me.

Anyway, so I was playing in my room and all I remember is hearing Mum's voice shouting in Bless's room. I sneak out of my room and look in through the crack of the door. I'm kind of terrified but I'm like ten so I want to know what's going on. Bless is like eight years old, so this is way before he did what he did to her. Dad was off on one of his disappearing tricks again so it was just the three of us. So there is Mum shouting like mad at Bless who is just standing there, looking down at her feet, these fat tears rolling down her face. Mum is going 'What is the point of you, stupid child? I am at work all day long. I still have to make dinner for you ungrateful children and you cannot even have the sense to tidy up your mess. Why are you still standing there child? Go do it. Do it now!'

As Mum leaves the room I dive back into my room so she don't see me. Then in like two minutes Bless comes straight into my room, these tears tracks all on her face. I'm thinking to myself she better get on with it before Mum comes back, and I start clearing up my own mess. But the weird thing she does next is that she starts to tidy my room with me. Then before I can say anything, Mum is back up the stairs and straight in my room and she is angry! She starts proper letting go at Bless. 'You stupid girl. What are you doing that boy's room for when you haven't even tidied up your own room eh? Are you a slow child eh? Do you not have the brains that God gave you?' And then she is pulling her out of my room by her little stick arms back into her own room. Later when it has all calmed down a bit I go and find Bless and she is sitting quietly in a corner of the room playing with some fluff on the carpet. I go over to her and nudge her with my foot. 'I don't get you sis, why you do my room when you know it's just going to make her madder?' And she looks at me with this face I will never forget and says, 'She was already mad at me. I didn't want her to get mad at you too,' she goes and turns back to picking at the fluff on the carpet.

'Bless. You are too good for your own good, sis. You have to stand up for yourself,' I say into the phone.

'It's okay. I d-didn't really like it there anyway. Don't worry. Love to Kira,' she says and I end the call.

In a way, no matter that it was horrible what had happened with Bless, part of me was glad to be thinking of something else. As I got closer to home my mind drifted back to my own life and the visit with Spooks. That day part of me believed, I mean really believed, that my plan might have done the trick. It was perfect in a ways. Here was this little fool from South causing all kind of problems for crews in the North. Stealing customers. Dealing on next man's patch. It should have been enough to shut this ting down. With Spooks on the inside feeding vine to his crew on the outside about where his own sister was at, it was open and shut really. Really and truly it should have been five minutes before they shut that boy down. Didn't even matter that he didn't know where she was. It would have been enough of a thing that he had been roughing up big man's patch. Reason enough to put the boy out and I wouldn't have felt bad about that, no way.

Jamil being dead isn't a bad thing, not even now with

everything that happened do I ever think that. Trust me, he was bad, he was waste, but that doesn't mean I was the one who iced him. For real though, back then I did wish that Glockz would shoot him. I can't lie and say I didn't wish that because I'm only telling you truths here. But that doesn't mean I was the one who did it.

Long adjournment: 15:50

Before: HIS HONOUR JUDGE SALMON QC

Closing Speeches:

Trial: Day 32

Friday 7th July 2017

APPEARANCES

For the Prosecution: Mr C. Salfred QC

For the Defendant: In person

Transcribed from a digital audio recording by

T. J. Nazarene Limited

Official Court Reporters and Tape Transcribers

IN THE CENTRAL CRIMINAL COURT   T2013/0...

Before: HIS HONOUR JUDGE SALMON QC

Closing Speeches

Trial Day 12

Friday 5th July 2013

APPEARANCES

For the Prosecution   Mrs. .... QC
.... Habermann   ....

Transcribed from a digital audio recording by
T.A. Reed & Co. Ltd.
Official Court Reporters and Tape Transcribers
....

15

So I been thinking about my speech overnight, about what I said to you yesterday.

It's funny in a ways, when I think about it. Coz if Glockz killed Jamil, then you could say I was like the whisper that started that shout that ended in him dead. My vine that caught him up and strangled him. I put my hands up to that. I spread the word about Jamil being the one who took Kira. But I had to do that, to keep her safe, you feel me?

So what I should be saying now to you is that because of the words I said to Spooks it must have been them Glockz boys that wasted Jamil as revenge. Case closed innit. Goodbye and good life and hope I never see you again.

I won't lie to you, in the night, I thought to myself, you know what, just stick with the plan, make it easy and simple for everyone. Just go over what I said to you, in my statement, in court when I was giving my evidence. That all I'm guilty of is that I loved Kira so much I had to start a rumour. That I didn't know for sure, but it probably was them boys that wasted JC.

143

But then I thought that if I carry on not telling the truth again now, how do I know for sure you will believe me? Maybe by lying I lose my one and only chance of letting you judge what really happened. Because as dark as the shit is, some part of me hopes that even if you knew the proper whole truth you could still do the right thing. And maybe me going down for the right thing is better than me getting off for the wrong. I still have to live with this don't I?

At the beginning of my speech I told you about the other thing, the thing that could get me killed the second I leave this courtroom. I think I always knew that I might have to tell you about this thing. And I tell you it scares me just even thinking about telling you it. So what is stopping me? I don't have no brief telling me what I need to be saying. He ain't here to cloud your mind and cloud my mind with his words. There's just you and me, and the truth. And this ghost of a lie hanging over our heads. But I think maybe finally, I don't believe in ghosts any more.

This is a hard decision for me, you get me. Because I'm kind of guessing about what you might be thinking and as far as I know you might have been thinking to believe me if I had just kept my mouth shut about the other stuff.

On the other hand you might have gone away, thought about everything in like proper detail and then said, 'What about rah rah rah he didn't answer that?' And then gone, 'Guilty.' Thing is: can I take the risk? I don't think I can take the risk. To my mind I've got this one chance and it's my life at the end of the day. This is hard man. Shit. Because believe, if I tell you this next thing, that might make me even guiltier, you get me? Shit.

Okay . . . Listen yeah?

A few weeks after I met up with Spooks I was at my yard with Kira. She was kind of beginning to warm up a little by then. She felt better now that she knew I had met her brother up and that he was still alive. Plus I told her that the heat was off of her and that the Glockz boys weren't really interested in her any more.

'You're just a random girl to them innit?' I said. 'They got dozens of girls here there and everywhere and they got their own trap-house now anyway so they ain't really looking for that kind of girl no more. They want girls to be making the drugs up and what have you. They producing now. As long as you're off their radar I honestly don't think they give a fuck any more.'

'What about Spooks though? How was he when you saw him?' she says, all quiet. Then out of nowhere, the door goes bang bang bang. Shit. I started flapping like a caught chicken. My first thought is Glockz! They have come for her. That fucker Jamil has opened his mouth already. Shit. Where can I hide her? Shit nowhere. My yard is like the size of a two-man cell.

Bang bang bang again. I run into the kitchen and look for the gun that I had stashed there. I find it. It's still loaded but at least I knew it worked from the time I shot that boy in King's Cross. The door goes again.

Bang bang bang.

The Baikal goes down my waistband. Kira has gone into shock and has started rocking on the bed. I take her by the arm and put her into the toilet and shut the door. I tell her to lock it and she must have snapped out of it long enough to do it because I hear the click of the latch. Bang bang bang! Louder now. 'Don't open your door whatever happens,' I say through the toilet door. I don't know if she hears me or not.

Bang bang bang! Then, someone is shouting something out but I can't hear what. I go to the door. My heart is proper racing. I ain't got one of them little peepholes thing so I don't even know how many there is of them. If I don't do something though, that door's going to come down for sure and we'll be finished. Shit! I decide that I'll open the door quickly. If there's more than one of them I'll shut it again and get my gun out ready. If there's only one? If there's only one, maybe – I don't know. I'll decide later.

I pull open the door quickly just long enough to take a look and then shut it again. Huge man. For a second I think it's Shilo, Jamil's hench. Then I hear my name being called.

Break: 11:00

16

'For fuck's sake, open the door, man. It's me, Curt.'

I open the door. I'm still breathing hard but not as hard as before.

'Shit man. You proper had me going there,' I goes and he comes in without really asking.

'What you doing round these ends boy? You lost?' I say, kinda now laughing but still confused to see him. As he squeezes past me I can feel the muscles in his body slamming into my flesh. The man is a wall.

He takes a seat at my little table in the kitchen-diner and hunches over as he does.

'Bro this is serious. We need to talk,' he says, lifting his eyebrows.

'Sure,' I goes. I push the door shut and then sit opposite him. 'What's happening?'

He looks down for second at the table and then meets my eyes. 'They want her back bro. You have to give her up.'

'Kira?' I say. 'Blood, what the fuck makes you think I got her?'

He says nothing.

'Was it JC? He's full of shit. Don't be believing nothing that comes out of his mouth,' I say throwing my arms out wide.

'Then tell me where she is?' he says, not moving a muscle.

'How the fuck do I know where she is? I was the one looking for her,' I say and get up from my chair. I try to make it sound natural but I ain't no actor.

'All I know bro is that she is gone and they want her back. And if I tell 'em you ain't got her they ain't just going to take my word for it. They're going find you and start asking questions innit bro.' He still doesn't move.

'What questions?'

'Like are you gay?'

'What?' I say sitting back down in my chair and facing him.

'Well if you're not gay, why does your crib smell like Selfridges perfume counter?' he says and looks at me in the eyes once again.

I take a deep breath and wonder whether I can style it out. Then a voice comes out from behind me –

'It's okay. I'm here.'

I look round and it's Kira, standing in the doorway. Her arms are hugging her body but her eyes are steel.

'You're going nowhere,' I say and then I look straight into Curt's eyes. 'You ain't either blood. Not until we work this out.' Then I get out the Baikal and put it on the table.

'What the fuck man?' Curt says. 'You taking a gun out to me? Have you lost your senses bruv?'

'I can't let you take her Curt. I cannot do that,' I say and I know he can see from my face that I am serious.

'This ain't worth losing your life over man. She knows. Let her go.'

'No.'

Curt gets up with a sigh and walks over to my fridge and pulls out a beer. He sits back down and flips the lid off with his teeth and takes a long sip.

'She's going to be okay. They're taking her off the streets now. They just want her to work in the trap.'

'Are you kidding me? She ain't being no one's trap bitch,' I say and look over at Ki to reassure her. She starts to shake her head slowly.

'I'd rather be on the streets. I'm not making drugs for anyone ever again. No way,' she says, pale.

I take a grip on Curt's giant arm and look straight at him.

'No. Turn your mind, you get me. You need a plan B coz plan A ain't flying,' I goes. 'And anyway, why the fuck do you care about what happens to her? You ain't really Glockz. Why do you give a fuck?'

'They're coming here any day bro and I ain't even lying to you, they are pissed. If they see you here or her, they'll burn this whole block down, believe.'

I take another breath and look over at Kira.

'Then we need a new plan A,' I say, and get up and lock the front door.

*

The thing is yeah, it was all very well sending out the message that Jamil had Kira but the fact was that I had misjudged him. Jamil was doing so much trade for the Olders that he was now their number one boy by a street mile. He and his two boys were shifting more gear than whole crews put together. Each week he was coming back with bigger and bigger orders. And he always paid, on the nose, you get me?

Now this may not mean that much to you, but to a drug dealer, payment is everything and not everybody, believe it or not, gets paid. Let me try to explain this . . . If you were shifting ten kilos of gear in kilo loads, you could expect to be paid about ninety per cent of the time. And the ten per cent you maybe didn't get paid, you didn't get paid because you got ripped off or taxed by someone even more gangster than you thought you were.

If you were shifting shit to soldiers in twenty gram loads, you could only expect to be paid about sixty per cent of the time. Why? Because forty per cent of the time the kids you gave your shit to sell for you, smoked it. Then all you could do is punish them, but that did not get you paid. It just got you vexed. But the upside was, if you off-loaded to crews in those smaller deals, your profit was like three hundred per cent rather than the fifty per cent you might pick up dealing in bulk. You following?

The thing with Jamil was that he was buying in twenties at first but it wasn't long before he was buying a whole kilo. But here was the other thing. He was buying bigger deals, but he was still paying twenties prices.

Okay, that must sound confusing.

Basically what you need to know is he was buying enough rock to get it at a third of the price but paying full price. Does that make sense?

So he was buying a kilo but paying for it as if he wasn't buying in bulk, without asking for a discount. That was crazy. Why would you do that? Because as I said before, he had some brains.

On the outside he was saying that he didn't really give that much of a shit whether he was making five grand a week or ten grand a week. To him it was all fucking pocket money anyway, he would say. Once he'd bought a ride and some garms and a few watches or whatever, there was a limited amount he could do with more cash anyway. He couldn't stick it in a bank because people would want to know where he got it from. All he could really do with it was fill up his safety deposit boxes that he had. The rest was just hidden, literally under fucking mattresses, you get me.

He was just biding his time truth be told. That's what he kept saying to anyone who would listen. He was making the contacts and setting himself up so when the time was right he could do it properly. For now, what he needed most was back-up. He knew he was paying top dollar for every kilo he bought. He also knew that meant that as far as the Olders were concerned, he was more or less laying golden eggs for them. And he knew that meant he was basically untouchable. It meant that he was protected.

Now it might be strange to hear that he was paying twice what he needed to. But really and truly that boy weren't making no losses. He was still cutting, you know diluting the drug, and he was selling retail prices so he still made a margin. But for him it was worth it to be paying the extra because of who he was paying the extra to. It gave him proper protection. Ain't nobody was going to mess him up if he was connected to them Olders as their main buyer.

This meant that whenever Jamil came across anybody who he couldn't deal with alone, and by alone I mean using his mans Shilo and Binks, he could just pick up his phone and call in the Older tanks. This put him in a different league. Where the best the others could do if they was in trouble was to call up their mandems from their crews and cause a small-time gang fight, what Jamil could do was something else. He could face down a gang without even having to call it. Because he knew, and anyone who stood in his way knew, that if he called in the Olders they were going to settle the shit in old-timer style.

Now maybe I need to explain this a bit more to you if you don't know about it. There is a big difference between some crew made up of boys having a stab-up in the park and a man's crew.

In a boys' gang, someone fronts you up and you maybe stab him. Then he goes back to his gang and his gang comes out looking for your gang. When they find them, there's a riot. Everyone gets a good beating and then goes home. Minus teeth, or fingers or a gang member if they are really unlucky. Don't get me wrong though, it is still scary shit. You do not want to be in the middle of something like that when it goes down because people are bringing swords and army knives and even shooters to them parties. And people do get hurt. It is serious.

But with the Olders, it was a different kind of a game. These were men as I said before who had been in prison for long and knew their way around. These were people who had actually seen hundreds of thousands of pounds in cash in their own hands. And when someone came to them and tried fronting them up, they knew it wasn't for no feud about who called whose mum a slag. If it happened it was going to be to steal their whole stash. Drugs, money, guns, the lot. And when someone comes after you for what you have spent ten years on the block for, ten years of their life, they ain't going to just stab you up. Nah man. These guys will torture you.

They won't think twice about killing you. They won't even think once about it. And believe, if your mum or your nan or your sister is in the way, they will kill them too. These guys aren't the Krays. These are proper hard men who will kill your mum. And to them, Jamil was like a massive bag of cash and a massive bag of drugs all rolled into one. No way were they going to let any posse fuck with their bag.

So, when I started putting the word around that Jamil had taken Kira, even if the Glockz wanted to, they didn't have the balls to do anything about it. Jamil man, they couldn't touch him. He was protected up to the top. That wasn't the real problem though. I didn't need them to *do* anything about it, I just needed them to *believe* it. If they *believed* that Jamil had taken her they could be vex about it and then forget about it. And most importantly, stop looking for her.

As it was though, now that Jamil was getting to be a top shotter, they preferred to believe him over rumours that I had planted. I can see your faces doing that thing again, jury. Right so 'top shotter' is like our word for top drug dealer. Nothing to do with shooting. Better not be getting them things wrong innit.

Anyway, with him being a top drug dealer, his word was more gold than mine if you like. So they would believe him over anything that some nobody like me might be telling. And it weren't long before Jamil started saying he had heard that I had Kira. Jamil knew about her going missing like everyone round my ends. From me. They all knew I was looking for her like a mad man. I'd been tapping everyone out over it, I was desperate, you get me, and I didn't care in them times, who knew I was looking for her. I wanted people to know. But when I found her and then stopped looking JC got the idea that she must be back. It was just a fucking guess but when he saw me that day in the street and called me out about it, that's when he knew. It was my fucking reaction. It told him everything he needed to know. That's what Curt told me. 'Your face, blood. It gave up the game.' That was when he decided to warn me. They would rather believe that and cut me up than believe Jamil had her and risk their own lives. It didn't basically matter whether I had her or not. It was still better for them to fuck me over just as one of them things. Just for face. They had do someone over for the shit. And if they were too scared to do Jamil then they would be just as happy doing me.

Now, obviously, to you guys it looks proper guilty on my part that I now have a better reason to kill Jamil than even Mr Prosecutor thought I had. In other words that I killed him because he was telling mans that I had Kira. Like a revenge kind of thing. And I know that don't look good for me right now. It *does* give me a reason to want him dead. Fuck I probably did want him dead at that time. But this is the truth. I wouldn't be telling you this stuff against me if it wasn't true, is it? Besides the thing on my mind wasn't getting revenge on Jamil. He was still a nobody really in my eyes. The thing on my mind was getting the Glockz the fuck away from Ki. The rest of the story isn't that much better for me, I will tell you that here and now. Just remember though that my life is in your hands in a way so just hear me out innit, please.

Break: 12:00

17

12:15

It was Ki who came up with the plan actually. I was dead against it, I ain't even going to lie to you, but once I thought about it I knew it made sense. The fact was that Jamil was being ripped off by the Olders and he knew it and everyone knew it. It was like a joke everyone was in on. Now I know boys like him from old. Underneath all the front he was just a wannabe. He was still only a plastic gangster and the thing that mattered to him most of all was the same shit that mattered to all of them boys. Face. Or as Ki put it, 'It's one thing to be ripped off and to pretend you want it that way. It's another thing if his mandems start calling him out about it.'

It was just a matter of time really. Someone was bound to rub his face in it one of these days and what Ki thought was that it might be better for us to do it and to do it sooner rather than later.

I didn't really like the idea of Ki putting together this plan. It weren't that it was a bad plan or a good plan. It was that I didn't want her to still be in this. She was just starting to get back to herself. Every now and then she would open up a bit about what had happened to her. And when she did I felt like the distance that was between us got a little bit shorter. That was really in the end why I let her get involved at all. It seemed to make her more alive. It gave her something to think about. And Kira needed stuff to fill her brain. She was one of them kind of people. Not like me. I'm more a PS3 kind of guy. Switch it on and switch me off. Unless you got a ride you want to sell me I don't need random stuff in my head to keep me interested. So where was I? Oh yeah plan A. The new one.

To kick it all off we needed to find JC. Curt man, I don't know why he felt he had to help us. I mean I know we had been tight but this wasn't his shit and to be honest with you this could have fucked him up a bit with the Glockz. I still didn't know what his deal was with the gang. He was a straight-up-and-down non-ganger all his life – like me – and suddenly he was into a proper crew. It didn't make a lot of sense to me. But the way he told me it then was that he wasn't really *in it* in it. And he was doing his best to get out anyway.

It didn't take me and Curt long to track Jamil down. You could go to any one of the estates round my ends and he had either just left there or he'd be on his way there, in his M3 with his goons hanging out the windows. We decided to go to the Aylesbury. You know the one. It's the one that you used to see at the beginning of the Channel 4 thing innit. Ki told me that it was named after like a rich little town or something which proper would make you laugh if you saw this estate. Hah. Whatever, that's where we decided to go because that was the one we knew best because of Curt living there at one point before he went up to North London.

We walked over there and just hung about for an hour or something before he finally rolled up. It was like five or six o'clock, just about the time that Jamil started his evening shift. We stood by the side of the road waiting for his ride to pull up. Then just as we was talking about maybe jetting, we saw him. He had his usual mandems Shilo and Binks with him, with their heads sticking out the back windows like dogs. He parked up and in a few seconds we could see them as they came bouncing down the path like they were big men.

Curt tapped me on the arm and pointed at them with his chin. 'Check it bro. You think they need some fruit to go with that bowl?' he goes and laughs his bear laugh.

'Idiots innit,' I say.

We hang back to where we knew they basically have to pass us to get by. Jamil comes up first with his boys directly behind him. He sees us and then as he gets close he nods at me.

'Blood,' he goes.

'Blood,' I go back.

They walk by close enough for me to be able to smell the unwashed smell on them. And then just after they have passed us, Jamil turns round like we knew he would. He's that kind of fucker who just can't resist a little dig or something.

'How's Kira?' he says over his shoulder.

'Don't know what you're chatting about boy,' I say and turn to face him.

'Ha,' he says laughing, 'I'm fucking wid you innit. Don't be so serious.'

'I am serious, boy. If you know where she is I wanna know, innit,' I say and put extra emphasis on the 'boy'.

'Don't be boying me. Who the fuck is he to be boying me?' JC says, screw-facing.

He starts looking at his mans as if to bring them into his beef. Shilo takes the signal and walks up to where we are and gets in my face.

'Don't be fucking boying him, man. You boy him and you're boying me. And nobody boys me.'

I take a step back to get away from his breath which smells like a dog's. As I do Curt steps into him.

'Fuck off boy,' says Curt with his arms out like Jesus. He is almost as big as Shilo but in a straight fight I'd put my house on Curt. But I ain't sure Shilo knows what a straight fight even is.

Suddenly Binks is right there. He puts his hand in his pocket and pulls out a lump of metal. I swear down, the shooter was this big. He comes right up and starts pointing it directly into our faces. All I can see is the barrel. It's the size of a drainpipe. I follow the hole straight down into the darkness of it. There is hell in there. I flick my eyes to his face. He's saying nothing with his words but he's saying enough with everything else. That boy was ready to shoot us there and then. I have to do something or this thing is over.

'Yo yo, easy Binks,' I goes. 'We just being friendly.'

Jamil changes colour for a split second, as if he is just realizing how this could go down. 'Yeah put the fucking shooter away, we ain't getting rolled for this waste man,' says Jamil pulling Binks' gun arm back gently. He turns to me. 'You want to be careful about what you fucking say in front of my man innit. He'll shoot you up for jokes.'

'We ain't even looking for beef,' I goes. 'Actually I was just seeing if I could put some business your way.'

He pauses for like a minute like he's trying to think it all through. He ain't sure whether he's being messed with or not. Then finally his eyes go bright.

'Well why the fuck didn't you say so? And so it's no hard feelings blood, first one free,' he says smiling now and reaching into his pockets for a ball.

'Nah man. Not that kind of business.'

'Well I ain't selling fucking trainers.'

'Nah, I mean it is this kind of business but he wants to buy a block innit,' I say pointing at Curt with my elbow.

'A whole kilo?'

'Yeah.'

'Fuck off,' he says and turns as if to go.

'Serious,' I say and just then Curt makes as if to walk off like he's had enough. It feels like I am juggling balls.

Any minute now I think one of them is going to slip out of my fingers.

'Nah man, hang back,' I goes to Curt then I turn back to Jamil. 'Man's good for it.'

Curt stops and waits looking from me to Jamil. He is playing this just right. Jamil and his mans stop in their tracks. It's like they can see money flying around. Binks especially is proper panting.

'Lay it down for me,' says Jamil and then in that moment, I know he's hooked in.

Curt and Jamil huddle together a little closer and start speaking low at each other. At first it's just general chit-chat about prices and shit and then when we notice Jamil beginning to relax, I give Curt a little side-eye and we start reeling him in.

'Nah, let's fuck this off,' Curt says eventually. 'Fifty gees for a kilo? This guy's taking the piss.'

'Take it or leave it man. You'll get fifty a gram after you cut it up innit. That's doubling up easy. I got to make my own slice though too you get me?' says Jamil, arms folded.

'What purity you giving me though? Eighty per cent?'

'Fuck off. Forty.'

'Forty per cent and you want fifty K? Do I look like I just came out my mum? I can get eighty per cent for fifty K no problem. What kind of fucking slice you carving up blood?' Curt leans over him using his huge bulk to intimidate the man.

'No way you can get eighties for fifty K. No fucking way.'

'I can even get *you* eighties blood. Sixty K if you want it.'

'I'm selling, not buying,' says Jamil pretending he's all cool about it but you can tell from his face that he is interested.

'You got to buy though innit? You gotta buy and either you ripping me off or you being ripped off. Simple as that. Tell you what though, I never took you for a kid. Mandems telling me you connected and you just a kid selling street deals. Soldier innit,' says Curt and then he nods at me and walks off. 'Let's bounce.'

As we walk off I see that witness who came into court saying that she heard me arguing with Jamil. I didn't even know she was there till I saw the CCTV. But when she came into court I realized that I know that girl from time. She's okay, you know. Now I can understand why she might have thought that it was a bit on top at this point. There were plenty of loud words being spoke and bare waving arms so I don't blame her for what she said. In fact to my mind she is kind of a witness in my favour. What she is saying kind of proves what I am saying. There was an argument. Well kind of an argument but what she don't say is what it was for. What I can do that she can't do is to say that.

Anyway, there is a few seconds as we are walking away when I am thinking to myself have we blown it? Curt is whispering at me, telling me, 'It's okay, it's okay, he's on the hook', and to keep walking, but I'm not sure. Then as we are nearly on the road, Jamil comes jogging up, shouting for us to stop.

'You got a deal then blood,' he says. 'Fifty-five K. Eighty per cent.'

'Sixty,' goes Curt, 'I ain't unloading a kilo for five K.'

'Okay sixty,' Jamil says not missing a beat. 'How long you need?'

'You got the dollars? Next week then. Where you want to do it?'

'Nah, tomorrow man. I got the P right now. At one of my yards,' says Jamil and points vaguely in the distance like his place was just there.

'Nah man, too soon,' says Curt all calm. 'Okay three days. My yard. I got a trap going round the block. These are my digits. Check me laters,' says Curt getting out his BB, you know, BlackBerry, as he's speaking.

There's a few seconds where no one is talking. Jamil's got his head down typing in Curt's number. Shilo and Binks are just watching but you can tell they're feeling useless. Finally Jamil looks up. 'Who's your crew?'

'Glockz innit,' Curt says.

'Guess your crew don't mind getting their girls jacked if you hanging with him,' he says, pointing his head at me.

Curt shrugs his huge shoulders like he doesn't give a shit one way or another.

'Unless you Glockz too?' he says turning to me.

'Nah man, I ain't rolling with no crew. I'm just giving my mans a bit of a favour. I ain't part of this. And for your FYI, I ain't got Kira. But I am looking for her, blood. So if you know anything . . .' I goes and with that

I was gone leaving the two of them to work out the details.

Later that day Curt met me up and told me it was on. 'All we need now is a trap,' he says.

Luncheon adjournment: 13:00

18

So just before lunch I was telling you that Curt says we need a trap. By the way if any of you lot have like a spare sandwich or something the food in the cells is proper rank! No, no I was kidding I'm okay really. Just got to like lighten this tension. I been pacing as much as a man can pace in a cell that small. It feels good to tell you the whole truth, but it's making me proper on edge innit.

Where was I? Yeah we needed a trap. I can see you all looking confused. I know it's quite a lot for you to take in but I need to make sure you got me. Right so the thing of it was this, if we could make Jamil think Glockz had done him over, then Olders and Glockz would start some kind of war, and then the pressure would be off Kira. The plan was supposed to be simple really, which I could laugh about now if the shit hadn't got so dark.

Ki's plan was we would dress up some blank yard as a trap-house, a drug factory set up in an empty flat, which basically meant putting a lot of white powder around like we was cutting up gear. Just to give the impression of a legit set-up. Then when Jamil came and saw that the place looked right, and started to relax I would come out of the shadows and knock him out. Then we could tax him and take his sixty grand. And when he came to, Curt would send him on his way with a Glockz sticker on his head.

It was perfect really for all kind of reasons. For one 'taxing' is a known thing that happens. Drug dealers get ripped off by other dealers. It's a common thing that we know about on the streets. You lot don't know it because who reports to the police that they just got their class A jacked?

Anyway this was a sure-fire way to get his Olders sure fired up. Nobody was going to fuck with their number one shotter you get me? And then nobody would have any time to be worried about Ki. Like I was saying, the Olders were fucking brutal and we fully expected them to do a job on the Glockz and we weren't even sure whether any Glockz would be left after that.

Believe me, I really and truly did not want to get involved in all this gang shit. It terrified me. I heard all the same shit everyone heard about growing up. Trust me. I didn't want to be anywhere in smelling distance of that. But if you was in my shoes right then you might have done the same? Have any of you, jury, ever loved someone? I know it sounds like a stupid thing to say. But have you? Really and truly? It's a funny thing, love. I never knew it until I met Ki. But love is a thing that can make you do a thing for them that is exactly the wrong thing for you. It messes your order all up.

I loved that girl, you get me. I would have done

anything to make her even a little bit safer. Even if that meant messing around with the gangs I had tried my whole life to stay out of. But to do that, to keep her safe I needed Glockz to back off. But the only way they would do that was if they was taken out. And if not taken out exactly, if they was in a war with the Olders then that would give them some proper shit to worry about.

And it also meant this. Jamil wouldn't have no one to run his mouth off about Kira to. He wouldn't be telling Glockz who had their girl if he thought they had just jacked him. He would have no reason to. And if Glockz ran into Jamil any time soon, they would be less than impressed about Jamil getting the Olders on to them. Then, who knows, they might have to ice him and then the only person who knew about Ki was out of the picture. It was a perfect plan. That was Kira though. She was a person who had a head for a plan.

I told you lot that this would make me guiltier though. This is like I was planning the murder of other people. And I can't really argue with you there. I got to admit if you asked me I probably would tell you that I properly believed a few people would get killed. In fact I could have practically guaranteed it. But these were gang members at the end of the day. And in my mind they must have done some shit that they hadn't paid for yet and if I was the one paying them out then that was just life. Like I always said, you got to pay for your shit one way or another. No one needs to walk away free of charge.

One of the things that they shove down your throat every day is that people are equal. People believe this shit even though it clearly isn't true. You even know it ain't true but you still believe it. Or you say you believe it. But if you are honest with yourself you don't believe it any more than I do. It's bullshit. In my eyes a drug dealer isn't equal to a normal person. He ain't even equal to most criminals. Most criminals do some shit and deep down they know that the shit they are doing is wrong. You rob someone, you know it's sly. You thief something out of a shop even, you still know it's wrong even though you might tell yourself they got insurance. You know it's wrong because it's not your shit you just took.

A dealer fucks up people's lives and doesn't give a shit even while he's doing it. He don't give a fuck if he's selling to adults or children. He don't care if a child becomes a prostitute at the age of twelve just to get a score. It ain't none of his business. He's just after the dollars. As far as he's concerned if mans stupid enough to take it, mans deserves what comes at him. So do I feel guilty about hoping that some bad men were going to rough up some other bad man? No. Not a fucking bit.

Sure, life is life and all that but at the end of the day, if they live, they probably take out twenty good lives each. A way you could look at it is I am saving lives. It wasn't how I was looking at it exactly at the time, but to me they weren't really lives worth crying over. You could show them someone who is now a crack addict because of them and they would be like, nah man, they a crack bitch because of themselves. Even if they sold the drugs to them in the first place. It's not a real human being is it? Where is the human in that being? Nowhere. But at the end of the day, as long as I didn't pull no triggers, whatever shit went down is not on me. That's how I see it. You pay for your own.

So getting back to the thing of it, one of the problems in the plan and there were a few of them, was that Curt was going to be exposed. Jamil knew him now and if he had to he could name him and pick him out. And if he picked him out to the Olders they'd probably merk him. Kill him.

If Glockz found out that Curt had taxed someone like Jamil and they wasn't in on it, they would probably ice him too. I wasn't that happy about two lots of very bad men looking for him. We discussed the situation back at my yard the day after the meet with Jamil. But the funny thing was, Curt weren't that bothered about it.

'I need to get out of this shit anyways blood. It's all getting a bit on top, you know what I'm saying?' says Curt and pulls up a chair around my little kitchen table.

I take up a seat next to him and Ki stands behind with her hands on my shoulders like she's giving me a massage but has forgotten to do the actual work.

'They're going to find you though whether you want to get out or not,' she says.

'Yeah well they ain't going to look for me in Spain is it?'

'Spain?' I goes. 'What the fuck you going to do in Spain?'

'The way I'm thinking about it, I ain't putting my head on the block without a little something innit,' Curt says and gets up and helps himself to a beer in the fridge.

'I don't get you,' I say and look at Ki for some clue. She doesn't seem to have one and pulls up a seat next to me.

'When we tax Jamil, I'm taking the dollars. Sixty long is going to set me up in a bar or something out there or if not there I'll keep moving,' he says and takes a long swig of his beer. He looks at me all the while to see whether I'm going to start arguing about the money.

'Fair enough,' I says. I weren't interested in the money anyway. For me taking the money was nothing but a pain in the arse anyway. What would we have done with it? What could we have done with it? I just wanted Ki safe, that's all that was on my mind. And since Curt was helping us out it only felt right he should get whatever he wanted out of it. We couldn't do it anyway without him.

'So where we going to set up the trap-house?' Ki asks. Her eyes have got some colour in them again. They ain't quite like the diamonds they used to be but they are getting a bit of sparkle back. I reach over and touch her arm. She doesn't flinch. Which I think is the first time since this all happened that she hasn't.

'I still got my old yard. There's a few people using it from time to time, but I'll get it cleared and we can set it up,' Curt says. He drains the last of his beer then scrapes back his chair and gets up. I think he's leaving but he walks towards the sofa, sits down heavily on it and then switches on the TV. He just wanted to change the subject, I reckon. You could tell he was tense. We all were.

The next day when we got to Curt's old yard my heart proper sank. There was no way we could pass this place off like a den. It was just too normal. Sure it was a bag of shit, but it was a dump like a student house is a dump. It still looked like a place that someone lived in or could live in. The door opened to a big square room with steel-framed windows. There was some curtains up but curtains like you never see these days with flowers over them and made of some shiny material. There was a mattress right in the middle of the room with a duvet on it and against one wall an old table with drop-down edges which had all plates on it. There was all kind of rock posters on the walls from fuck knows when and the place smelled rotten. It smelled really and truly like the inside of my trainers.

To the left there was a small kitchen which still had like cabinets from the sixties in it with no handles on the doors just like metal tracks going along the tops and bottoms that you pull at. There was one of them ring cookers which probably once was white but right then it was mainly the same colour as the inside of the oven. The sink was probably there somewhere but you couldn't see it for takeaway boxes and bits of rotting food.

To the right of the main room there was the one bed-room. It had a window in it but it looked out on to a brick wall so there was not much light. It didn't matter anyway since the room was just full of random junk that you probably didn't want more light to see.

There was an old flat-pack wardrobe which looked like it was trying to go back to being flat-pack again. An old mattress was stood up against one wall but had slipped so it looked more like it was sitting against it than standing. The middle of the room had all kinds of shit in it like a bike and one of them frame things for drying clothes and just boxes of tapes. There was even a bit of pushchair or something in amongst it.

There was a bathroom off to the side. That was it.

It wasn't what was in the place that was the problem it was just the normality of it all. It didn't give you the feeling that people could be cooking up crack in there. It was too boring. That's the worst thing about council blocks, worse than all the noise you hear at all times of the day, worse than the leaking pipes and the fact that all the stairwells smell of piss. For me the worst thing was that right there. It was fucking boring. You live in a place like that and all you want to do is spend all your time out of it. In more ways than one.

'This ain't going to do it,' I goes. 'Fuck.'

We sat on the mattress on the floor, me and Curt. I was half wondering whether something was going to crawl out of the duvet so I couldn't really relax, though. I could tell he was thinking the same thing that I was, both about the rats and the yard, and he shifted on the mattress like it was alive and then got up.

He stood in the middle of the room and stared at the yellow ceiling as if there was some writing up there that spelled out what to do next but he couldn't read it. We was fucked and he knew it.

It was Ki though who came up with the goods. She looked around for a few seconds and then she started coming alive.

She started walking round the place quickly waving her hands in the air as if she was creating stuff out of it. I looked up at her. She had this look in her eyes that changed her face. It was the same look she always had when her brain was in gear. The whites went really white. The pale irises became dark and dangerous. I knew then whatever she was about to say, she was about to say it fast.

'No this is perfect,' she says. 'It just needs work. You got pans?' she adds walking into the kitchen. She comes out making a face and then says, 'There are three big ones in there under all that crap. Get 'em, clean 'em and start clearing all the crap away from the stove.'

'What, you want us to clean it up?' says Curt with a kind of puzzled look in his eye.

'Not exactly. Just make it look like it knows what it is,' she says.

Me and Curt look at each other with like a what's-she-on-about kind of look. Ki shrugs her shoulders and lets out a sigh as if she is talking to idiots, which might not have been that far off the target.

'A trap-house isn't just a dump for no reason. It's a dump with a purpose. You have to think of it like, I don't know, a building site. There's stuff around. It's a mess. But the stuff has to be there for a reason. So unless you got better things to do guys, you better step to it. Now!' she says and starts walking around again with her hands making shapes in the air and shouting out orders.

Curt gets up, a little dazed. He's never seen her like this before and even though I have a few times before, she is on fire this time.

'Fill them with water, get them on the stove. We need that water boiling. Add some bleach. You got some bleach right? That table, put it in the middle of the room. You need a big space around it. That table is your workshop. Everything else in the room – and I mean everything – must go. Get it into a different room. Just pile it up. No, leave the mattress. Windows. Pull those curtains off. They don't look right. Tape the glass all up with newspaper instead. Tape up that ventilation brick up there. Now powder. You need something that looks like it's a cutting agent. Vim. Curt, run down the shops and get some Vim. If there's no Vim get something called scouring powder. And some baking soda. As much of it as you can get. We need lots of white powder. Epsom salts. Anything like that.'

'Fuck babe,' I says properly stunned. 'Where the hell is all this coming from?'

'There's a shop down the road, I saw it when we were driving up.'

'Nah babe. I mean all this. Like how do you even know what it should look like?'

'You don't want to know,' she says straight away. Then after a pause she sighs and says, 'I got taken to a couple of traps when I was with those bastards.'

'Why they take you there?'

Ki ignores me as if she hasn't heard me and then says just as Curt is out of the door, 'You need some girls. In masks.'

'Okaaay,' I say, 'maybe I can find a couple.'

'No clothes.'

'What?'

'So they don't steal nothing,' she says and looks at me dead in the eyes.

Shit.

'Ki. I'm so sorry,' I say, and I am.

Break: 15:05

19

So just before the break, I was telling you about the trap-house we were making.

Anyway the trap-house we made wasn't no trap-house that would fool anyone who had ever seen a real one, but we were counting on Jamil never having seen one. Of course he was picking up a kilo from the Olders when he had to, but word had it that he met them in their Mercs in a car park. They trusted each other by now so it wasn't really a problem for them to do business like that. But they weren't about to let him into their factory.

For this to work though, we needed to persuade Jamil it was a legit set-up. It didn't have to be perfect but it had to be good enough to pass a casual look. The plan was to get him through the door, past all the powder and the operations, and into the back room. As long as it felt right, he wouldn't ask no questions we reckoned. He was still a boy after all. He was still a plastic.

When the day came we had the yard looking like it was a den. The place smelled of bleach and all other kinds of chemicals and there on the table in the middle of the room was a pile of white powder, soda mainly, some scales, some little plastic bags, a few razors, that kind of shit. The windows were all covered and the single bulb in the middle of the ceiling made a giant glow on the table but shadowed out edges of the room. I thought it looked the part, but then I'd never seen the inside of a crack house before. Curt was happy with it though. And Ki. And they knew what was what, though for different reasons of course, even if I didn't.

The only problem was the girls. There weren't no girls we could count on who we wanted to bring into this shit. We thought about all the girls we knew but the only ones who would be willing to do this kind of shit were basically drug whores and they were too fucking unpredictable. There was no telling what the fuck they might do. I decided that we would just have to do without them. There was no other choice.

'We could just say they're on a break or something innit?' I say.

'A break? This ain't fucking McDonald's man. Those bitches don't go on no breaks. And they definitely don't go on no breaks at the same time,' says Curt as he gives the place a once over.

'Well there ain't nothing we can do now is there? He'll be here in about ten minutes. Ki you better make tracks. Now Ki!' I shout out at her in the kitchen where she is boiling up some pans of water.

'And give me them masks,' I go, 'at least maybe we

can have them lying around or something.' These were the mouth masks that if this was a real trap-house, we would be wearing to stop the powder getting into our lungs while we were cutting it up. I had bought them for the girls to wear but as I say, we couldn't find no girls.

'And the aprons,' I add.

I spend a few minutes trying to get the plan straight in my head in the little time I have got. We got the room ready. We got masks and aprons though we got no one to go in them. I got the gun.

The Baikal makes me feel a bit like I don't know who I am but at the same time I feel almost complete with it. A part of me doesn't know how I will be able to live without it in a way. The fucker is still whispering to me but me and it have come to an understanding about it. I ain't going to use it. It's just there as a back-up, like a third man. Although it is possible I might give him a whack on the head with it. You know, if needs be.

Just then Ki walks in wearing a baseball cap pulled down low over her eyes and one of them white masks over her face. For a second I almost laugh out loud as if she is just pissing about. Then I look again and see the rest of her and immediately I start seeing all kinds of colours, not just red.

'No fucking way,' I say. 'No you ain't doing it.'

She pulls her mask down. 'You don't know what I have done. You do not tell me what I can do. I am doing this.' Then in a different voice she adds, 'Do you even have a choice?'

I look at Curt hoping that he's going to say something, but he has this look like, she has just done the only obvious thing there was to do.

'Come on man, tell her,' I say.

'She's right bruv,' he says and puts his palms in the air.

'Well at least stop fucking looking at her, dude,' I say and throw her an apron.

'I still haven't agreed to this Ki. Put the fucking apron on please while I think.'

'There's nothing to think about,' she says and right then there's a knock on the door.

'Fuck he's here,' I say and dart into the back room and get flat behind the door. I touch the Baikal to make sure it's still there and then I look around for something to put in my hand. I find the metal bar bit of a dumb-bell in amongst the wreckage in the room and weigh it in my hand. It feels solid, but too heavy maybe.

My heart starts doing its thing. Bang bang bang. I wait for a minute and then hear the front door opening. Fuck this shit is too quick. Then I hear Curt's voice. Then Ki's. That is the strangest part. Ki should have her mask on, bent over the table. She should not be saying anything. She should be playing the role of a beaten-into-submission trap girl, not chatting up the punters. I start worrying for real now. I should have pulled her in here with me. What was I thinking?

I steal a look through the crack of the door but can't really see anything. Curt's massive body keeps getting in the way to block the view. Just then a voice is calling out and steps towards my door. The bar is clenched hard in my fist. I can feel the blood leaving my hand and the fingers throbbing, ready. Curt should be coming into my room first. Then Jamil. I need to hit the second head I see. Just then I see it. There is Curt's head leaning into my room, the light from outside making a stripe of colour. Something is wrong. He is calling my name. He shouldn't be doing that. Nobody is supposed to know that I am here, hiding in this room. With a fucking gun in my pocket. Am I being set up?

'Fuck man! False alarm. False alarm. Put that fucking thing down man.'

'Shit,' I say and start deep breathing. It takes me a while to catch my breath again. Finally I say, 'Who the fuck was it?'

'A Blessing.'

Break: 15:40

20

So, yeah, it was Bless. At the door. Man I was furious.
My sister? What the hell was he doing bringing my sister
into this? It was bad enough that Ki was here and now
her? Shit, we had like two minutes and we had no fucking way to get rid of her. I couldn't leave her here. And I
couldn't send her back out in case she bumped into them
coming in.

'Bro. What the fuck we going to do with her?' I say
pulling Curt to one side as I step out of the bedroom
and into the main room.

Curt says nothing but points his chin behind me to
where Bless is standing. She is already undressed and
has a mask on. I can't even look at her. This is fucked up.
How has this happened? Shit. I look at the floor when I
speak to her.

'Bless. Bless. What the –?'

I am proper vexed about seeing my sister there. My
mind is going round in circles. I'm angry and I'm scared
you get me. I look over at Ki at that time to see if she's
going to step up for me.

'It's okay,' she says. 'She's fine. I will look after her.'

181

'Ki what the fuck? Bless? Curt man, what the fuck we supposed to do with these two now?'

'Bro do we have a choice? Boy's going to be here in like two minutes.'

And that was that. There was really no choice. I couldn't have them in the room where I was going to jack Jamil. There was barely enough room in there for me with all the crap in that room. And besides it was the last place I wanted either of them to be. In a room with a shooter. And a shotter.

'Listen, Ki, promise me, as soon as he is in that back room, you throw your coats on and you leave. Straight away. No waiting, no watching, no nothing. Just please get the fuck out, both of you. Please.'

I am almost crying now and I don't know whether it's the tension of waiting to smash someone over the head or the worry of what might happen to the girls. Then the knock comes for real.

Curt is supposed to let them in. Jamil and his mans Shilo and Binks would want to have a quick check of the room, we knew that. They'll check Curt for weapons, Curt will check Jamil. The two bodyguards will then leave. Curt will then come into the back room. Jamil then follows. I bang Jamil on the head. We take the money. Job done.

How Curt told me afterwards about what actually went down was this. Jamil and them had come in as expected to check the place out. I could hear them in the room chatting shit being all loud and proud. At one point Jamil looks at one of the girls apparently and says to Curt, 'You might have to throw these bitches in, innit.'

'Fuck off,' says Curt, 'they're working.'

'Just a quick suck off for my boys in one of the rooms innit, while we doing business?' says Jamil.

'Hey I ain't having your boys in here while we dealing. I got to watch my back blood,' says Curt.

'How you know we ain't just going to roll you over right now?' Jamil says with a cheesy grin.

'That's easy,' says Curt. 'You can't score at these prices and if you want more, you need me. And anyways blood, you roll me and you a dead man. Now get these fuckers out of here and let's do some business.'

Shilo walks out and Binks hangs back a bit to say loudly how they'll be just outside. I am in the back room waiting but even I can hear that bit. Two guard dogs really just making noise. I hear the bolt going on the front door. Then as quick as anything I hear Curt bringing Jamil to me. As they near the door, I hear Curt:

'You got the dollars?'

'In the bag,' says Jamil.

'I want to count it first,' says Curt.

I'm thinking now about Ki and Bless. Somewhere in that room in masks. But no clothes to hide behind. And here I am, with a gun and I am so scared. I hate being here.

Then there is a second where it's like time has stopped. Then what I hear next makes my blood cold.

'Count this,' says Jamil and pulls out a gun.

I can't see the gun at first. All I can hear is that suddenly there's loud banging on the front door. Shilo and Binks are trying to kick the door in. I can hear Ki crying out and then there's the scrape of the table as it goes to block the door. Curt is trying to calm Jamil down. I am hearing what I can and making pictures to fit the sounds but it's patchy and I really want to step out so my eyes can catch up with my ears. Then I hear Curt's voice.

'Easy man. Take the fucking gear if you have to blood. But unless you are prepared to shoot me here and now, I will be coming after you.'

'I am taking the gear blood. And you ain't coming after no one. Do you know who's even got my back? Your shit lickle crew ain't going to do fuck all. Now give me the block man or you eating bullets.'

I hear Curt sigh heavily. 'In here,' says Curt and pushes in through the door I am standing behind. Light floods into the room. I see Curt with his hands out come into view. Jamil follows. Curt suddenly leaps away and jumps on top of all the shit that's in the room and looks at me to do something quickly. But for some reason I feel as if I am walking through jam. Nothing about me can move quickly enough. I see Jamil's face which starts to change colour as if he has realized what is going to happen next. He hasn't seen me yet, but he knows this is all wrong. Then I see his shooter. In my head all I can hear is my own voice, saying 'nine mil'. He brought a gun. For some reason I never thought he would bring a gun.

Just then a spark ignites somewhere in my body and starts the motor. I drop to the floor and swing the metal bar I still have in my hand at Jamil's legs. It's too risky to hit him higher in case I catch the gun and bullets start flying. Jamil screams out then falls down flat. In a second Curt is on top of him, crushing him with his huge weight. It's only seconds before Curt has him knocked out cold. Jamil's gun is still in his hand. I pick it out. It's nice as guns go, nickel-plated Browning. Where the fuck he get that kind of shooter from? I stick it in my pocket. Right next to my Baikal. I almost feel sorry for my shitty gun next to this one. Then I ain't thinking about that no more. Suddenly the only thing in my head is the girls and I am ashamed I forgot them for even a second.

I look at Curt and we run to the front door where there's still the sound of it being kicked in hard. The lock has already gone and the door is splintering. The table has been pushed flush against the door and the girls are doing everything they can to stop it flying open. I don't even see how they got there. All I know is that every scrap of soul they got is trying to keep that door shut. A gap starts to open up as the men behind it are pushing it. Then I see the nose of a gun poking through. Binks is calling out for Jamil, his voice all jumpy and high. As soon as they realize Jamil ain't answering back, the kicks to the door get harder and more violent. The door jumps open and shuts again as the girls push against it. Curt runs across and sweeps the girls away with one arm.

'Go and sit on that idiot,' he says and nods at the back room. 'He's out cold.' Curt takes care of the gap that the men are trying to make by slamming it shut with one huge heave and then sits with his back against it, breathing hard.

I throw their coats at the girls as they head to the back room and then remember something and run after Ki to hand her the Baikal. It's not as pretty as the Browning but I know mine works. 'If he even moves,' I say. Then I run back to help Curt who though he has his whole weight against the table is now straining against heavy kicks to the door. I know we ain't going to be able to hold it for long. I ain't even that sure the door ain't going to split.

I need to think but it's getting slow again in my head. More jam jamming up the parts. All I can think is that the door ain't going to hold for much longer now anyway. I know Ki is watching Jamil but I have no idea what Bless is doing. When I caught a glimpse of her face earlier I swear she was looking at me like this might be the last time she ever sees me. The door bounces again and I know we have to do something quick.

'On three, pull the table away. They'll come tumbling in. You put your hands up high and surrender. I'll get behind the door. They won't be expecting me. I'll take their legs out,' I say whispering, showing him the Browning.

186

Curt nods. He stands and yanks the table back. As they come crashing in, he flings his arms in the air. The two men come tumbling in, tripping over themselves as they do. Their faces are like the perfect picture of surprise as they fall to the floor on top of each other. I am behind the door and they see only Curt with his hands up. Their faces change as they jump to their feet. Binks is holding some fat weapon and has it pointed straight at Curt. The image of it for a second seems almost funny. This skinny guy holding a gun that big makes him look like a cartoon. He's all edgy and has a look like a person who's had too many drugs.

'JC!' he shouts out, keeping his eyes on Curt but spinning his head round the room frantically.

I aim my gun. They are both moving around the room looking for their boy, making it hard to keep them at the other end of my barrel. Shilo is the easier target. He's big. Bigger than Curt even and he moves slow like an elephant. He lumbers over to Curt, probably planning what to do to him. It's going to be seconds, if that, before they see me. Or worse, seconds before they are in the back room where the girls are. Just the thought of them now makes me desperate to go to them. I can't see them and that's making me even more nervous.

Binks then comes in my eye-line but he doesn't see me. I line him up but each time I get ready to fire he moves again. He's twitchy but all I need is one second of still. I get it when he turns suddenly and sees me. He raises his arm with the huge gun and points it at me, I don't want to kill him. I just need to stop the guy. I look at his legs and in that split second I pull the trigger. I pull it once but three rounds go off. Bang bang bang. One catches him in the leg and he drops and hits the deck.

Shilo, who by now is nearly at the door to the back room, looks round stunned. Then in half a second, Curt's huge right hand comes hammering down on top of Shilo's head like he is dunking a basketball and he goes down hard. It's like seeing the Hulk knocking out the Hulk's brother.

Binks' gun has gone skidding across the floor like a delayed reaction. I run over to it and pick it up. It's heavy like a hammer. I walk over to Binks who is clutching his leg. There is blood spurting out of it and his screams are filling the air. I have to shut him up or who knows what is going to walk through that door next.

I pistol-whip him across the head and I'm expecting him to go out cold but instead he starts screaming louder and suddenly he doesn't know what to do with his hands. They go up to his head from the pain of the whack and then the blood from the leg comes squirting out again in jets and they come back down again to stop the blood. I hit him again. Harder. This time though he goes proper out.

Curt starts calling out for tape and I run to the kitchen to get the parcel tape we been using to tape up the windows. Curt starts winding it round Shilo's arms and legs and then he starts on his face. At first I think he's taping up just his mouth but then I see that he's taping up his eyes too. He throws over the tape to me and I start by taping up the bleeding leg. I ain't trying to save him. I just don't want blood everywhere. Then I copy Curt and tie up the legs the arms and then the face. It's not till I have finished off the last of the tape that I suddenly remember the girls. Curt starts walking towards the room as if he has read my mind but then just before he opens the door there is the sound of a gunshot.

I get up and start running to the back room. I can hear Ki screaming. I get there just as Curt has walked into the room. That's when we see it. Ki is holding the hot Baikal and Jamil is on the floor. Dead.

Long adjournment: 16:45

IN THE CENTRAL CRIMINAL COURT   T2017229

Before: HIS HONOUR JUDGE SALMON QC

Closing Speeches:

Trial: Day 33

Monday 10th July 2017

APPEARANCES

For the Prosecution: Mr C. Salfred QC

For the Defendant: In person

Transcribed from a digital audio recording by

T. J. Nazarene Limited

Official Court Reporters and Tape Transcribers

21

10:15

That picture of Ki. That look on her face. That is going to be something that I ain't ever going to be able to forget. Her face had lost all its blood and her wide-open eyes seemed just blank. Like the life was all gone. Like when that boy's life was draining out of him, hers was draining out of her too. I took the gun from her hand and felt its heat burning. That fucking gun. I knew what happened. It had been whispering at her like it had whispered at me. *Shoot. Shoot.*

I asked her what had gone down.

'He, I don't know. He woke up and he went for my gun,' she says crying. 'I kept shouting for you. But you didn't hear me.'

I look at Curt and he shrugs his shoulders at me.

I hold her close to me. 'I'm sorry. I'm so sorry, babe. I didn't hear you with everything else that was happening'

I take the gun from her hands and put it in my pocket. It's still warm. I take her by the hands and lead her out of the room. She says nothing. I don't even think she blinks. As we walk into the main room I remember the two men taped up on the ground and spin her back round to the bedroom again. I hold her face in my hands.

'Ki. Listen to me. Curt is going to go out now and get you a cab. Then in a minute I'm going to walk you both outside. Listen to me though. I want you to keep your eyes shut till I say. Okay? Curt?' I say to him and he turns and leaves straight away.

I look around to find Bless. She is turning round in circles and mumbling to herself.

'Bless. Bless! It's going to be cool. You too. Hold on to me and keep your eyes shut.'

Bless suddenly snaps back into herself and seems calmer and turns to Kira.

'Kira, it's going to be f-fine. I'm going to be with you all the way. Come on now. Let's get you out of your c-coat and into your clothes. Come on baby.'

I turn my head away as they dress and then wait another two minutes before taking them both by the hand and rushing out of the flat as quickly as I can. The scene is like a thing from a movie. Two men out cold on the floor. Blood in places it had no business being. Door with cracks all through it. Shit everywhere. Binks looks like he's asleep but he's moaning like he's having a nightmare. Shilo is knocked the fuck out though, face to the sky.

By the time we get to the street Curt is already standing by a waiting car in the dark. I help the girls in and give a twenty pound note to the driver and give him the address, just trying to sound normal. I nod to the girls at the back and say to the driver, 'Just split up from her boyfriend,' and he nods back to me like he's seen this a lot.

Curt and I run back up to the flat. Shilo and Binks are still there on the ground but they are both coming to now and making noises. The blood around Binks' leg has changed colour and seems to be drying. That tape must have stopped it. Curt and I nod at each other and then go to where Jamil's body is waiting for us. That's the immediate problem, not the two boys groaning in the other room, with their faces taped up like mummies. We had to move him out of there before his mans woke up and realized he was dead.

It was already late at night which was a good thing because it meant that we could move him without being spotted or whatever. Curt and I agreed we would take him one arm each and walk him to his M3, which we knew was probably nearby. Jamil had a gunshot wound in his chest. There was a bit of blood but not nearly as much of it as Binks who'd been shot in just his leg.

'His heart's still pumping, that's the reason,' explained Curt. 'Fuck though bruv, you look like you been shot too. You can't go out again like that. You better hope that driver didn't see that.'

I look down and realize that Binks' blood is all over my clothes from when I was taping him up. It was dark outside though so the driver probably didn't see anything.

I look at Curt who is pacing the floor as if he was trying to work out what to do next.

'Listen,' I say, 'I'll tape JC up to stop the blood. You don't need no blood on you and I'm already covered. Then we can zip him up in his coat and drag him out.'

'Plan bruv,' says Curt and I get to work.

It's pretty messy work taping up a bloody dead man. A little bit of blood makes a lot of fucking mess. I can't tell you how many times I scrubbed myself clean when I got back home, but however many times it was, it wasn't enough to get rid of the tiny speck they found under my nails when they arrested me more than a month later. And when I say I scrubbed, I mean I scrubbed until my own skin was beginning to bleed and then I couldn't tell whether it was his blood on me or my own. I basically soaked myself in bleach that night but no matter how hard I tried I couldn't get the feeling or the smell of the dead boy off my skin.

Once I had taped him up and wiped him down with bleach, I went into the main room and scooped up a handful of baking soda that'd been laid out everywhere and covered all the wet bits on him with it. I more or less covered him in powder until he was dry. The smell of it helped to cover the smell of the blood too. Anyway, I finally zipped up Jamil in his coat and to my mind, I thought, if you didn't get up too close, he didn't look too bad. For a dead boy. I pulled his hat over his eyes and called Curt over.

'Good,' says Curt. 'Now you better get that shit off you.'

I take off my top, which is bloody and covered in powder at the same time and throw it in a bin liner. Just as I am wondering what I am going to wear, Curt hands me his hoodie. It was his hoodie, you get me. An XXL black hoodie with Chinese-style writing on the back of it. You remember. The number three evidence the prosecution has been going on about. *That* hoodie. I put it on without giving it a second's thought. The same one Curt had been wearing three days before when we had met up with Jamil on the block. The witness that saw me that day, must have seen Curt and me and confused who was wearing what. I don't know how that shit can happen but apparently it can.

'Gloves man,' says Curt and hands me a pair of them yellow washing-up gloves. He also puts on a pair and together we stand there for a second looking at each other, wearing these ridiculous gloves. Then without saying anything we take him by an arm each and stumble down the two flights to the ground floor main entrance.

Just before we open the front door, I look at Curt. He is breathing heavy but other than that he seems like he's okay. Calm in a ways.

'What about those two upstairs?' I go.

'They ain't going nowhere. That tape's not coming off any time soon,' he says and heaves the body out into the cold air.

It was the hardest thing man. It was like dragging a bag of cement and trying to keep it upright at the same time. We dropped him a couple of times on the way down it was that bad. Every time we did I kept expecting him to scream out. But he never did. Like for once he was taking his licks like a man.

Once we were at the bottom Curt held him up while I stuck my hands in his coat pocket and waded through used tissues until I found his car keys. Then we stepped out into the cold air, and looked for his wheels.

'Where the fuck are his wheels at?' I say looking around.

'Just press the button, maybe it's got one of them bleeper things.'

I did and suddenly two amber lights wink at us from the other side of the street. There it was, his gleaming M3 right under a tree. Don't know how we missed it.

Now what I really should have checked if I had been thinking straight was his phones. I really should have got rid of them. But I ain't got a murdering kind of a mind, you get me. This wasn't planned or nothing. This was just supposed to be taxing, end of story. Get Ki safe. That's all it was about. Anyway that was my bad luck really. Doesn't matter now though does it? You know the whole story now innit? Oh shit and the hair. My hair in his car. I just never even thought about it. Who would think of hair when you practically ain't even got none on your head? Maybe I should have put plastic on the seats before I sat down, or fucking hoovered the car up afterwards but I just didn't think of them things with all the other things that were crowding my mind. That's how they find you though. What's that thing people say. You can think of some things. You can think of nearly all the things. But nobody can think of all the things all the time. Whatever. You know what I mean.

Anyways we parked up round the back of one of the estates we knew and dragged him out of his car and round the back to like a shed thing where they keep all the bins. We had no clue what to do with him so we just proper dumped him. Like he was just another bag of rubbish. And when he landed on the ground, the thing I remember most is how he made a muffled kind of a sound like he wasn't even really there, like he was far away from his body already. That's the only thing that kept me able to even do it. That I knew it weren't even him there any more. It was just his past.

We put a bin liner over his taped-up body so he didn't stand out and looked back at him. I said a kind of prayer under my breath and tried to make it real but all I could see was rubbish lying there. I remember thinking then about that dust to dust thing and I knew that he was gone.

After we left him, we had to lose the wheels. We didn't want to go too far though because we had Shilo and Binks to deal with still. So I drove a little bit until we saw another council estate and then parked up.

'Here?' says Curt.

'Why not here?' I say getting out.

'This whip? Here? It'll get jacked for sure,' he says, heaving himself out from the seat.

'Exactly,' I say and head towards the main road, making sure I leave the doors unlocked and the key in the ignition.

We dash the gloves into a nearby bin and jump on the bus and back to the trap. We walk up slowly to the big front doors, looking at everything. Just in case. You never know what can come at you. But it all looked cool to us. Everything like it was. We bounced up the stairs and listened at the door for any sounds. Last thing we want is to be jumped by two very fucking vex boys, you get me. I have my ear pressed to the door but all I can hear is Curt's breathing. I give him like a thumbs up and he puts in the key and turns it. As we open the door I half expect them to be gone. But Shilo and Binks are still there, fully awake now moaning and squirming in their taped suits. We ignore them and start cleaning the place up. We basically threw bottles and bottles of bleach around the place until the whole place smelled like a swimming pool. Nothing can survive bleach apparently. Kills ninety-nine per cent of all known shit, everyone knows that. It was only once we had washed the place down that Curt finally looked at me and then at the groaning men on the floor. He pulled me into the back room out of earshot.

'What the fuck do we do with those two clowns?'

'Cut 'em loose,' I say. I just wanted the thing to be

over right there and then. I wanted them out. I wanted Curt out. I wanted me out.

'What if . . . ?'

'They don't know fuck all. They was out cold,' I say.

'Well, eventually they will start to wonder where the fuck their bossman is at though.'

'We tell 'em we delivered him up to Glockz. They might even drop the word to the Olders and start the war themselves.'

'True say,' he says and then walks back into the room and starts to pull the tape off their faces. They scream like girls. Then Curt leans his big face right into theirs and gives them this look.

'Listen you motherfuckers, next time I see your ugly faces, they'll be chewing steel you get me,' he says and drags them to their feet. One under each hand.

'Where's JC?' says Shilo rubbing his head.

'He got some business with Glockz innit. They took him. Now if I was you, I would maybe want to get the fuck out of here before Glockz comes back for your arses.'

Binks is coming to life now and starts getting all jumpy again. Then he looks down at his leg and screams out. 'You fucking shot me man,' he goes to me, crying like a baby.

'Yeah man,' I goes, 'I fucking shot you.'

They make as if to leave but Curt grabs each of them, by the collar.

'Wait the fuck up boys. Curt got some questions for

201

you. And you better think before you give me any bullshit or you gonna follow JC up North.'

Even I am afraid when I hear Curt talking about himself as if he's some next man. I look at him and he nods like he's saying, 'Yeah I know.'

Break: 11:00

22

11:15

So the rest is just details really. We were pretty surprised
that Jamil pulled that shit in the first place you get me.
It weren't even one of them things. It was like, yeah
we expected him to think about trying it on but we
thought even he wasn't stupid enough to cut off a supply
chain at less than half the price of what he was paying the Olders. It was like he hadn't even thought this
shit through.

The thing that amazed us most of all though was that
the bag he brought with him had actual money in it. Not
the full sixty grand but half of it. It was like he weren't
even that bothered about losing the cash. Why risk taking all that cash if all you was planning on doing was
taxing the drugs in the first place? It didn't make sense
to us at first. It couldn't have been as a just-in-case kind
of thing, because there was only half the cash there.

We found out from Shilo that there was no plan to
tax the drugs. The plan was to hand over the thirty gees.
Shilo and Binks would start banging on the door causing a commotion and Curt would be too para to count
it all out and would just hand over the drugs. They had

apparently been actually shouting out 'There's police here!' or some shit, just to hurry the shit up. Anyway then Jamil would be gone with what he thought was a kilo of white and we would be left short. Short but not so shafted that we might want to go to war with the Olders over it. It wasn't a bad plan. But they hadn't counted on Curt. He weren't there to hand over anything without getting his paper first. And when Curt didn't get shook like he was supposed to, JC uploaded his shooter and started a thing which no one could control.

So it was Ki who did it. Now I realize that this shit is all new information as far as you are concerned. I know this, and I know that is not allowed. My QC told me this. He told me again and again. 'You can't say new information. It's against the rules of evidence.' That is why you can see the prosecution QC squirming in his seat. He don't like it. And I don't like it really and truly. I know there is going to be consequences at the end of my speech. Shit is going to happen. But I can't help it. It is the truth. I can't keep you in the dark. These things need light. No matter if it hurts me or Ki.

And I tell you the last person I wanted to get into this is Ki, but since she is far away by now, I figured it was safe to tell you lot about it.

Okay the prosecution might say, why did I not tell the police all this stuff about Jamil in my interview and they could have checked it out. But the truth is that I did not want it coming on top of Ki. This whole thing was for her benefit and I wasn't going to be putting her in the frame for it no matter what. Especially not while there was a chance they could arrest her for it, you know what I mean.

In fact at the time we was doing our best to make sure none of this shit came up at all. We wanted to bury it good and proper. Who the fuck would believe my story anyway? What? Honest officer, we was setting up this drug dealer who was giving it about my girl who some next drug dealers were looking for and we were going to rip him off so that next man's dealers would kill those first dealers and rah rah rah. Besides even if they had turned the place over, although they would have found a lot of shit, they wouldn't have found what they were looking for. They wouldn't have found any evidences. We ended up making that impossible.

After we cleaned the place up, Curt dumped all the shit, the powder, the bleach, the clothes and whatever, while I went back to my yard to see about the girls. I had no idea what sort of state they was in, so we made a plan that I would go straight there in a cab with the cash and Curt would meet us once he'd got rid of what he had to, including JC's silver Browning. We looked all over the place for my Baikal but it was nowhere to be seen. At the end, we figured maybe Shilo or Binks had taken it, somehow. Or maybe it got caught up in the other shit we had bundled together for dumping. Either way it didn't matter to us as long as it was gone. Sure I had touched it. And sure Kira had touched it but neither me nor her had any criminal records so the Feds didn't have our prints anyway. So whilst they might pick up some marks from it, if they found it even, unless they had us, they wouldn't be able to do no matches. Just as long as we didn't leave nothing that could lead them to us. And we didn't think there was. We was being careful. Or you know, we thought we was.

When I got home, only Ki was there. Bless had finally agreed to go home to Mum's after Kira had convinced her she was feeling better. Ki did seem better truth be told, in the way of not being so shell-shocked. But something else was in her now. She was talking a hundred miles an hour and making lists in her head and then spilling them out of her mouth.

'What did you do with him?' she says at one point.

'Better for you not to know,' I say and start looking around for something strong to drink.

'What about the others? Did you do something else to them?' she says. Her body is shaking as she is talking. But like a nervous energy thing rather than a fear thing so I feel a bit more okay about her. Kind of.

'Nothing, babe. They fine.' I find some rum and pour out a shot for us both into some mugs. She takes a sip and makes a face.

'What about your clothes?' she says clocking the massive hoodie I'm wearing.

'Ki. It's fine. Curt took care of it. Just. I don't know. You got to just park all that shit away babe. Nothing going to link you to this thing. I swear down.' I take her hands and she looks down at mine.

'Blood,' she says.

I look at her blankly. She never calls me that.

'Your hands. Nails. There's blood. You have to wash it. Wash it all off. There's a nailbrush there under the sink. Do it. Do it now!' she goes getting all frantic again.

'Okay,' I say, and swallow the rest of the rum and head to the bathroom. I spend the next twenty minutes scrubbing as much as I could of the whole night into the plughole. But the shit just clung on. All around me all I could see was shreds of that night.

Anyway I had just got out of the shower when the doorbell went. Ki went and let Curt in. I dried myself off and then joined them in the kitchen. Curt was a bit wired but the spliff he was toking was getting the better of them nerves. Ki still looked white.

'Shit I am worried about the yard man. If those boys let on about the place to anyone, we are fucked. Especially you,' Curt says passing me the spliff.

'Why?'

'The place is dripping with blood man.'

'But we bleached the place down,' I say getting up from my chair.

'Don't matter that we washed the fucker down. Blood and DNA has a habit of hanging about.'

'You're watching way too much *CSI* man. Anyways they don't have my DNA on record innit? Or Kira's.'

'Sure enough. But they do have mine. And if those jokers Shilo and Binks get caught up in something and they name you for this murder? Any DNA in that place that matches yours or Kira's is going to get them out of a hole and you in one.'

'Fuck,' I say and sit back down. I hadn't thought about that at all. It wasn't just what DNA the police had on record it was also about if anyone lined me up for the murder. Then I would be fucked. It was Curt's place so he could explain his own DNA. But mine wouldn't be so easy and I didn't fancy having to say that I was anywhere near it. Let alone that Ki was.

'So what do we do now?' I say.

Ki then gets up from her chair to go and open a window to let some of the spliff smoke out. As she comes back to the table she looks at us both with something like fear.

'There must be something you can do,' she says.

'What like?' goes Curt.

'For a start,' I say, 'we need to get out of London. Maybe even out of the country. I'm thinking like Spain even.'

'And do what there? Live on what?' says Ki raising her voice at me. 'What are we, the Great Train Robbers?'

'Well, we got that bag of cash that Jamil brought,' I say. 'Should help us all to just keep low for a few months. Just till we know that they ain't looking for us.'

'Which brings us back to the DNA, fam. What the fuck we going to do about that?' says Curt taking a long drag of his spliff.

Then I get a brainwave, or half of one.

'Get your mandems back in the flat,' I say.

'What the fuck for?'

'You want it to be occupied if the police ever turn up there. If it's empty, it's just going to look like a crime scene. If there's people there, it just adds more shit into the mix,' I say.

Curt considers this for a second and then nods slowly at me.

'I'll get on it,' says Curt and picks up his phone.

'Wait. There is a better thing you can do,' says Ki, the edges of her eyes white again.

'What?' we both say.

'In a way it's what you just said,' she says looking at me. 'Add more shit into the mix.'

We look at her puzzled until she makes it clear.

'Drown the place in DNA.'

Everyone has a mate round my ends who either is a barber or who knows one, so getting hair clippings was easy although I did get some strange looks. But barbers are weird anyway so you have to be doing some proper bare weird shit before they draw the line. Anyway, once we got enough of it together, Curt and I went up to the flat the next day with a bag of clippings and scattered it around everywhere. It was disgusting, true. But if there was hair DNA to be found, there would be strange results coming up from any test you get me? Sure the police might find my DNA if they happened to look, but if there's DNA from a hundred boys in that place then no way would they get a case to stick. I mean I ain't no lawyer or nothing but it sounded tight to me.

*

Getting blood was obviously a bit more difficult but we did. At first we spent the afternoon getting bits of meat from the halal meat shop and smearing the walls with it but you can't get much blood from butchered meat it turns out. Then Curt remembered that he knew someone who used to work in a chicken slaughterhouse and later that evening we had a gallon of chicken blood in a bucket. I asked him what he told the guy he needed it for but all he said to me was, 'You don't wanna even know blood.'

I tell you what though, that shit smells like dead chicken blood should smell. But we took it and even as it was gelling up, we rubbed the whole place down with it. Then, once that was done, bleached the place all over again. Trust, whatever any CSI or whatever found there, it was going to confuse the shit out of them. That was for real.

We spent the next day on edge. I can't even tell you. It hadn't really hit us at the beginning that somebody had ended up, you know what I mean, dead. Even when we was dumping the body on the estate, it still didn't hit us. It was only once all the work was done, all the hair and blood and cleaning up, it was only then that it hit home. I remember it vividly.

We was sitting at my yard round my table, Ki was still in the zone. A hundred things to do. Number one on the list of which was booking tickets for us all to Spain. We could only get two tickets out straight away, the third one had to wait for another couple of days. We agreed that Ki and Curt needed to get away the quickest. Ki because she was now in the frame for this as the shooter and Curt because he had no other place to go. His yard here in South, the one we had made into the trap, was way too hot. His yard up in North London was being banged on every hour by Glockz who were now starting to get on top. His phone had been ringing off the hook with threats and even his mum was chasing him down. So they needed to jet urgently.

'The shit is getting hot on top, fam. I can't even tell you. Glockz chasing me down every two minutes,' Curt says after ditching yet another call.

'How the fuck those boys nail you for this so quick?' I say.

'Probably them two innit. They must have gone running straight out of the trap to the Olders. That was the plan though,' he says walking to the fridge and picking out a pasty before dropping it whole into his mouth.

'But so soon? And not knowing your name. I mean,' I say turning to face him.

'Yeah you think you need to know my name to pick me out?' he adds holding his arms out so that he looks twice his normal size. 'We should have fucking iced them bruv.'

'Fuck man,' I say. 'That ain't us. We ain't about all that shit. Sure a boy got merked but that was not something we like aimed for. That shit just went wrong. And I know you Curt. You're not a gangster no matter if you linked in with this crew.'

He throws himself into a chair next to us at the table.

'Yeah man, I know. I'm just prang innit bruv. Glockz

211

is heartless and I don't want to know what they got planned for me.'

'It's okay bruv. We getting you out of here soon. And for as long as you need. Or as long as thirty gees can keep you in meat.'

The cash weren't exactly straightforward though. We couldn't just stick it in a suitcase and jump on a plane with it. It needed chatting out properly. Then, as we were physically handling the money, counting it up and dividing it up, the whole thing hit us. One by one. Bang. Bang. Bang.

'He's dead,' says Curt.

I look at him like he's gone mad. 'We know,' I say slowly.

'Nah man. I mean he is dead,' he says, rubbing his face. 'I mean he was alive one moment. Now he is just gone. Everything that he knew is still here. But he himself, he is just gone. This money here, was here and it's still here. He was here with this money. Now the money is here and he ain't. He's just like disappeared. He is like proper gone, you get me?'

At first I carried on looking at him as if he had lost his mind. Of course he was dead. We had just spent the whole of yesterday covering the flat with hair and chicken blood. Did I get him? No. I didn't get him. And then just as I was about to say all that, I did. For the first time I got it. It just slotted into place like a piston into a cylinder bore.

Weirdly it was Ki that got it last. Then again, the shit she had been through kind of turned the world on its head. You have to forgive her a bit for that. Also, she was the one who was doing all the follow-up shit. She was the one booking the flights. She was the one getting the passport details. She was the one watching the news for updates and trawling the net for any information on Jamil aka JC, R.I.P., and whatever. I suppose for her brain, the thing hadn't properly finished happening yet. It was still going on. Then when she made the final flight confirmation and sat back and looked across at us. She got it too. Bang. Those white lights in her eyes were gone and suddenly she was sobbing. Crying enough tears. Enough tears. Enough for all of us I reckon.

But then this next strange shit happened that changed everything.

Ki and Curt were going to be flying off the next day. It had to be quick. So quick that we was happy to pay nearly four times the normal cost of the ticket. Anyway I planned to go with them to the airport to see them off. We were all pretty on edge still and I don't think that we maybe had three hours' sleep in three days.

In fact those three days felt like three weeks. Every second seemed to stretch out so that you could fit a hundred thoughts into every one. Thinking was the thing we did mainly. Nobody spoke if they didn't have to. It was like if you did, you somehow were bringing Jamil into the room. It was bad enough he was in my head twenty-four seven. All taped up. Covered in bleach and powder and bin liners, sitting by those bins like a sack of cement. But I couldn't bring him into the room. None of us could.

Nothing in those three days had any, like, innocence to it. If someone switched the TV on it was like we were looking for news. If anyone went for a shower it was like they were washing the blood off. Even the washing up felt like we were doing some wrong shit. It was like the more we were skirting round it the more it just came up and slapped you in the face. Once it just got too much and I came right out with it.

Curt and Ki were sitting with the TV on. No one was watching it really, it was just background. Ki was looking like someone had died. Which weren't really surprising but I couldn't handle seeing her like that.

'It ain't your fault Ki,' I say into the air.

'I don't want to talk about it,' she says staring at the TV.

'It could just as easily have been me.'

'But it wasn't you. It was me,' she says turning to look at me.

'Yeah but what I'm saying is it could have been. And at the end of the day he pulled out a gun and if you do that you got to be prepared to be shot.'

'Is it really that easy for you?' she says, eyes blazing in her pale face.

'For real. I'd have shot him if I had to.'

'But you didn't. I did. And you haven't even asked me why I shot him.'

'I don't care why. He deserved it.'

'It's all so black and white for you isn't it?' she says standing up. 'It isn't for me. A man is dead because of me.'

'Nah, Ki. A man is dead because of *him*.'

'I killed him though. Do you understand that? That's the bottom line.'

'It ain't that black and white either though is it?' I say standing up too and taking hold of her elbows to pull her near.

'No it's not,' she says breaking free, but the heat is all gone from her voice suddenly, 'but you don't seem to believe in grey areas.'

I start getting angry now myself. I don't understand why she thinks like this. 'Why though? Why didn't he deserve to die? Did Curt deserve to die when he was going to shoot him?'

'That's my point. Nobody deserves to die for what they done. They might deserve something but not that,' she says slumping back into the sofa. She pulls her bare knees into her chin and closes her eyes.

'So then what did he deserve? What did he deserve for all that crack that he's been pushing on people? Slapped arse?'

'Fuck you,' she says softly as if her battery is all but dead.

'Nah, Ki. Fuck you. He never paid for that shit that he did. Now he's paid.'

It stayed pretty tense after that. Truth be told we were all winding each other up. It was too small a flat for that many people to be living in twenty-four seven. Let alone after one of them had just killed someone.

So when the day came to leave the house, we were all

relieved in a way. We were on edge, true, but we would still rather have been out. The shit was just claustrophobic.

We still hadn't really heard anything about the murder, just rumours really but no police and nothing on the news. Anyway Ki had booked an early morning flight so there was less risk of being spotted just in case.

Ki woke me and Curt up with some coffee and then put some toast under our noses for breakfast. But it was early, man, and besides no one was in no mood to eat really. The bags were already packed and waiting all fat by the front door ready to be picked up. We had decided that we would leave the cash with me for now since they couldn't exactly take it as hand luggage. Later on when they had settled down we would think about how we could maybe get it over. The best we could come up with was that maybe I could send money over to them like Mum did with her fam back in Nigeria, through one of them money shop places. A bit at a time until some better idea came to us. Ki looked it up and it seemed like we could send something like two grand over without any questions.

When they were dressed and ready they both gave me this look like maybe they wouldn't see me again. Even though I was going with them to the airport, Curt gave me a giant's hug and says simply, 'Bruv, soon.' I swear down I nearly start crying but then I turn to look at Ki. She just has jeans and a sweatshirt on but she looks so clean and beautiful that it makes me die on the inside for a reason I can't understand. I look at her hard and try and remember what she looks like right then so I can keep it with me and bring it when I need it.

'Ki,' I goes and then she runs up, squeezes me tight and starts sobbing. She cries and cries till my shirt is wet at the neck. If I could have carried her out of there and away to somewhere secret, trust, I would have.

She was so small at that time. I felt her just crying and shaking in my arms and it was like she was just a child. The shit she had been through in her life. For what? For just trying to survive and be a – and be a good person?

You people man. Looking at me like – like that. What do you know? Sh-shit she had been through.

I don't even know why I'm crying in front of you. Do I think it is even going to make a difference to you? Talking to you like I'm ever going to convince you? What, so you can listen all polite while I go on and then at the end of the day send me down? F-fuck you all man. I can't do this no more, Judge. They can do what they going to do innit. Guilty if they want.

Long Adjournment: 13:15

(Short day. Juror personal commitment)

IN THE CENTRAL CRIMINAL COURT   T2017229

Before: HIS HONOUR JUDGE SALMON QC

Closing Speeches:

Trial: Day 34

Tuesday 11th July 2017

APPEARANCES

For the Prosecution: Mr C. Salfred QC

For the Defendant: In person

Transcribed from a digital audio recording by

T. J. Nazarene Limited

Official Court Reporters and Tape Transcribers

23

10:15

So, like, I just want to say sorry. I don't know why I went off like that yesterday. It was just remembering Ki in my arms – it's just – anyway.

I just need to look at my notes for a second.

Back to that day.

Nobody was in the mood to do that long drive to the airport so we decide just to get the tube. We leave the flat and next thing I know we were sitting on the tube looking at each other's faces, waiting for it to leave Elephant and Castle station. Then we were off. The train was racing down the tracks and hitting all the stops quickly because hardly no one was getting on at that time in the morning. Ki and Curt had their bags on their laps and were quiet, just staring ahead, their eyes doing that flicking thing as the stops rushed by. Every now and then a couple of people got on. They were either workmen on their way to a building site mainly, or every now and then a late night raver just getting home, eyes still like glass from the E's.

We get to Piccadilly Circus then we change lines to the dark blue line to take us to Heathrow. The platforms are filling up a bit as we get off so we have to bundle our ways past the crowds which are like the London crowds everyone knows. Some drunk people. Some homeless people. Some students. Some working people. Small pieces of the whole world right there underground. We cross to the right platform then wait a minute before the tube comes into view and finally screeches to a stop. We still ain't said a word and as we get on and find seats next to each other we still don't do more than just look at each other until the train pulls away again.

We watch the stations flit by one by one. Green Park, Hyde Park Corner, Knightsbridge, South Kensington. All these names which don't mean nothing to people like us except richness. A kind of richness that even money won't ever get us closer to. We know the names and we know the places, but we ain't invited.

Then as we pull up to Earl's Court in the corner of my eye I see a boy waiting to get on with a girl. It doesn't mean anything to me. Just another couple. Then as the doors were waiting to open, I notice Curt start to stiffen. 'Fuck,' he goes, 'I know that boy.'

The doors open and the boy gets on with his girl behind him. Curt buries his head in his giant paws but anyone who met Curt even once knows that he is impossible to miss. It was like an elephant trying to hide himself with his trunk. The boy saunters in and then sits opposite us with his legs wide open. He has on an Avirex flying jacket which makes him look bulked up on top, but you could tell by his stick legs that there weren't nothing underneath that leather. The girl he's with is all heels and short dress. It's obvious that they've just been out clubbing somewhere. They have that dazed half-drunk, half-whacked-out-on-E's look about them. Suddenly the boy notices Curt.

'Yo,' he says and leans over with his arm out and touches Curt on the knee.

Curt pretends like he's noticed him for the first time and says 'hi' by nodding at him. The boy takes this as a sign and gets up and sits next to him.

'Dread you know mans scoping you on the street. Bare people looking for you.'

Curt shrugs as if to signal he ain't interested but the boy can't be stopped. 'Even your General's putting words out. Where you been at?'

Curt folds his arms and gives out this look that could knock a person down.

'Hey that ain't even my crew no more man. I ain't no one's soldier you get me?'

The boy physically backs down and puts his hands up. 'It's cool man. So you want me to keep it on the low bruv?'

Curt nods and then says, 'What's even the beef though? You know anything about it?'

'Yeah some Pagans giving Glockz a bit of heat innit,' the boy says smiling again.

'Yeah? What about?'

'Some Somali boy got shot up and these big mans — Olders — on the war path you get me. They reckon it's

223

Glockz who shot their boy up and Glockz reckon you might know something. Boy says he was in some yard doing a deal and got shot when it went mash up.'

Curt nods, trying to look all 'whatever man' when he suddenly twigs.

'Boy said? What boy said?' he says.

'The Somali boy. The one who was shot up. JC, I think he's called.'

'No man. Back up. The shot boy said it?'

'Yeah.'

Curt looks at me baffled. Then he turns back to Avirex. 'The way I heard it is that the boy was merked.'

'Nah, man. He was shot up but the bullet went straight through. Survived. Shit this is my girl's stop bruv, I'll see you about. Don't worry though I'll keep it low,' he adds, winking, and then pulls his girl off the tube waving us goodbye as he does it.

Ki and me look at Curt. No wonder we couldn't find nothing about the murder in the news. Fucker was still alive. Curt thinks for a moment then stands up and swings his bag over his shoulder.

'Let me look at them tickets,' he says to Ki who fishes the printouts out of her purse and gives them to him. Curt gives them a once over and then rips them up.

'What you doing bro?' I say raising an eyebrow at him.

'We don't need these no more. Five-O ain't going to be on us now is it? Come on. Back to your yard. Some shit's going to kick off soon though.'

'What? We aren't going to Spain now at all?' says Kira following us off the tube, confused.

'If this shit is true, we don't need to run from no police if no police are looking for us,' says Curt as he walks across the platform to catch the train going back where we came from.

'How do you know the Feds ain't looking for us?' I say following him.

'Because no way would he have said anything to police about a drug deal gone wrong. And anyways, he's scum but he ain't a grass innit,' he says and gives Ki a look which tells us that he is talking about Spooks.

'And what about the gangs? What about Glockz? What about the Olders?' she says still worried.

'Olders ain't after us though are they? They after Glockz. JC would have told Olders it's them. Glockz might come looking for us but I reckon they got more bigger problems than us,' he says and just then the tube falls into view and we all get on. It is still early in the morning but by now commuters are just starting their days and the train is fuller than before.

'Anyway,' Curt says in a low voice just as the train doors shut, 'if there's no Feds on this then Bless and your mum and my mum and your brother are all in shit.'

Ki and I look at each other. We know he's right.

Break: 10:45

24

We basically couldn't believe it but we got confirmation of it the next day through some vine. Jamil was alive. Well I say through some vine but in this case the vine was Blessing.

Bless knew we were all planning to jet. Ki and Curt to go first as I said and then me following in a few days. We decided that linking up with Bless though was just too dangerous. At the moment we had deniability for her. Nobody really saw her. She didn't shoot no one, she had her mask on throughout and was out of the flat double quick. And on top of all that she weren't really a candidate for trouble. She was just a girl who lived with her mum. She didn't even go out really. I'm not sure anybody even knew her to be able to line her up. So the last thing we wanted to do was to uproot her from Mum and go on the run with her. There was just no need, you get me.

But once we realized that there was no police on this thing, it was a different thing completely. With no police sniffing around to frighten them off, the gangs would start doing what gangs like to do. Glockz would

226

come looking for Curt. Olders would come looking for all of us. Jamil would have lined us up for that. The added problem for me though was Bless and Mum. If we were in Spain when Olders came looking for me, when they didn't find me, the next place they would knock on is Mum's house. Just for the shit of it.

So there it was, catch-22 again.

If there was police on our backs, no need for gangs to start chasing down our families. When Trident or whatever police unit they are gets involved then the gangs back away. They don't want no Five-O looking into their business you know what I mean? But if there's no police and no life sentence, the downside is that there is a good chance that gangs would want to kill us. And our families. This is why we had to come back. I wasn't sure which was worse. It was one of them things. Might have almost been better to call the police and be done with it. Then again I ain't a person who can do a life sentence you get me. Or Ki of course. She ain't one of them people at all. Trust me.

Anyway once we got back from that tube journey I got on the phone to Bless to tell her that we weren't going away after all.

'Good' she had said, 'I'm g-glad.' Then she hung up as if there was nothing more to be said about it.

We arrived at the flat and Curt and Ki dumped their bags. There was nothing to do now but wait. You see the thing of it was that we didn't know what the next move was till we got a bit more vine. Were Glockz actually looking for Curt? Had Jamil told the Olders about me and Ki yet? Was he even alive? Was that shit the boy told us on the tube even for real? If he was alive, exactly how alive was he? Could he even talk?

The three of us spend the rest of the day trying to work out a plan B or even a plan E or F you get me? The first thing we needed to know was if Jamil was definitely alive and if he was, what had he told the Olders?

'Maybe even he didn't tell them anything,' I say to the others while we are eating our pizza-from-the-freezer dinner.

'How you figure that out?' says Curt who trails long ribbons of cheese from pizza to mouth like it's elastic.

'Well he's just been taxed and his mandems been shot up. He's lost money and more importantly rep. Maybe he wants to keep that shit on the low.'

Curt decides that eating pizza the normal human way is too difficult and puts two slices of pizza together to make a sandwich and puts the whole thing in his mouth.

'Mm maybe,' he says, 'maybe.'

'Or maybe not,' says Ki who gets up from the table and slides her dinner into the bin.

We end the night with nothing really decided except that we need more info. And just this other thing. That if he has told the Olders about us already, we need to find a place to be. Quickly.

By the time Curt starts to snore on the sofa, we know it's time to turn in. I nod my head at Ki and we quietly go to the bedroom. That night while I am trying to think of a place maybe we could stay, Ki turns in the bed so that she is resting on one elbow and faces her head towards mine.

'Can't we just go to Spain?' she says softly.

'No man. We can't. Or I can't. Mum and Bless. They're in a risk situation,' then it occurs to me for real. 'But you can. You can go. Why don't you go? You settle yourself wherever and we link you up laters,' I say sitting up suddenly.

'Shut up,' she says with a sigh, 'you know I'm not going without you.'

I lie back down and stare at the ceiling for a while. It's not long before I hear Ki's breathing telling me she is asleep. It ain't long after that that I fall asleep, Ki's head on my chest.

My dreams are all messed up that night. Ki was some kind of bird with all these colourful feathers and she was trying to fly away. But she couldn't because I had a string around her neck and every time she pulled away the string got tighter. It was like she was choking herself or maybe I was. I woke up before I killed her though. That was something at least.

The next morning there is a knock on the door so gentle that I almost don't hear it. I had woken up to find a space where Ki should have been and for a second I remembered her as that bird. I shake that vision from my head like it's old cobwebs and I go into the kitchen to find Ki making breakfast. Then there was that quiet knocking. Nearly like a tapping. In fact it's only because

Ki looks up from buttering the toast to say, 'Is that pipes? Or is it someone at the door?' that I hear it at all.

I look over at Curt for confirmation but nothing about his face tells me he is even awake. He's chewing handfuls of toast by the table but his eyes aren't really alive yet.

Tap tap again. Why didn't I get one of those peep-hole things on the door? I remember thinking I have to get that sorted out even though I was in a panic. I wave at the other two to hide somewhere and I creep to the door in my socks, trying not to make any sound. Then there it is again. Tap tap tap. My heart though, is going boom boom boom. I wait. I put my ear to the door. Just then a voice comes whispering through.

'It's me. Bless.'

I open the door and there she is, tiny, but wrapped in a cloud of puffa jacket.

'Quick come in,' I say and pull her by her wrists which are poking out through the sleeves like smooth twigs.

'What are you doing here?' I say.

'It's about that b-boy Jamil,' she says, eyes wide.

Just then Curt comes wading out of the bathroom where he has been hiding. Ki follows. Both have the same expression on their faces. Puzzled. That's what you could call it.

'Hi guys,' she says at them and receives a hug from Ki who in turn strokes her face as if she is a child.

'Bless. It's not safe, why you here babe?' says Ki who then looks at me for answers. I don't have any to give.

'Don't I get a hug?' says Curt suddenly and lopes towards her. Bless's cheeks flush red as he comes close but I don't know why. Maybe she is nervous. Curt has a habit of making people nervous.

We look at her and wait until she speaks.

'It's J-Jamil. I heard a rumour.'

'What rumour?' I go.

'He's alive, and c-coming out of hospital tomorrow.'

'Shit. How do you know that?' I say.

'Just a rumour. Just kids talking. Th-that's all they're saying. He's been seen and he's c-coming out of hospital tomorrow.'

'That boy on the tube wasn't chatting shit,' I say to Curt who nods slowly to himself, still chewing toast.

'Look you have to go now. It's dangerous,' I say holding her by the shoulders.

'Don't worry, I'm g-going. I didn't want to phone,' she says and turns to go. 'Oh. Mum said come for dinner. Bring the horse too,' she says looking at Curt and going red once again.

I look at Curt who beams this wide smile at the thought of Mum's food.

'Maybe,' I say, 'we'll see.'

Jamil was alive. Not only that but after Curt made a few calls we found out he was up and about already. Word was, exactly like the boy on the tube had said, the bullet went straight through and out the other end. Apparently he would have bled out if it hadn't been for all that tape we had wrapped him in. Anyway, turned out that the morning after we left him some bin men found some heavy bin bags in that estate. Just rubbish they thought.

Anyway, they were just about to dump them in the crusher when it looks like one of the bags starts moving. Poor fuckers got proper shook and dropped him and the boy nearly died a second time. There was proper commotion all round that estate. Feds everywhere. And then next thing you know he was in ICU. Then a normal ward for a few days. And then, just like that, he was out. The Feds were just sniffing round as they do but they weren't in on it properly yet because Jamil hadn't blamed anyone for it as far as anyone could tell. They must have tried getting a statement off him but the man was a drug dealer at the end of the day and he wasn't going to grass anyone up if he wanted to keep his rep up on the streets. Curt was right about that. The question was what was going to happen next.

Ki and I kept ourselves holed up in my flat for the next day or two. When we needed to get anything in I got up early and went out. Gang-bangers like a lie-in and on no street in London will you ever find a soldier on the streets before lunch. So as long as I was up early I knew I was pretty safe.

Curt wanted to keep moving around rather than stay at his own crib because he knew that he could be a target and they might be watching it. But he didn't have many options so he ended up staying at mine more than he wanted. He still had some allies in Glockz who were able to give him messages and pass on intel, and although at the moment Curt wasn't really being lined up for the shooting, his name was being passed around.

Then one day about a week after the shooting when we were all at my yard doing the usual, PS3 and pizza ting, trying just to get through the day, Curt gets a call in from Guilty, his General. He freezes when he sees the number. His hand floating over the phone, unsure about pressing answer. But then after about a dozen rings he gulps, answers the call and looks at me eyebrows high. He's been avoiding this call for days but knows that he has to take it this time.

Curt puts the phone to his ear and nods. A few seconds go by and he nods again as if the person he's talking to is right there in the room. Finally he speaks.

'Nah blood, nothing to do with me – mans just lining me up for it innit because I jacked him time ago – I ain't hiding out bruv. I'm in Wales innit – cousin's funeral – nah, for real blood – yeah okay. Check you when I'm back innit.'

He put the phone down and breathed again. He looked like he'd just dodged about a hundred bullets. Once he was the right colour again Ki asked him whether he was in the frame for it as far as Glockz were concerned but Curt didn't think so.

'Nah, I ain't hot yet. Guilty's pissed off for sure but it ain't coz of this. It's coz he thinks I've come out of the life. He thinks I've left Glockz.'

Me and Ki breathe a joint sigh of relief.

'But I got to come out of the dark soon if I want to stay cold,' he says. 'And sooner rather than later.'

I didn't really like the idea of Curt going back to

Glockz. As far as we knew they might have just been waiting for him to come home before icing him. But at the end of it all, we knew he was right. He had to go back and show his face. At least that way he had a chance. If he kept avoiding them they might start to get sus and that was the last thing we needed.

The night of the call from his General, Curt stayed with us. He was feeling a bit wired and wasn't in the mood to go and find some place to sleep. And anyway he still had his luggage at my flat so it was just as easy for him to crash here.

The next morning as he left Ki hugged him hard and told him to be safe. I looked him in the eye and asked him if he was sure he wanted to go.

'Ain't got no choice. If I don't go back now, they going to merk me for sure. Anyway I got some friends there, proper safe mans, and if there was a real danger I think they'd have told me.'

'Okay, bruv, if you're sure.'

'I'll be in touch if and when I get some more vine innit,' he says and then swings his travel bag over his shoulder and walks out.

In a way I wished I didn't have to send him back there. But it was the only thing that made sense. He had to go back there or they'd start to get suspicious that maybe he was in hiding because he had done the shooting. Then there was the inside line.

We needed Curt to be tight with Glockz so he could give us the heads-up if things started to heat up for us.

Well for Ki especially. If they were planning to come looking for us, we needed Curt to tip us off and also maybe to send them off down blind alleys, you get me. But that's not to say we weren't worried for his life. We were.

The next twenty-four hours or so, Ki and me waited for news from him like we was waiting for results from the clinic. Curt had ditched his sim which meant that there was no way we could get hold of him. We just had to wait for him to find us. At the end of that day having heard nothing from him I was sure he was dead. The next morning though, he called.

'Yo bruv,' he says, 'got to make this quick.'

'Shoot,' I say, 'well, you know, not shoot. But. Sorry man. Go.'

'Well, good news, bad news.'

'What's the bad?' I say with my heart so deep in my mouth I can hardly get the words out.

'Jamil's got me lined up for the shooting. He ain't remembering much but he does remember me.'

'Shit. What's the good?'

'Well two goods actually. First thing is that Guilty ain't buying it. Second is that nobody has mentioned any girls being involved.'

'That is good,' I say proper relieved, 'so why isn't Guilty going for it? Why he don't got you lined up for it?'

'Dunno. He thinks JC trying to play him against his own crew. Listen, I will swing by laters and catch you up. Right now though I got to bounce,' he says and I am left looking at the dead phone in my hand, my mind all buzzing.

I called out to Ki to tell her the news but saw that she was on her phone. Finally she hung up.

'Your mum,' she says, 'she is insisting on dinner.'

'Shit,' I say. 'Don't worry, I'll think of something.'

I don't want to be leaving this place if I can help it and I certainly don't want to be painting signs for the people who might be looking for us where Mum and Bless are living.

'You won't have to because I told her we'll be there. Tomorrow,' she says with a half-smile. 'Bring the *boss*,' she adds in a Nigerian accent.

That's all we needed.

Actually maybe it was what I needed, some normal back in my life. I couldn't do this much longer. These walls were suffocating me.

Luncheon adjournment: 13:00

25

14:00

Anyway this is how eight days after the shooting, me, Kira, Curt and Bless end up sitting around my mum's table eating dinner like we are just any family.

Except we ain't like just any family and this ain't just any dinner. I was paranoid about going out of the flat. We could be seen at any minute once we were out and about, and if we were then we were toast. So far nobody had come knocking but *believe*, as soon as they had even a slight thing about where I was, they would. Then there was Mum and Bless. I didn't know whether anyone knew where my mum lived but so far they hadn't been tapped so I could only hope that they didn't. So that being the case, the very last thing I wanted was to be seen, let alone at my mum's door.

I wanted no part of it. Mum was cool with it. I told her we couldn't do dinner. I told her it was dangerous for Ki but that was all I said. She didn't ask too many questions. She knew Ki had been missing that time and deep down she would have known that whatever I was doing, I was doing to keep her safe. Mum, as I said to you, loved Ki and the last thing she would have done was put any risk on her. But it was Ki herself. She wanted it.

We had it down like a military op. First of all dinner weren't going to be at dinner time. It was going to be at breakfast time. You remember I said, gang-bangers don't like being up early since they spend all night dealing. The plan was that Curt would do a drive-by in his whip round Mum's in the morning and see what was what. If it looked hot, then the plan was off.

If it all looked cold and nobody seemed like they was watching then he would park up round the back entrance to our flats. There was like a long alleyway there that led to the main road. He was going to park up to block the alley. We would come running down. Jump in the back and shoot off. Sorry. I didn't meant to say 'shoot off'.

Curt's ride has tints in the back so once we were in we would be invisible more or less. Then we would do a couple of loops of Mum's house and if everything was still cold, he would drop us round the back of the house. The back gate would be open and then we'd be in.

Although it all went to plan the shit was still tense. Kira and I had hoods pulled right up the whole journey. In the back of Curt's Range Rover Sport I had my eyes peeled back for any sign of something. There was only working people and some schoolkids up at that time but even the postman makes me sus you get me. Even when we had done a loop of the house I wasn't sure and wanted to do another.

'Nah man, we can't,' says Curt with a sigh. 'We do any

more circuits and some nosy neighbour fucker's going to be all over the phone to Five-O. We look proper shady man.'

Only when we were all sat down in Mum's warm kitchen did I finally relax.

'Mum, come and sit down with us and eat,' I say to her back as she fries more food at the stove. The smell of fried food in the morning feels surreal but since we haven't eaten since lunchtime yesterday, my stomach ain't fussy.

'How can I sit down eh? If I sit down who will feed the horse?' she says and turns back to her cooking. I think that she is smiling but I can't see her face. I did see it though when Curt walked in through the back door and she looked as if she was going to cry.

I look back around the table. Bless looks like she has made a special effort for me and I am almost touched. I haven't seen her looking so, well maybe pretty isn't the right kind of word to say about your sister, but yeah pretty. I haven't seen her look so pretty in a long time.

She is wearing what looks like a new dress. It's like a dusty soft pink colour which kind of makes her cheeks glow. And Ki too. Some of that worry seems to have washed off her face and she looks at me for the first time in ages like she is glad of me. Her eyes are so intense I can't hold their gaze. In my head I change the subject like I am changing gears. It makes a clunk in my ears as I do it.

'So Curt what about Guilty?' I say trying to make sure Mum ain't listening too hard. I didn't need to worry truth be told. She never listens to us. She treats us like we are an alien race. 'You people. You don't even speak in English any more.' I tell you what though, just as well my mum ain't in the courtroom at the moment. She would give me some beatings for that terrible Nigerian accent innit Bless? Oh shit. That is her coming back into the court now. So where was I?

Yeah, at that moment Mum walks over to the table and dumps like a hundred pieces of fried chicken on the table. Curt looks like he's choosing between speaking and eating. In the end he picks up two drumsticks and chews off huge chunks before remembering that we were talking. He wipes the grease off his mouth with his sleeve and when Mum has shuffled back to the stove he carries on.

'Yeah so JC been shouting his mouth off to the Olders about how I was the one who taxed him. Word got to Guilty.'

'Shit,' I say.

'Seen bruv. Seen. But here's the crazy thing. Guilty goes to me, "Fuck dat little Somali fucker. He's been fucking around in our patch for long. He's getting iced next time I scope him."'

'Is it?' I say.

'Yeah for real. And get this, he then gives it all, "And I am pretty fucking sure that that fucker was the one who grabbed the bitch from under the bridge. No other fucker would have dared. Mans thinks he's gangster but man's just a pussy boy with Olders watching his back. Thinks he can fuck with mans, mans got a bullet coming for him."'

'Shit,' I say pushing my chair back from the table and slapping my leg.

'Yeah so I go, "Fuck brother, I'll waste him for you. It would be my pleasure."'

Curt starts laughing and then before you know it all four of us round the table are laughing so much that there are tears. It feels like we can't even stop it.

Eventually Mum turns around from the cooker with a big spoon in her hand which she starts waving at us.

'Eh eh. Stop it for goodness sake. You know what they say. As much as you laugh now is as much as you will cry later.'

Once 'dinner' was over we realized that we couldn't just leave. It was proper busy out there and too dangerous. So we stayed. It felt like a kind of lazy Christmas. We just hung back. Took off our shoes and lay on the sofa or on cushions on the floor as Mum brought us snacks and tea. It felt nice. It's hard to explain. It felt like someone had pressed a pause button on our lives and we could escape it for a while. Be normal again. I didn't want the day to end.

By the time we left early the next morning to go home, I was feeling better than I had in long. I think we all did. Bless saw us to the door and hugged me and Ki goodbye.

'Bruv? Come on we better jet,' I say.

'Nah man. I'm cool here,' says Curt looking sketchy. 'Here. Take my keys, I get 'em laters. I think I will just hang back here for a while if that's okay with your, erm, mum. I ain't seen her in a while. You know.'

'Sure,' I say and then look over at Bless who quickly slips off to the kitchen where Mum for some reason is cooking again.

'You going be able to get back okay?'

'Yeah' he says, 'I'll just get a cab.'

'So,' I say drawing Curt close, 'you think we might be in the clear?'

'Yeah it's possible. Guilty don't believe the rumours about me being there at the trap-house. Shit I think he partly wishes *he* had done the taxing. He hates Jamil like you wouldn't believe.'

'And what about if the Olders get heavy? What then?'

'Nah man. Glockz is proper. I don't think they going to back down from no Olders. Yeah there's going to be a war, but I think we are sweet, as long as we keep our heads down,' he says and turns to go back into the kitchen.

'Swing by tomorrow if you can. We still got some details to tie up innit,' I say to his back and then leave.

And I tell you what right now. I swear down at that moment I thought that was it. Over. We were in the clear. But I had not counted on what kind of mans Jamil was linked up to. It was that that changed everything I reckon. A man who people just knew as Face.

Break: 15:00

26

So the next day Curt comes by the flat so that we can sort out a few things. For one there was all this money in my yard we had to do something with. I didn't really like the idea of it being there to be honest. I wanted it gone and as far as I was concerned it was Curt's money to do what he wanted with.

I got the money all tied up in elastic bands while Ki made us all some breakfast. As I was laying it all out on the table I squeeze a look at her and she seems beautiful again. I mean she was always beautiful, just she seemed to have got her shine back. She wasn't even wearing anything special, just some grey leggings and a silky purple top which left her arms bare. But I tell you her face in the window-light, for just one minute looked like an old painting. Beautiful I mean. Not old.

I let Curt in and he came and joined me at the table.

'Shit. I almost forgot about that,' he says nodding at the piles of money.

'Yeah well you decided what you going to do with it? That's enough paper right there. I can source you some phat wheels bruv if you're interested. M3, RS4 whatever you like.'

'Nah man. I got plans for that.'

'Like?' I say, intrigued.

'I'm buying my freedom, blood. Get the fuck outta this life you get me.'

'What the fuck you chatting about freedom for? You ain't a slave are you?' I say and grin at him.

'Nah man. That's the price. Sure I told you this. I told Guilty last year that I wanted out and he goes, "Sure nigger you are free to go. For fitty thou,"' he says and makes five lots of tens with his huge fingers.

'I don't get it,' I say and truly I didn't. 'You got to *pay* to leave?'

'Shit yes you got to pay,' he says and levers himself up from the chair to get a beer from the fridge even though it's like ten a.m.

Pay to leave? This was sounding more Mafia than Camden to me but he knew shit I didn't. I leave him to his beer and I go and dig out an old rucksack I can put the cash in and then start loading it up. By the time I am finished I am surprised at how heavy it is. But the process of slowly loading the money into the bag starts me thinking.

'Hey, one thing I never got,' I say, walking back into the room, 'is how you got mix up in this gang shit in the first place. I remember them days when you'd rather take a knife than get all ganged up.'

Curt takes a glug and then sighs all heavy. 'It's a long story man. Another time, maybe.'

At that exact minute, his phone rings and he answers it after a few rings and listens. As he nods and 'yeahs' into the phone, Ki comes to the table with a pile of toast on one plate and about a dozen fried eggs on another.

'We need more food,' she mouths so as not to disturb Curt's call. I nod back but I'm not really paying her any notice, for all the listening I'm trying to do is to Curt's call. I see Curt's face changing colour. When he finally puts the phone down I get the feeling that whatever was being said on that call wasn't going to be one of them good news bad news things. It was all going to be bad bad news.

'Bad bad news,' Curt says finally. 'We are in shit.'

Ki sits down at the table as if she is in slow motion. The colour leaves her face.

'What do you mean?' I say trying to keep my heart from hitting my balls.

'So that was Guilty.'

'Yeah I guessed, and?' I say.

'Well, you know these Olders JC is linked up to?'

'Yeah.'

'Well these ain't just any Olders.'

'What do you mean?'

'This crew ain't just a regular fucking Olders crew.'

I look at him blankly.

'This is Face's crew,' he says and then I understand.

Ki looks at us both then, her face still innocent.

'Who's Face?' she says slowly.

'Face,' says Curt as he puts his head in his hands. 'You

want to know about Face? Okay then let me tell you a story about this motherfucker.

'So one day last summer Face was up at a club with his Lieutenant when some Pagan stabbed up his left-hand man while he was in the toilets.'

'So?' says Ki. 'One gangster stabs another one. Standard.'

Before I can explain Curt cuts back in.

'No man. It was a big deal. Stabbing up a man's Lieutenant is properly serious shit. A General and his number two are basically like brothers. You know how it is,' he says to me. 'One will take other man's bullet. Even his jail time if he have to.'

I nod but truth be told I ain't really as down with all this as Curt is.

Curt takes a swig of beer and then continues his story. 'Anyway this dude gets stabbed and Face is wild. If he had been there next to him I ain't even sure the shit would have happened. But he wasn't and now his two was nearly dead. And Face was on the warpath.

'So where he might have spent some time trying to find out who had done this, this time he didn't have to do shit. He found out the next day.'

'How?' says Ki leaning forwards.

'Easy, the man himself fucking advertises it. He goes and makes a load of T-shirts with the man's face on it with the letters R.I.P. and hands them round his crew.'

'Shit yeah I heard about that,' I say suddenly remembering.

'Face though ain't no ordinary gangster. He is like a genius you could say. He is like a strategizer. And to cut a long story up, Face guessed the guy was going to try and ambush him. And he knew that the other crew wouldn't be starting no shit unless they thought they could win.

'So Face played it smarter than the other man. He got a few of his young soldiers, Tinies, together and sent them on a mission to track the guy's movements.'

You looking kinda blank at me again. Is it Tinies? Yeah okay. So 'Tinies' are like soldiers-in-waiting. They are just kids really but the gangs like 'em for all kinds of reasons. It's messed up but the shit is what it is.

So back to this story Curt is telling.

'He wanted to know where mans was on any given day. Which clubs did he go to? Where was his ride last spotted? How many people was he with? Where did he go when he left a club? Where was his base?'

'But hang on,' says Ki, 'he's using kids?'

'Shit, yeah he was using kids. Face was the first one to use kids. "Get some respec' or get some holes". That was his like recruiting line.'

'No, I mean he's supposed to be this genius and he is using children?'

'That *was* the genius man. Because they was just kids,

247

no one gave them a second blink. They were more or less invisible. No gang expect trouble to come from ten-year-old boys in school uniform.

'And that is how in a week Face found out where mans lived. Then one morning, very early, like before even the sun was awake, Face pulls a balaclava over his head and goes into his house with two of his men. They drag him out of bed and lash him to a chair and then they spend twenty minutes heating up the end of a wheel brace with a blowtorch right in front of him.

'And all the time it was heating up, Face is whispering at him, "Where's your P? Where is it at? Where's your stash? Give it up."

'Then, when he don't get no answers, and once the iron was glowing hot, he takes it and holds it like an inch away from the man's eye.'

'Curt,' I say at this point knowing what is coming, 'I think that is probably enough.'

'No. I want to know,' Ki says, eyes wide open.

'Well what can I tell you? He holds the iron in front of man's eye, slowly heating the air in front of it, until the eye goes pop. After that, with all that shit coming out of his eye socket all over his chest, man pretty much drew him a map to where the stash was. Something like a hundred grand came out of that taxing, in drugs and dollars. And guns. But that wasn't enough as far as Face was concerned.

'When mans stopped screaming, Face sends his boys out of the house and then he takes his balaclava off and shoves it into the tied man's mouth. At that moment he must have known it was game over because Face had shown himself. No way could he let him live now you get me.

'"This is for my number two," he goes, and takes up the blowtorch and puts it on a blue flame. Then when he had done what he needs to do, he shoots him three times through the head.

'The very next day, every member of Face's crew is wearing a T-shirt with a picture of a man's chest with the letters R.I.P burned into it. Nobody from the dead man's crew did a fucking thing to retaliate. Within two weeks the whole crew failed. The crew became basically R.I.P., you get me. That is who Face is.'

'Put it this way, if Face finds out you and me were there when JC was taxed, we are smoke,' I say.

'Yeah, about that,' says Curt before this has even sunk in.

'What?'

'JC has started remembering more shit.'

'Like what?' we both say.

'Like how it was some *links* that put a hole in him, a girl. A links that had grey eyes.'

Anyway, I look over at Ki who has now gone pale. At first she doesn't say anything. She just gets up and starts to walk in tight rows up and down the room.

'This is not good. This is not good,' she says over and over.

I get up and put an arm around her but she shrugs it

off and carries on pacing up and down the room. I know this is bad. For one we have to bail from this place. No way can we stay here. Then there's Mum and Bless. What if this Face brer came looking for them when he couldn't find me?

'Don't worry Ki. You're safe here,' I say but even as the words are coming out I look around my flat and know it ain't true. The cheap front door and the loose windows bleeding sound in from the streets below tell me I'm a liar.

'Yeah girl. No one knows where you are. It's still cool,' Curt adds and looks at me with a kind of 'sorry bruv' look.

'It is not cool,' she says still pacing.

'Listen,' I say stopping her and taking her shoulders in my hands and looking her directly in the eye, 'they don't know you are here.'

'Or you know, if it gets hot, you just jump on a plane,' says Curt.

Ki meets my eye and holds my gaze. 'It's not me I'm worried about. It's my brother. They'll get to him,' she says in a voice that sounds like a scream in a box.

'What do you mean?' I say. 'What's Spooks got to do with this?' Then I realize what she means.

Long adjournment 16:31

IN THE CENTRAL CRIMINAL COURT   T2017229

Before: HIS HONOUR JUDGE SALMON QC

Closing Speeches:

Trial: Day 35

Wednesday 12th July 2017

APPEARANCES

For the Prosecution: Mr C. Salfred QC

For the Defendant: In person

Transcribed from a digital audio recording by

T. J. Nazarene Limited

Official Court Reporters and Tape Transcribers

27

10:00

Just yesterday at the end I was telling you that JC was starting to remember shit. A girl with light eyes. It was the kind of line nobody could forget and the girl was a girl that nobody could forget. And when people called her to mind, they would call up everything they knew about her to squeeze where it hurt.

Ki was right. First place the Olders would go was to Spooks if they couldn't find her. Once they worked out who the girl with the light eyes was, they would know all about who her brother was. Even if they didn't know where she was, they knew where he was. And it didn't matter whether Spooks knew where she was or not. That wouldn't stop them applying a bit of pressure to his pressure points, if you get me. We all knew that, and right then we ran out of things to say. Curt left a short while later. Part of me wished I could leave too.

I spent most of the night trying to think of things to say to make Ki feel a bit better but even I knew that nothing was going to work. She was doing her thing where she went and hid in her own mind. It was the best

253

thing probably, I thought, so I left her alone. I weren't allowed in that place in her head. I ain't even sure I wanted to go there even if I was. Sometimes you just had to let Ki do her thing and wait till she came out again.

The surprising thing in the end was that the next morning when I woke up I found her in the living room reading a book, like nothing had happened. It was almost as if she realized that the shit was what it was and there was no sense worrying about it. I knew better than to stir it all up again so when she smiled at me and asked me if wanted coffee I just nodded and smiled back.

Of course I was worried that in the next days she would sink down again but the next few days could look after themselves. It had only been a couple of weeks since the taxing so I had no idea whether this was healing or some next shit that was going to send her down. All I could do was keep them fingers crossed. I smiled at her again. She looked at me calmly and I tried to do the same. To be calm. To double out the calm in the room even when I knew there weren't no good reason for it. I felt like a dad making a clapping sound so his kid would forget that he fell down and scraped his knee.

What I remember most was this look she had. It was more than – what do you call it? – resignation. It was more like a look that said she weren't so worried about Spooks any more. She looked like she did when she knew what was coming next. You know, like, in control. She handed me a mug of coffee and smiled casually.

'You not having one?' I say.

'No. I'm going out for a few hours. I'll be back by one.'

I rub my eyes and look at her puzzled. 'Out where?'

'Just out. I need to get some space.'

I begin to wake up a little more and then when her face comes back into focus I say in a panic, 'Ki, you know you can't go out. It's too dangerous.'

'Err excuse me? Who do you think you're talking to? I'm not asking. I can go and I am going. I could have gone while you were asleep. So you just have to deal with it.'

'But you'll get seen.'

'I won't. I'll pull my hood up and wear some shades. It'll be fine. Besides as you keep saying, there's no gangsters awake at this time,' she says and just like that she leaves.

I tried keeping her back but it weren't no good. I took her arm and looked at her like I wasn't in any mood for messing about. But she gave me a look back that was twice as heavy and slid her arm out of my grip.

'I will see you later,' she said before she left. And I prayed she was right.

'Where are you even going?' I say to her back as she pulls at the door, but she doesn't answer. She doesn't even look back.

*

The rest of that morning I am basically wired. I try her phone a few times every hour but it goes straight to voicemail. I send her some texts but I get nothing back. Where has she gone anyway? It can't be just a walk or she wouldn't have said she would be back at one. I couldn't think. Maybe she was at a friend's. Maybe she went to see Mum and Bless. I didn't really think so, especially after the hassle of the last trip and all the things we had to do to make it safe. Anyway I racked my brains but I knew that my brains didn't have the room for much racking so eventually I just give up and stand by the window looking out for her to come back.

One o'clock comes and goes. Then so does two. By the time it's three I am really starting to worry for her. That makes it what six hours or something she has gone? It feels like the first time she disappeared all over again. Fuck. I shouldn't have let her go man. I should have kept her in even if I had to hold her down and lock the doors. I stayed by the window for the next hour nearly, still calling and texting with no answers either way. Then as I am gazing out of the window I see her. But I nearly don't. Which is more fucked up than it might seem to you lot. You see to get into my estate, there is really only one way you can get in if you are coming from the street. And that is a place I can see right from my window. I can't miss it. It's like directly in front of my view. But where she came from, and why I nearly missed her, weren't from there. It was from around the back. I caught her just coming into view from the side. And if I can explain it to you, it is not a place she should have been. That is the place where like kids chill and blaze or deal or whatever. There is no other reason to be there – you can't even get out to the street from there. You can get to the estates at the back but you going over some rough ground to get there. It didn't make no sense to me. Not one bit.

When she came through the door I was in a mind to call her out. I weren't angry exactly, just you know, confused. I couldn't think of a thing she could say to explain it really, unless she would have said she went out to score, you get me? But something about the look on her face made me stop. She seemed worried and calm both at once.

So I just casually go to her, 'Where you been Ki?' I say, expecting her to give me some bullshit.

What she says next though throws me.

'To see Spooks.'

'What? Are you mad Ki? Fuck knows who saw you in that prison.'

'I had to,' she says, as if it was obvious, and takes her coat off.

'Had to? Do you even know what you've done?' I was furious. How could she put herself at risk like that? How could she put Mum and Bless at that kind of risk?

'Just leave it. I had a visiting order already and, you know, I had to see if he was okay.'

I turned my back on her trying to just settle myself down, I was so angry I didn't know what I might say or do. Eventually when my blood stopped making my face red, I turned back to her.

'What if you were seen?'

'I wasn't,' she says as she moves past me into the kitchen to put the kettle on.

'So was he? Okay?' I say at last, still simmering about how risky she has been but wanting to try calming myself.

'Yes. He's fine. They're moving him next week. Protected wing.'

I look at her then but her face is giving nothing away.

'Okay, you've seen him now. No more of this bullshit please, Ki.'

'Plus I had to get some more books,' she says, holding out an Oxfam bag with a dozen paperbacks in it.

Man, sometimes for a clever girl Ki did some stupid things. Actually going into a prison to see Spooks, in a prison full of gangsters, some of who are probably on the lookout for this very girl? Shit. It wasn't like you would have missed her. She walks into a supermarket and everyone looks at her. Imagine what effect she would have had on a room full of men in a prison. It was like – I can't even say what it was like. It was like a beautiful girl walking into a male prison.

Then I remember seeing her from the window. How she came round the back. From that place she shouldn't have been in. I was about to confront her but Ki wasn't really a girl you'd want to just accuse straight out. I had to play it gentle like.

'Just tell me one thing though. Which way did you come back?' I say eventually, not sure if I want to hear her answer.

For a second she has this look like I have caught her out doing some shit she shouldn't have been doing. Then the composure comes back so I ended up feeling like I had misread it.

'I got a lift from one of the visitors.'

'What visitor?' I say, thrown back by what she just said.

'Someone at the prison. It's okay. I know him. He's a friend of Spooks.'

'Spooks? You got a lift from a friend of Spooks? Ki, you must be off your meds or something man.'

'I said I know him. He's safe. He's been more of a brother to me than Spooks.'

I don't know what to say any more. She's never mentioned no second brother friend of Spooks in all our years together, but I can't control Kira. But I need her controlled if she is going to be safe. Then I remember the route she took. It didn't explain that.

'What way you come back?' I ask again.

'What way?' she says back to me.

'Yeah. What way?'

'Oh' she says and then quickly her face lightens up. 'Don't worry. I got them to drop me to the other estate. No one saw me coming here. I cut through the back.'

'Ah,' I goes and at that time, that was good enough for me. It's only later when I am turning it over in my mind that I wonder about the books. If a visitor gave her a lift back, how did she get the books? Did he take her to Oxfam? I suppose he could have. But then did he wait for her and then drive her back? It didn't make no sense I could follow.

Break: 11:00

28

11:30

I get the feeling you lot are waiting for the ending. And one of the last things my brief said to me was 'Don't let them lose interest' and I don't know if you lot are maybe losing interest. But I am getting there, really and truly. Just give me a little more time yeah? So where was I?

That's right. The Spooks thing. Anyway it was the day after that whole thing that Curt comes knocking on my door.

'So it looks like the shit is heating up,' he says. 'Face's lot is combing the ends looking for Guilty. This thing's about to happen.'

'Good,' I say, 'about time.'

The way we figured it, the sooner those two mans knocked each other out, the better. It had been nearly ten days now of being locked up in my flat. The walls felt like they were closing in and all the space in between them felt poisoned. We hadn't had a clean breath since this whole thing began except for that day at Mum's. We needed it to be over. All it needed to end was for it to start. The two gangs take each other out and we are home free. We just had to hope that with that kind of war going on Face would be too busy to be wondering about the girl with the light eyes. With luck one of the Glockz might even finish him off you get me?

Things even have begun to feel more positive in my mind. I look over to where Ki is sitting on the sofa and it's obvious she is much calmer now that she's seen Spooks. She seems even like nearly her old self. I feel like she is more in focus, less faded. The edges of her are becoming sharper.

I look across at her and say, 'A few more days, a couple of weeks maybe and this shit'll be over babe.'

She looks up from her book and hooks into the conversation like she's been listening all the while.

'Face and the Olders are way too bad for Glockz from what you say,' she says calmly.

'Bad? Face by himself would be bad enough. But with a crew behind him? This shit is going to be dirty. Those boys are medieval,' I say.

'Well isn't that a problem for us?' she says, putting the book down next to her on the sofa and blinking slowly at me.

'What you getting at Ki?' I say, hating the way that she saves her punchlines like this.

'Is Guilty going to die?' Ki asks.

'He's getting iced for sure,' says Curt, interested enough now to put his spliff down.

'If he's dead,' she says cool as, 'who's going to take care of Face?'

We pause, just looking at each other and breathing in the silence.

What Ki was getting at was that the plan only worked if the two gangs cancelled each other out. If Face survived and Guilty got killed, Face would still be looking for us. The only thing that interested Face was the money and it would only be a matter of time before Face realized that Guilty didn't have the money. We had the money and that meant just one thing. With Jamil whispering into Face's ears, about who was behind the shooting, Face would soon come looking for us. All of us. Me, Curt and Kira.

Of course we already knew this in a ways. But what me and Curt had hoped though was that in the crossfire, Face might catch a couple of bullets. Maybe, we thought, it would be enough for Face that he had won a gang war. You know maybe he would be happy with just that and a chance to do his own taxing on Glockz.

'We can't do shit about that though,' Curt says at last. 'Face and his crew are like Terminators. They unstoppable.'

'But that don't mean they can make bullets bounce off them,' I add, wondering if maybe there could be a way of stopping Face's crew.

Curt rubs his face with a huge paw and then says softly, 'I don't know man. Maybe they can.'

Ki pulls her cardigan round her shoulders and then stands up straight after thinking a moment.

'Then we have to do something,' she says, 'to slow Face and them down.'

Slowing down Face was one of them easier-said-than-done tings. How were we supposed to slow down Face? For one thing we were in hiding. We couldn't even roam the streets freely you know what I mean? We were stuck in this place. For another thing, Face's Olders crew was proper big mans gang. Guns and shit. I mean proper guns. MAC-10s. Sub-machine gun kind of gun. What could we be doing against that? I said something like that to Ki.

'Got any ideas?' I then add looking at Ki.

'Me?' she says.

'Well, maybe I mean all of us,' I say quickly looking at Curt.

'Point taken,' she says as if asking us to come up with ideas is like the stupidest thing she has ever heard, 'but I tell you one thing I am not sitting here just waiting to be killed. And we have Mum to think about too or have you forgotten that?' she adds.

'And Bless,' Curt says under his breath. Ki and him exchange a look like there is something they are not telling me.

'Yes and Bless,' she says picking up her phone which has pinged through a message. 'Look I can't think cooped up in this place. I have to get some air,' she says quickly.

'You can't leave. It's too dangerous,' I say but with a look that shows her that I am not having any more of this bullshit where she just walks out for hours like she did when she went to see Spooks.

'It's okay. I just need somewhere quiet to think,' she says though and begins to put her coat on. I need to work on my look I think. It's like she is trying to not understand my daggers.

'Blood,' I say to Curt with my hands out urging him to do something.

'Not me bruv,' he says.

'It's okay. I'll go somewhere quiet.'

'Like where?' I say concerned. I do not want to risk her getting seen. Not now that it's so hot. Not hot hot, it's England. I mean hot like the heat is on us.

'Maybe the church,' she says.

'The church? Round here? On Sunday? You crazy?'

Ki stops as if she is taking in the sense of what I am saying. Church in Camberwell on a Sunday is busier than McDonald's.

'Why not try the mosque?' says Curt, 'that ain't going to be busy on Sunday is it? I'll drive you down there. I got to drop in on Bless anyway,' he says and then adds after a beat, 'and your mum.'

Luncheon Adjournment: 12:50

29

So Curt was going to drop her to a mosque. Sounds messed up right? I mean a mosque? Something about it felt shady to me. All that weirdness you read about. Now since I been locked up in jail I know a bit more about Islam. Except in here we call it Prislam. Most people just join it to get better food. Other people join it so they can hook up with their mans in a bit of peace and quiet. A few do it to get their shit together. It was only really the odd Pakistani or Somalian that joined it for real, you know to actually pray for salvation.

Back then though, I didn't know anything about it really. I knew the basic stuff like prayer mat and Mohammed but nothing more than that. As far I saw it then, it was just a thing that terrorists and guys with them long beards and no moustaches did.

But was I happy about Ki going to a mosque to find some peace and quiet as she called it? Not really truth be told. It was way too dangerous for her to be out at all. I mean I get it. She was cooped up in this tiny flat with only me to look at. It was horrible. I didn't know it then but it was worse than prison in some ways. In prison you get out for some air every day at least. But back then in that flat, it was bare claustrophobic. Bare claustrophobic.

And then the mosque of all places. That didn't seem to me to be a safe place for a person. In my head it was going to be one of them places with the minuets or whatever they call them. You know with the towers and the wailing. And men. For some reason in my head it was only men in them kind of places. Where there are only women when they are made to be there by the men. Like the opposite of a church innit, where the men are only there because they been dragged there by their mums and wives.

On the other hand there weren't no chance that she could be recognized in a mosque since we didn't really know any Bangladeshis or whatever.

Anyway long story short Ki leaves with Curt and before I know it she is sitting in a mosque doing some of her thinking. I am left by myself again in the flat. Checking my phone every minute. Looking out the window every two. I feel sick every one of them minutes that she is not there. How she even getting back? I don't even know whether Curt is picking her up or what.

In the end I get so bored of just waiting I do what any guy would do. I pick up my PS3. I did have *Call of Duty* in my stack and although I was pretty good at that, I felt like I'd had enough of guns and all that shit to last me a lifetime. So it was *FIFA*. My Chelsea team was hench, trust, it had the best players money could buy.

I had Ronaldo, Messi, Agüero, Bale, Silva, Suárez, Neymar, you name it. I had so many strikers that I didn't really have much room for defenders so I had people like Fàbregas and Touré in the back. It weren't like any team you'd see in real life, but who wants real life when you're trying to escape it?

The thing I noticed though when I played it that day that I didn't notice before was that you can only properly play it when your head is clear. I don't mean that you need to concentrate. You don't. It's just that when you're like worried about something, you can't use it to run away from your life. It's only good for getting out of your life when there's not that much in your life in the first place. I reckon that's why, when you are doing your time, after your trial is over, people play PlayStation. Yeah, believe. It is true, there is PlayStation in prison. But like I say, it's only good if you got nothing else to do and you need your life to move on as fast as it can.

I turned it off and walked around the flat looking for something to do. I had already washed all the dishes. The cooker was clean. There was nothing to do but wait. After a while I walked into the bedroom and poked around. On Ki's side of the bed there were books stacked in a pile on the floor and I picked one up. *To Kill a Mockingbird*. I flipped it over and read the back. A few words jumped out at me. Kindness and cruelty. Love and hate. It looked like the kind of book that she would read. A book of opposites. Like me and her. I opened the first page and started to read but I couldn't get the story going. It was the same thing as the PS3. My head wasn't clear enough to hang on to the words. Every time I got hold of something, my mind started to slip back to Kira. In the end I can't do anything except to stand by the window just to watch out for her or anyone else I need to worry about. I don't like the idea of her being out so long. I worry that it might happen again. She might get taken. And I ain't sure I can live through another one of them dramas again. Then it gets dark and I start getting edge. I can't stay in here much longer so I decide to go out. Just for a bit of air. The darkness probably give me enough cover I reckon.

When I am outside, I decide to cut through the back. That place I saw her the last time she came back. I don't know why exactly, I guess I was just curious about it still. It didn't sit right with me and I just wanted to get my eyes on it. I weren't even sure any more if there was a cut through to the other estate. It had been ages since I went round that way. I get to the bins and there is a low wall there which I jump. And then I'm like in some kind of waste grounds around that other estate. There's nothing really there but some old faded cans and bottles and random bits of rubbish. It looked like a kind of place where they thought about having a garden when they made it but then couldn't be bothered. I cross it in about five minutes of fast walking and then think about what I do now. There is nothing to see here. Then suddenly there is.

A car.

*

Now the thing with me is that I know most of the cars that go up and down my ends. It's not that I know every car, obviously, it's more that I know when a car is there that doesn't seem right to me. It kind of just throws me off a bit like when you walk downstairs and you think there's an extra step but there isn't but your foot moves like there is. Anyway I see this one car pulling up directly outside but on the far side of the street and to me it doesn't look right. Or maybe it's not even that. Maybe that is whatever it's called, hindsight, that I'm saying it. But thing was I noticed that car. *I* noticed it but my guess is that not many people would have. Not even people who are quite interested in cars would have noticed it. You would have to be really, really proper interested to have noticed it because it's a kind of car that is designed not to be noticed.

What it was: a late-model ice-blue Alpina D3 two-litre bi turbo estate. What that basically is to anyone looking at it is a BMW 3 Series Touring. Just a normal BMW estate to look at. If you saw it, you wouldn't notice anything about it. But what it actually is, is a company called Alpina; they take a BMW and change it.

The main thing they change is under the bonnet. So they take a naturally aspirated engine and turn it into a supercharged engine. It's all about creating high torque at low revs. Anyway the point is you can't really tell unless you get up really close and check for the badge that says Alpina on it. But if you know about them, like really know about them like I do, you can tell from the wheels. They put twenty-spoke alloys on it. Nineteen inches on this one. This car was a car for someone who knew cars. So I noticed it. And in my head I was just going, I reckon that's probably worth twenty-five thousand pounds or whatever. But what shocked me was that after a minute of being parked up, the back door opens. And Kira gets out. She leans in to get something from inside and then starts to head in my direction. I can't see what it is but it looks like a black sheet or something, which confuses me. I quickly duck in behind a van that's parked up in the car park before she sees me.

I crouch down and watch her pass me by. My eyes follow her as she fiddles with the black sheet thing and then starts to walk in the direction of the front of my block. Shit. I think, I need to get back before she does. Something in me needs to see what her face is going to tell me as soon as she walks in that door.

I realize I only got about five minutes to trace back the route I came from and beat her home. But it's only when I start to run that I remember that I haven't had to run for years. I make it to the flat in about two minutes, my lungs pumping hard.

I open the door to the flat and my mind is still running even though I'm not. What the fuck is going on? Why she in a car like that? I poke my head round the door and see that I have beaten her back. Now I just need to think of what to say to her. So I wait. And then after a few minutes I hear the door.

When she comes in she is a changed person. And I don't mean spiritually speaking. I mean she was a proper changed person. I didn't even recognize her. In fact I almost screamed. I thought for half a second like I was maybe in a nightmare. It was only when she took the head bit off that I realized it was Ki. In a burkha. I swear down. The full Darth Vader.

'Oh fuck,' I go as soon as I see her face. I feel like I almost had a heart attack. She smiles at me like one of them smiles like *don't I look silly* and I ain't even sure whether to laugh.

'Yeah, yeah,' she says, cool as and takes off the rest of it. 'Besides, I thought you'd be happy.'

'Happy?'

'What's a better disguise than this? I can go out every day,' she says hanging the whole shimmery black outfit on a peg by the front door.

'Well I ain't sure if —' I say but she cuts me off by showing me a palm.

'Shut up anyway. Listen I think I'm on the way to finding a way out of this mess,' she says and those eyes are back, gleaming. This is like the old Ki coming back and right then for that moment I completely forget the whole Alpina thing. I can't make it make any sense right now so I park it up.

'Shit, a way out already? You are good Ki. I give you that. Smart. Always said it. Hit me. What you got?'

'Got? Nothing yet. I said I am on the *way* to finding a way. I just need some time. Give me a few days just to think it through properly. After that I will tell you what I got. Now to change the subject. What do you think is going on with Bless and Curt?' she says smiling one of them smiles. You know the ones.

'What you chatting about gal? Ain't nothing going on. He just dropping in to see Mum. Eh stop that smiling I swear down,' I say and at that point I push her on to the sofa, both of us laughing like little kids.

Well that was really the turning point right there. The day she came back from the mosque. From that minute everything changed. I should have been on it. If I had a brain like hers I would have seen it but as I told you before I ain't got one of them kind of minds. Black and white my brain is. Hers . . . hers is all kind of colours.

Break: 15:00

30

So then every day for the next four or five days Ki is at
the mosque for hours at a time. She puts on her burkha
thing and leaves taking nothing but her phone with
her. I try asking her why, why does she have to go there,
to the mosque, but she just passes it off as one of them
things.

'What, you want me to go to the park or the library or
something dressed like this?' she says as if it is the stupidest thing she has ever heard.

'But why you have to go out at all?' I say after the
third day. 'Can't you do your thing here, in the flat?'

'No I can't. I need to think. I need room. I need some
peace. How can I think with you breathing down my
neck all the time?'

'I know that,' I say. 'But can you not see that it is
dangerous for you to be out there? Dangerous for you,
for Mum, for Bless, for Curt. Everyone, Ki. Is it worth
it for your breathing room or whatever you want to
call it?'

'It's okay babe. I'm wearing this,' she says tugging on
the side of her burkha. 'I'm invisible.'

274

I even tried to walk her down there myself but she wasn't having it at all. It was too dangerous she told me. Turning my own lines back at myself.

Then she would come back and each time she would have this bright-eyed look about her like she just been washed in light. Like she was alive again. But that weren't the only thing. She began to look sketchy you get me? Jumpy and nervous. And whenever I asked her whether she was any further with her plan she would just say, 'Soon. Just give me a little more time. It's coming together.'

On the fourth or fifth day I started to get worried about Ki. Proper worried. I half questioned whether the pressure that Ki had put on herself to come up with a plan was what was bothering her. God only knew how we were supposed to get ourselves out of this shit. And why did I think Ki would have the answer anyway? What was she supposed to do? Think up a plan that would take Face out of the picture somehow – just like that? It was one thing maybe to bring down some next crew, but Face was premier league. There was no way we could face off Face. Mouse can't fight a snake, I said to myself. Mouse can't fight a snake.

But the more I thought about how impossible it was, the more it became obvious what had to be done. How it was going to be done was another thing, but at least I knew what it was that needed to be done.

I stared out of the window and noticed that the

skies had gone dark like they were brewing up for a storm. I hoped Ki wasn't going to get caught in the thunderstorm. I was pretty sure she hadn't taken an umbrella. I found myself wondering whether burkhas were waterproof. Then thinking about Ki, getting caught up in the rain, just a simple thing like that got me wondering about her moods when she came back.

She had this look painted across her face like she had found enlightenment. She didn't seem worried no more. And each day she seemed less and less scared and more and more focused. Those grey eyes would slip all lazy under her lids and I could almost see her brain mashing up the problems and sifting out the solutions. Was it the pressure of being cooped up inside the flat that was making her strange or was maybe some shit going on at that mosque she was going to? It made me wonder. After all, those places know how to churn out the nutters don't they?

I didn't really think of myself as following her exactly. I was more just making sure that she was okay in my mind at least. Who knew what went on in those places after they finished the prayers? Did they all meet up in some room with a wall chart and start planning their next terrorist attack or was it was just tea and cakes? Who the fuck could tell? Not me at any rate. I just wanted to be sure they weren't mind-fucking her you know what I mean. She had enough shit going on without having to help some shoe-bombing sisters of Islam put their shit together.

The nearest mosque to our place was just a short bus ride away in a straight line. It wasn't one of them domes and minuets places that I had in my mind. It was more like some grim little community centre that they had converted. Although I didn't know for sure that was where she went, that was my best guess. I don't know why I didn't ever ask her. Maybe I was worried she might have thought I was crowding her if I started to get all up in her face about exactly where she went.

Anyway half an hour after she had gone on this fifth day, Friday I think it was, I decided to go after her. Like I say, not to follow her or check on her, but just to make sure she was okay.

I pulled on a hoodie low over my eyes and jumped down the stairwell to the communal doors. I pushed open the heavy metal doors and the light hit me, like bam. And then all the smells that I had nearly forgotten. It was strange to be out in the proper daytime. It felt like I hadn't really seen real daylight for time. The closest I had got to the outside was that day with the Alpina but that was more or less night-time. I looked up at the sky which was getting darker by the second and pulled my clothes tight to me. I ran to the nearest bus stop and put my head under the shelter just as the first drops of rain started. For some reason I couldn't quite work out, I felt really uneasy. Like some bad shit was going to happen.

I jumped on the first bus I saw and sat on the lower deck away from the kids at the top who were making the kind of noise that people without real problems can make. All I wanted to do was to make sure she was okay, I said to myself as I stared out of the window. The ride was a short one maybe two stops. Then I saw the low, square building come into view. I rang the bell and then got off and jogged up to it keeping close to the walls to try and avoid the rain. It still had the words 'Community Centre' high up on the bricks, just above the words 'Camberwell Community Mosque'. I took a deep breath and approached the main doors.

The prayers were still in progress when I got there so I hung back outside and waited close by in a doorway to avoid the rain. I didn't really want to be interrupting no prayers. You know you don't want to be fucking wid no Muslims breders when they in the middle of praying. They don't take to that kind of shit well from what I hear.

Ten minutes or so later the people started pouring out. Hundreds of them. Made you wonder how they could get so many people in one small place. I mean literally, there were hundreds of them. There were even more people in here than in my mum's church and trust, her church packs them in on any given Sunday. This mosque though must have been rammed with three times the numbers I even saw in a church. I didn't go in but I had a sneaky look in through the windows of the double doors.

It's just like it is on TV. Rows and rows of people, not an inch between them, all praying. I have to tell you, for a second I started to wonder whether there was maybe something in this religion thing. That many people all cramming into one tiny space, all praying? It's not like they even got chairs you get me. It's all just floor. You didn't go to a place like that just to get some quiet time or because your mum made you go but you could still doze off and think about at least getting a Sunday lunch after. And there weren't even no singing you get me. This was more like the gym. The kind of place you go to do your thing and then leave.

So anyway, I waited to see if I could see Ki when I realized that the only people coming out were men. I don't mean mainly men. I mean all men. Every single one. So when the last few stragglers were coming out I stopped one of the younger guys.

'Hey, is there ladies in this place?' I said keeping my eyes low.

'Sisters' entrance round the back,' he says as he's slipping his shoes on and then mingles in with the rest of the crowd heading out.

Who knew there was a ladies' entrance? Shit. I ran round the back just in time to see the door open. And then slowly at first, they start to come out, until there's maybe sixty of them out there. And then slowly it hits me. I'm a idiot.

Every second one of these ladies is in a black burkha. There are dozens of Kiras. All star-bursting into different directions to get out of the rain. Shit. I can't follow all of them so I decide I got no choice but to get back. Quickly.

I kept it on the low, head down, hoodie zipped up, eyeballed no one. In less than ten minutes I was racing

279

back up the stairs to my flat. Breath heavy with all the no-exercise I was doing at that time. I know to look at me with all these prison muscles I look like a superhero but in them days, cooped up in that flat, I was more Fat-man than Batman.

The thing that messed me up though when I got back in was that Ki still wasn't back. Maybe she was still inside hanging with a few of the sisters until the rain stopped, I thought. It was possible since I didn't actually go into the building. And anyway she weren't going in there to pray so maybe she was up in some room somewhere where maybe people go to meditate or whatever.

So when she did turn up an hour later, I didn't say anything. Nobody wants to be one of them type of guys who stalks his own girlfriend innit?

She breezed in holding her burkha over one arm and came into the kitchen bit where I was heating up some soup for lunch. She gave it a jokey, 'Honey I'm home,' draped her burkha over one chair and sat on another by the table.

'Hey come sit, we need to talk,' she says and smiles at me.

I sit next to her and I can feel the heat coming from her body. Then she puts a hand on my leg and suddenly a waterfall opens in my mind. The thoughts come crashing out just like that. Her face close to mine. Her eyes locking me into her. The scent of her skin. My head begins to spin from the memory of her, of us. Of how we were before it all became messed up. It has been so long since she touched me at all that I have almost forgotten that we were a living thing once. A fire-breathing thing. I look at her and she smiles that smile of hers. A smile from before.

For a second it makes me forget that anything was wrong. Then something niggles me and I snap back into reality feeling like when you fall asleep and then you are awake.

'Those things waterproof?' I say, indicating the burkha.

'What? Erm no.' Then she realizes what I'm getting at and adds, 'Oh I got a lift. Anyway shut up about that and listen for a second. I think I've worked it out.'

I stare blankly at her for a second until her look reminds me. We have more serious stuff to worry about than this.

'Sure,' I say. 'Yeah well I think I worked it out too,' I add and pull up a chair next to her.

'Oh yeah?' she says, 'Fire away genius,' she says still smiling. 'And while you're at it pour me a bowl of that delicious-looking soup you got going on there.'

This was one of those moments where the old Ki seemed to materialize. It was almost as if she was back to how she used to be. If I could only hold on to her and keep her here I knew everything would be okay.

'Well,' I say as I pour her soup into a mug, 'the way I figured it yeah, is there ain't no way Guilty going to be taking down no twenty-man crew, all of them carrying. Nothing we can do going to fix them numbers you get me?'

'Go on.'

'But –'

'Yeah?' she says, curious.

'Can a mouse eat a snake?'

She looks at me like I have lost my mind. 'Are you feeling alright?' she says with a kind of half-smile.

'Look Ki, what if the snake had no head?'

'Err – what?'

'What if the snake had no head?' I say and realize that I am sounding a bit crazy even if I know what I mean.

'Then sure,' she says slowly but you can see from her face she thinks she's talking to a retarded person.

'Then that's what has to be done. We need to find a way to take the snake's head off.'

'What are you talking about?'

So then I explain it to her. All about how I was asking myself how can a mouse beat a snake, and how he couldn't unless maybe the snake had no head. And then even as I am saying it, it sounds stupid so I stop midway.

It takes a minute but then she smiles to herself and says, 'You are a genius after all.'

'No need for sarcasm,' I say.

'No. I'm serious. That is just what I have been thinking.'

And that's when she says them words that change our lives. Once a thing like this is said, it can't be unsaid. It gets a life of its own. Like planting a seed. All you can do is step back and watch it grow.

'We have to take out Face. Once he's gone it's game

over. And we can get some normal back in our lives. Stop all this hiding. Living like we are fugitives.'

'That's it! That's what I was getting at!' I say amazed that for once I'm not completely stupid. Then it hits me what she just said. '"We"? I never said nothing about we,' I say suddenly not liking what I think she means.

'Who then? Guilty? You think he can do this?' she says looking right at me.

'Yes I do. We can set Face up somehow and let Guilty take him out. One on one. Element of surprise.'

'Guilty?' she says with her eyes all wide. 'From what I hear about Guilty, he can't even take the bins out. No babe. We can't risk leaving this to him.'

'I don't know what you've heard Ki or who you been speaking to, but Guilty ain't a person to fuck with. Mans is brutal.'

'It's not about that. I don't care if he's brutal. I care about if he's smart enough to make a move on Face. And even from what you told me, he is not,' she says and I know she is right.

'Who then?' I say. 'Who's going to do it?'

'Us. We have to do this,' she says and leaves the room.

Long adjournment: 16:05

IN THE CENTRAL CRIMINAL COURT   T2017229

Before: HIS HONOUR JUDGE SALMON QC

Closing Speeches:

Trial: Day 36

Thursday 13th July 2017

APPEARANCES

For the Prosecution: Mr C. Salfred QC

For the Defendant: In person

Transcribed from a digital audio recording by

T. J. Nazarene Limited

Official Court Reporters and Tape Transcribers

31

This plan of Ki's I was telling you about yesterday, the plan to take out Face. I don't really know when it was that we basically started taking our lead from Ki or why. It might have been just that she was smart or it might have been that we didn't have any ideas. But what you could say was right about then, Ki was directing ops. She was the General in our little three-man crew.

I still wasn't sure what Ki meant about 'us' having to deal with Face. I mean I didn't think she meant like we literally had to do it ourselves. Just maybe you know put things in place so some next crew member from Glockz could do it. Or something anyway. Something that didn't mean that we physically had to do the thing.

Yeah I meant killing him. Straight up. But I was saying that I didn't think that she meant that we had do the killing ourselves. So you know, you ain't catching me out on that.

So yeah, I'll say it again, it makes me look guilty. But like I said I didn't think she actually meant that *we* kill him. So the next day, we arranged for Curt to come by so we could chat it out with him. We couldn't raise him on his phone and we figured that he was ditching sims as usual. But Ki tracked him down in the end by phoning Mum's, where he just happened to be.

'Come round,' I said, 'we need to chat,' and I put the call down. Ki gave me another one of them smiles that I am supposed to be able to decode but can't.

When he came Curt was proper on edge.

'Shit is going down,' he says as he pulls his coat off and slings it over a chair.

'Before we get into that,' I say handing him a beer before he takes one, 'what you doing round my mum's?'

'You mean round at Bless's,' says Ki smiling like this is a joke.

Curt nearly drops his beer.

'Nothing man. Just making sure they safe innit,' he says going kind of purple. 'Anyway, word on the street is –' he starts when suddenly Kira laughs out.

'What you talking like that for?' she says.

'Like what?'

'Like you're a seventies pimp from American TV?'

For some reason that makes me laugh too. 'Yeah man. What's with the jive talking?'

'Whatever,' he says, 'but shit is going down.'

'Like what kind of shit?' I say.

'Like the smelly kind. Face shot at Guilty this morning.'

'What? Is he dead? What the fuck man?' I say my eyes wide open and serious now.

'Nah man. He shot *at* him not shot him. Well not Face exactly but one of his Tinies. Four of them came on

288

bikes. They rode past the club just as he was coming out and one of them fired off like a hundred shots at him. Not a fucking one of them hit him if you can believe it.'

'Shit,' I say and look at Ki.

I know to you this sounds weird. Gangsters on bikes. But as I said before the whole drug thing is like an army. You know Generals, Lieutenants, Soldiers. Well, Generals and Lieutenants and some Soldiers drive cars. Other Soldiers, younger ones, the ones we, I mean they, call Tinies, they ride bikes.

You might have seen these young kids on bikes tearing your streets up. And to you it might seem like they just schoolkids. But what you should know is that that shit ain't always random, and these kids ain't always just school kids. These are drug dealers. They are soldiers-in-waiting, at ten years old. And when they ride, they ride in *formation*. Depending on how many there are, a couple might ride up front and scope out the territory. The man with the gun will be back a little, flanked on each side by another couple of out-riders. They shield him. They scope their target. They ride past. Boy with the gun shoots and rides off. The rest take whatever drugs and money they find and bang – they're gone.

And the chaos that follows afterwards with all of them riding off in different directions, that's not random either, it's thought out. Spread out. Don't get caught. If there's heat around, the gun will get dumped. No prints on it either since these boys are wearing latex gloves. These little boys, they are smart.

So anyway Curt tells us that some Tinies just tried to kill Guilty. And Ki goes mad.

'We need Face gone. Like now,' she says her eyes narrowing at us both. 'If we leave this much longer Guilty will be dead and we will be next. We have to move on this.'

'Is that all? Why didn't you just say so? Hang on a second while I call fucking rent-a-hitman,' I say. Ki gives me a look.

'Nah man it's okay,' Curt says after a while. 'We can do this.'

'How?'

'I'll let Guilty know that he's being set up and he can organize a trap,' says Curt, 'and then, you know, ambush Face. Or something.'

Ki and I both look at Curt and whatever it is we are trying to say to him he understands and looks down at his feet.

'Look we all know even though he is a bad man and whatever, Guilty couldn't even spell ambush. No. We need to do it,' says Ki.

'No fucking way,' I say. 'No fucking way'.

'We got no other choice,' she says and folds her arms into a tight knot.

I suddenly felt like she was slipping out of my hands. All I wanted was our life back again. I wanted days where we went together to Barnardo's while she picked out books. Evenings where we could just lie on the sofa and watch a film without having this weight on our minds. I wanted to be able to look in those eyes of hers and see myself in them. I wanted to recognize her again.

Look I knew that there weren't no way that Guilty was going to be able to take out Face using his own wits. Face was just too smart and would have outmanoeuvred him in a second. And I also knew that there was no question that Face had to be taken out, if we wanted to live. I knew from a theoretical point of thing that this was all true. But I still couldn't make the jump from what seemed logical on paper to reading about it in the papers. It seemed mad to me. Mad that we had to actually be talking about killing a person. Fuck we had already nearly killed one boy. By accident I mean. But this was some next shit.

For one I wasn't that happy about dragging Ki into yet another situation. She had had enough drama to last her a dozen lifetimes. She didn't need a planned killing to add to it. And as unbreakable as she seemed to be, I knew that even she had her limits. She might have seemed to the outside world like she was solid. Like a V8 engine. But you know you put any engine under pressure and it's going to break. You can red-line it every now and then but you don't want to be red-lining all the time. And she had been in the red for some time. Anyway, I didn't want to be driving her to her limits again. And the way that I saw it was that I was responsible for this whole thing. I couldn't get her into another thing.

Then there was the risk involved. Face wasn't just smart enough to outwit Guilty, shit a five-year-old could outwit Guilty. Face was too smart, even for Ki, maybe. Sure she had skills, but I knew the limit of her skills, high as they were. What I didn't know were the limits of his. How high did he go? And if this shit went sideways, it wasn't a game where we could reload and get another life and try again. If this went wrong and Face dried us out, we would die. No question. He would ice us in a second.

And then. And then there is the simple fact of life. It was a life after all was said and done. His life was still a life. I know that Ki had put a bullet in Jamil and nearly killed him and I know that we then dumped him as if he was dead but that was just more like an accident kind of thing. Ki shot him by accident. She never meant to kill him. I don't think she even meant to shoot him. And yes I can see that he survived her bullet and that was an accident too. They say I maybe helped him survive by taping up his bullet hole and that it stopped the blood loss. I don't know about any of that for real but what I do know for sure is that if I helped him live, that was an accident too. I didn't plan on saving his life, but I didn't plan on shooting him either.

But this thing was different. I knew that this guy would kill me, kill Ki, kill Curt, kill our families in a heartbeat. Did that make it okay to kill him? I don't know man. But still, unless he was there in front of me, holding a gun to me, I didn't feel right about killing him like this. You know, like planned. It was like shooting a dude in the back. It didn't feel right to me. To plan a killing of a living breathing human being ain't like an accident kind of thing. It ain't like causing a war so that someone else pulls the trigger. If you plan to do it, that is next level shit. That in my book is a murder.

Break: 10:45

32

Curt left later that day and we all agreed that we would think about what had to be done and meet up again the next morning. The more I looked at it, though, the more it looked as if this had to be done. But I still couldn't get my head around it. Why did I feel so bad about it? He was going to kill me if he ever saw me. And here I was feeling guilty about it. Was it that much different from shooting that guy under the bridge when I took Ki? Would I feel okay about it if the man was in my face waving a gun at me? Could I shoot him then? Did I have to wait for that to happen? Is it still like a self-defence kind of a thing if you know a person will definitely kill you if he gets half a chance? But you take your chances before he does? I don't know, truth be told. It's proper confusing me.

That night Ki and I sat up and talked some more about it. She had spent a couple of hours writing down some details about the plan in a notepad and made me read them. But the more I read them the crazier it all sounded to me. We needed a gun. We needed to know where Face would be at. We needed an exit strategy. And we needed more luck than a human being could expect to get in ten lives. Suddenly I couldn't hold it down any longer.

'We ain't doing it,' I said to her, throwing her notes down on the table.

'What do you mean?' she asks me.

'What I said. We ain't doing it. We ain't wasting two men without like a proper need for it.'

'Proper need? What about your life? What about my life? Is my life not a good enough reason for you?' Her eyes are electric again.

'Ki, your life is one thing. We got our lives. We can go away. Scotland, whatever. Spain, we were going to go to Spain. We still can. We got the dollars. We got a choice. Let's just go. I can't be doing no killing. And I can't be letting you get involved in no killing.'

'Me?' she says her voice climbing. 'Can't let me get involved in no killing? Shouldn't you have thought about that before? Before you went and pulled me out of Glockz with all guns blazing?'

'What could I have done?' my voice following hers upwards into the sky. 'Left you there? What choice did I have?'

'What choice do you have now? Really? You disappear and Bless will be killed. Your mum too. Face won't stop. You know that. He's a machine. It's just a matter of time before he sends his little biker boys round to your mum. You want to wait till they've fired off a hundred shots at your mum? Or are you hoping they might miss her as well?'

295

'Until he's aiming a gun at me, he's just a person, Ki.'

Suddenly she stops whatever it was she was doing and drives them eyes straight into mine.

'Is this what it is? You worried about your soul?' she says almost laughing but not in a way that made me comfortable.

'Soul? I ain't said nothing about soul. I'm talking about a life. A real human. You are talking about killing a person. Planning it and executing it. Executing him. We'd be the same as him Ki, if we did this.'

'We are nothing like him. He murders people for money. He murders people for kicks and licks. He is a drug dealer. You are a car dealer. You are not him. We are not him. Nobody will cry for him. Trust me. Nobody. Not even his mum. He wrote this ending. Not us. He did it,' she says her voice calming now a little. She takes a deep breath and then looks at me, her eyes a bit softer than before. 'Now do you want to look at the details again or not?'

'No, man,' I say, and snatch up the pad she is waving in my face. 'I've read it.'

'Good. We start going over this properly tomorrow. When Curt comes in the morning, you stay with him until you get this down perfectly.'

'What about you? Where will you be?'

'The mosque,' she says and picks herself up and goes to the bedroom, leaving me staring at her notes. This is going to be a disaster – I can feel it.

*

The next morning Curt comes knocking on the door just in time for breakfast. It is as if he can smell the eggs cooking. He nods a hello at Ki and pulls up a chair.

'So Ki got a plan?' he says to me but indicating to Kira who is plating up eggs for him.

'Yeah,' I say and show him the notepad.

He sits down at the table and starts to read. By the time he is finished he is smiling.

'Girl,' he says to her holding up the pad, 'respect.'

'You eat your breakfast,' Ki says in reply, 'I've got some last minute planning to do. By the time I come back though, you two need to have this memorized,' she adds and then before I can say goodbye, she is gone, her burkha under her arm.

'What's up?' Curt says looking at me, seeing that I am on edge.

'Nothing.'

''Kay. Then . . . what's with the atmosphere?'

'I'm stressing about Ki innit.'

'Why?'

'Everything man. This plan about killing Face. It is madness bruv. We can't go round shooting up no gangsters. We ain't in some movie.'

'Feel you bruv. But what is our choices right now, though?'

'Well we could just jet out of here. Go on the run.'

'Shit blood. You know you ain't leaving your sister. And your mum, I mean. We got no choices right now but to do this thing.'

'Okay. Let's say you're right. We don't have no choice. I get it. We can't run. We can't go Feds. We can't just wait to get merked. So we do this thing, yeah. So tell me one thing. How the fuck we going to do this,' I say shaking the pad at him, 'this plan? How we going to bump this Face man?'

'We shoot him. Just like Ki is saying.'

'Yeah. But how are we supposed to *find* him? It's not like we can phone his secretary to find out where he's at.'

'Ki innit,' he says as if the answer was staring me in face all along.

'Jokes blood, ha ha. Okay then. How is *Ki* going to find that out?'

'She just knows innit,' his face flat.

'What do you mean she knows?' I say proper confused now.

'She just knows shit.'

Curt takes a giant forkful of egg into his mouth and then cocks his head at me like now he's the one who is confused. Then he says this: 'Well all the bits of info she been feeding me has been checking out. It is all solid vine.'

I take a breath trying to work out what he's saying.

'What? Kira has been giving you vine? What kind of fucking vine, blood?'

'Just like, don't go there today – so-and-so going to be there.'

'Ki? You sure?'

'Yeah I'm sure. You think that Guilty dodged them bullets by chance? Kevlar bruv.'

'What?' I say surprised. Like proper shocked. I didn't even know what the boy was talking about to even ask all of the right questions.

'Kevlar. Body armour. Guilty had body armour on. He was expecting to be rushed by Face. That is how he swerved them nine mils,' says Curt smoothing down his shirt as if to show me where a person might wear body armour.

'Yeah man. I know what Kevlar is. I mean, what? You trying to say Ki told you that Face was going to attack Guilty?' I say not believing what I have just heard.

'Straight up man. Time and date.'

'Where the fuck she tell you she was getting this from?'

'Mosque.'

'What you talking about bruv?'

'Mosque. She's hooked up. She's getting whispers. As I say, it's all been checking out. Ask her yourself when she gets back. Shit I thought you knew. You didn't know?'

'No, I didn't fucking know,' I say.

I had no idea what the hell was going on any more. Ki is passing information to Curt to pass to Guilty about where Face is going to strike? Where the fuck was she getting this from? I couldn't really believe it was actually from the mosque. What was I? Out of my mum yesterday?

What, she goes down there one day and suddenly

she's hooked into vine with one of the biggest gang leaders in the country? Nah, man. I didn't buy that shit. And anyway, even if she was getting information from some next mans or woman for that in the mosque, how the fuck she know that she weren't being stitched up by the man himself? This was classic Faceman moves. He was the information commissioner you get me. And this false feeding of intel was exactly what I would have expected of him. It would have made just the kind of story that people would be telling about him in years to come. Just like Face and the R.I.P. shirts.

'Listen bruv, you wait here,' I say. 'I'll be back.' I look around for my keys and start heading out of the door.

'Where you going man?' he says puzzled, but not puzzled enough to stop eating eggs.

'I'm going find where she's at,' I say and leave.

Luncheon adjournment: 13:00

33

I hope you lot had a good lunch. Mine was Gordon Ramsay obviously.

So I decided to go out and look for her. The weather was still pretty U.K. It was grey with that rain that hasn't decided to commit to raining properly. I stuck on my hoodie and put my face to the ground and walked out of the block. I jumped on the bus and before I knew it I was there, waiting outside the bit where the women go in and out round the back. The whole of my journey there was a blank. I remembered none of it.

I am waiting wondering how this conversation's going to go. I know more or less what I need to say to her but what I can't do right then is imagine what she is going to say that ain't going to make this shit less mad ting than it is. And one thing that was frying me up more than everything else was why, whatever she was doing, she was doing behind my back. You know what I mean? She could have at least told me about it.

'Brother you can't wait at the ladies' entrance.' I look round startled and see that this guy who is standing there is talking to me. But he's smiling at me so I can tell he's not disrespecting. I move round to the front. It's starting to spit down so I stand just inside the entrance and wait. Through the glass in the doors I can see it again. Rows of people standing like bottles in an off-licence, all their shoulders touching. All of them moving as one, standing, kneeling, standing. Even when they are doing the 'I'm not worthy' pose, all of them go down and come up at the same time like there's a signal inside of them.

When they pour out at last, a few of them nod at me. I even recognize some of them back from the last time. Then one small guy with a white skull-cap thing and cotton dress thing, with a smile that makes dimples in his face, looks like he's coming straight at me. Just before I move out of the way he puts out his hand.

'Assalamalaikum brother.'

'Slamalaikum,' I go, or something like that.

'Imam would like a word,' he says still smiling.

'Who?'

'The imam. The, erm, priest.'

'What for? I ain't doing nothing,' I say making a face at him and then I turn as if to leave.

'No, he just wants to talk. Maybe you have some questions?' he says smiling still.

'Questions?'

'About Islam?'

'Nah, man. I'm just looking for someone innit,' I say and try and leave again.

'I seen you here last time brother. Maybe the person you are looking for is Allah?' he says still with that Buddha smile.

'Trust me I ain't looking for Allah,' I go and turn around for real now. Then as I go to walk away I feel this gentle pressure on my arm and see that he's holding it. I hold back my instinct to shrug him off and punch him in the face.

'Just come in for five minutes. Ask Imam anything you like and then you can get on with the rest of your day. Just five minutes.'

The crowds had all about gone so that there was only really me and him left. The rain was coming down heavier now and I guess right then at that moment, that's all it took. Plus it might not be a bad thing to have a look inside and see what is going on at this place where Ki has been hanging.

The imam wasn't the hook-hand-eye-patch-beardy-screamer that I was hoping for. He was just, you know, normal. He was maybe thirty with a trimmed beard. Not tall. Not fat. Just average. And he weren't in some box or nothing or standing on top of a flight of stairs waving a stick around. He was sitting in the corner just saying goodbyes or whatever to some regulars.

'Ah brother,' he says standing up and offering me his hand, 'Assalamalaikum.'

I gave my best try back at him.

'You're the young man Abdul mentioned. You've been waiting outside, he tells me. He thinks you had some questions perhaps?' he says. I look round for the guy who brought me in, but he has gone.

'Not really. I was just waiting for someone,' I say and start shifting about in my socks.

He carries on smiling at me and part of me begins to feel sorry for him. I feel like I need to ask him something just so he feels better about having brought me in. I search for a question I can maybe ask him.

'Actually I do have one question. Why does everyone stand so packed in tight together when they're praying? You need more space or something?'

'Muslims,' he says, 'are fond of saying that if there's a space between two people praying then the Devil stands in it.'

'Seen.'

'But that isn't what is really meant by that saying. It means that if you let people make spaces between each other when they are praying, then some people will say, "Oh I don't want to stand next to that man, he looks dirty or he smells," or something like this. The Devil is really in man's behaviour, not standing in the mosque with horns and a tail,' he says making a 'horns' sign with his fingers.

'But maybe sometimes people don't want to be standing next to some rank-smelling person. They want to be standing next to clean people,' I say back. If you ever been on a bus in Peckham you will know what I mean.

'Clean people are only dirty people who have washed. And dirty people are only clean people that have not yet washed,' he says showing me a smile.

'So we all the same then is that what you're saying?'

'No, we are not the same. But we can be.'

By the time I leave I know that Ki ain't here. She has gone already. I had missed her again. I was going to ask the imam about where the ladies hang out but I thought maybe I would come off as some kind of pervert if I did that so I just shook his hand and left.

By the time that I get back to the flat, Ki is there already and is deep in conversation with Curt. I walk in and see them both sat around the table and flipping through the notes that she has made. Ki looks up and starts to speak as if she knows what I am going to say.

'Look I know what you're going to say,' she says standing up and taking a step towards me, 'but I can explain it.'

'I doubt that. Because this shit is going to need more explaining than I think you got in the tank. But fire away Kira. Tell me. What the fuck is going on?'

'I didn't know for sure whether what I was being told was true. I had to, you know, test it out. That's why I told Curt, so he could get back to me if it all checked out. And it does!' she says her eyes going wide with excitement.

'Wait, wait, wait. You didn't know if what you were being told was true? Being told by who? Who, Kira? Who is giving you all this vine?' I say now with my voice at max revs.

'One of the girls in the mosque. I overheard her speaking to one of her friends. It was her. That is who I got it from. That's why I have been going there every day. To pick up bits and pieces.'

'One of the girls? Are you crazy Ki? Just some random girl starts talking to her mate and suddenly you know that a proper big man gangster is planning a hit on Guilty? You expect me to believe that?'

'It's not some random girl,' she says quietly and then her tone changes a bit, 'and anyway what does it matter if you believe it or not? It is checking out.'

'Are you even that stupid? You believe some girl you don't even know? How you even know that you're not being set up by Face himself? And who is this girl anyway. You still haven't said.'

'It's Face's girlfriend. Or to give him his real name, Faisal's girlfriend. Look whether you believe me or you don't believe me the fact is that I trust what I am hearing. She is not setting me up because she has no idea who I am. I don't even talk to her. I just sit close by and listen in.'

'So how do you know that she is Face's girl? Or that Face is this Faisal guy? Come on Ki you're smarter than that,' I go, getting angry now at how stupid this is all sounding to me.

Just then her phone pings up a message and she quickly clicks her phone and puts it back in her handbag. She thinks I ain't seen it. But I have.

'Obviously I didn't at first. But the more I heard, the more it sounded like it could be him. That is why I had to tell Curt. So he could check it out. See if it was real.'

Curt gets up from the table holding the pad.

'Listen guys. Right now it don't matter how Kira knows this shit. Truth is we need to stop him. He is getting too close to Guilty and we are next, believe. We can't just sit here waiting to be merked, innit.'

Ki sits down again and takes out the notebook she's been writing in. I try and catch her eye to maybe see if I can see in her but she avoids my look.

'Okay Curt,' she says flipping open the book, 'if we are doing this thing, we need to move quickly. Face is going to be at Charley Horse nightclub on Jake Street on Friday. We do it then.'

Curt nods as if she's just said, 'Let's go for a burger.'

'What just like that?' I say amazed that this is all so simple for them.

'Yes. Just like that. You've still got your gun. We go in at nine.'

I feel her being pulled away from me again. I can't hold on to her tightly enough. She just slips through my fingers. This time though I can't tell whether she is the one moving away or I am. She is talking at us in a way that makes this seem almost like a dream. I tune in and out until I can get a clearer signal.

'I've squared it with the door staff, they'll give me a pass in through the front. You and Curt go in through the back. I've arranged it so that the doors will be unlocked but pulled to. Give it a tug and you'll be in. When you walk in, there's a corridor and some steps leading up to the main club. It'll be pretty dark so use your phones for light. There's a door on the left. You wait in there. I'll let you in when it's time.'

Curt nods.

I'm still stunned about what I am hearing. Nothing seems real. It feels like I've walked in halfway through a film but a film that I was supposed to be in. It wasn't like I had forgotten my lines, it was more like I didn't even know I had lines. I snap out of this trance that I am in by shouting at Curt.

'Curt are you listening to this? Ki what the hell you chatting about?'

'This is still a surprise to you?' she says cocking her head and squeezing bright lights out of them eyes.

Curt steps in between me and Ki as if I might do something to her.

'Bro, what are our choices right now? I'm just about keeping Guilty out of the way of enough bullets,' Curt says, but he can't look at me so he's looking at his hands.

'Fuck,' I say, 'we can't do this.'

'Why? Why can't we do this? We can't not do this,' says Ki keeping her eyes on me till I can't look at her no more.

Break: 15:00

34

People talk about crossroads moments. You have probably spoken about crossroads moments, I don't know. But whatever you have heard about them and whatever you think your crossroads moment was, truth is, that weren't no crossroads you were at. That was more like a bend in the road or a place where the tarmac has come off. Mine, mine was a crossroads moment, right there, right then.

I don't know whether if I had done something different maybe what happened afterwards would not have happened. If I had spoken some different words even, maybe that could have changed something. But what I remember about that day is that I could see the roads crossing in front of me. Every way I could take pointed to somewhere I didn't want to go. They were all pointing to one hell or another hell. And these roads were the one-way kind. What I know is that if there's at least one place in four that you want to go or could even live with going, you ain't at no crossroads, trust me.

'Okay,' I say at last, 'we do this, we do it my way.' I

309

look at their two faces and there's no resistance in them so I carry on. 'First of all I don't know where my gun is at. I ain't seen it since the whole Jamil-in-the-trap-house thing. Second of all, Ki, you ain't going in no front door, you staying put here. Thirdly –'

'No. No. No,' says Ki. Something in her eyes shows me that she is not backing down. 'You cannot do this without me. You will be killed. Are you hearing me? You need me there to get into the club and you need me there to call you to let you know when he's alone. If you go walking into that club at any time and he sees you, any one of twenty guys will be queuing up to put you down.'

'Yeah well that's where your brain needs to catch up with mine for a change Ki, because ain't no way no phone is going to be working in that club. No phone Ki, no need for you.'

'Do you even know me at all?' she says smiling out of the corner of her mouth. She goes into her hand-bag again and throws Curt and me each a lump of black plastic.

'What the fuck are these?' I say.

'Two-way radio. Got them from the bouncers. They use one channel, we use the second.'

'When? When did you get these?' I say. This is all sur-real still and I still haven't caught up with her. Right then I don't know whether I can ever catch up with her. 'And what about a gun?' I ask. 'Where we supposed to get one from now?'

'Curt,' she then says looking over at him. He is by the window looking out on to the street, his hugeness making shadows on the floor. 'Can you do something about a gun too?'

'It'll be dirty but I can probably get one by Friday,' he says.

'There we are then,' says Ki. She has it all worked out.

'Just one more question,' I say. 'How the hell you know Face is going to be there?'

'I just do,' she says and as far as she was concerned that was the end of it.

As soon as Curt left, whatever life was in those eyes of hers went again. The shutters went down and every time I tried to engage her she just looked through me. Of course I knew that all of this stuff was proper stressful for her. It was stressful for me but if you peeled back my layers I could pretty much guarantee that you'd still have found the same old me. A little more wired, yes, but basically the same guy. Ki had changed. Don't get me wrong. I know she had a right to change after all this shit. But she was changing before my eyes in a way that I couldn't keep up with. It was Spooks, I was sure of that.

She changed most after seeing Spooks. That time when she came back for the first time in that burkha and gave me the fright of my life. That is when it happened. The change. Not change in a way that would have been obvious to anyone looking from a distance, but I could see it. It was subtle at the beginning, almost like all the colours she was painted in started to change just in tone. The greens were not so alive. The blues were less vibrant. Everything was muffled like one of those 1970s' photographs where the colours are what they should be, just not sharp enough or bright enough to look real. Now, though, the colours on her were all wrong.

I was worried about her and I tried to talk to her after Curt went but the thing about Ki if you know her, is that she's not a person to be talked round. That was not anything new. She was always like that. It was one of the things I hated about her.

For any other normal person you could maybe pull them out of their bad moods with a joke or something. Even if not straight away, you could eventually crack most people. Ki though, she was not somebody you could talk round. It was like she considered it an insult to her own mind. As if you were saying to her, 'Whatever you're feeling, it's not the right feeling so change it.' So talk to her all you like. There was no way you could bust her out of whatever she was feeling. I know, I tried it enough times. The best thing to do in those times was to just let the feelings ride themselves out. Let them just be until they did the job she wanted them to. My way was to just change the subject.

I tried that of course but she wouldn't even really talk to me. It wasn't one of them moods that she was having where she looked like she hated me. It was just blanks. Her mind was somewhere else, and with Ki if her mind was somewhere else, all of her was there with it. Ki was her mind. The whole of the rest of that day went by with almost zero conversation. She grunted a 'no' when I asked her if she wanted a sandwich but sat with me as I ate. Later though, when I switched on the TV that night she went to the bedroom and just lay there staring at the ceiling and mumbling to herself, working something out. I didn't feel like going to bed right then so I called Mum.

'Mum,' I go, 'did I wake you?'

'Of course you will wake me up if you call at this kind of hour.'

'Sorry. I just –'

'I am just joking you, foolish boy. How can I go to sleep with the two of them downstairs?'

'The two of who?' I say suddenly worried.

'Your sister and that boy.'

I ask her, 'What boy, Mum? Who is there?' I can't believe I haven't been more careful and I can't believe Mum doesn't seem scared at all.

'The horse boy. Your friend.'

'Oh,' I go, 'Curt.' Then after a second I go, 'Curt? What's he doing there?'

'You are asking me? How should I know what you and your horse friend are up to all of the time? He says he needs to speak to your sister so he is speaking to your sister. That is all I know.'

I end the call and decide I need to go to sleep myself.

Thank God for Curt though. It's just like him to look in on Bless and Mum. I felt safe knowing that he was there.

I go and lie next to Kira. She is still awake, looking up at the lights, muttering quietly. I put my head next to hers and I try to think about nothing and before I know it I have fallen asleep.

The next day she was a little more with it you could say but truth be told I think that was more to do with the fact that she was on the phone for most of it. She would step out into the corridor, the communal one on our landing and take these calls. They were proper weird calls too. I didn't know who they were from but I did get that they were not normal calls. Mostly she just nodded with the handset held against her ear. Occasionally she said, 'Yes. Yes. Okay,' but that was about it. Really quick calls. No hellos no goodbyes. Like I say, weird. When I asked her about them she told me it was the bouncers at the club and how they were old friends of hers from time back. Or someone else that had something to do with how we could get in or get out. 'It's just details,' she said, 'leave it to me.'

I should have maybe guessed what was going on, but I swear down, my mind don't work on them kind of levels. This kind of thing is just out of my radar. I feel stupid now, but that time, I swear I had no idea. When I think back I sometimes think I probably should have known something was going on. Because I followed her to the mosque again the next day. I mean actually followed her. This time I left within a minute of her leaving so I could see where she went. Actually see exactly where she went. I should have known then.

Long adjournment: 16:20

IN THE CENTRAL CRIMINAL COURT   T2017229

Before: HIS HONOUR JUDGE SALMON QC

Closing Speeches:

Trial: Day 37

Friday 14th July 2017

APPEARANCES

For the Prosecution: Mr C. Salfred QC

For the Defendant: In person

Transcribed from a digital audio recording by

T. J. Nazarene Limited

Official Court Reporters and Tape Transcribers

35

11:10

I followed her. That was the time when I should have known that everything weren't on the level. I mean I knew it weren't on the level but I should have seen more. I blame myself for that. But this was some mad sideways thing that I didn't see coming at me. It was like when a car pulls out straight into you and you don't know it's happened until you hear the crunch. And you say to yourself over and over, I should have seen it man. I should have seen it.

So anyway like I said I followed her, the very next day. I wasn't buying that whole Faisal crap. I wanted to see with my own eyes what I could. Maybe it would all check out no matter what I thought. Don't get me wrong I was hoping it would check out. I thought maybe I could have a quiet scout around this time and see whether there were any guys hanging round who might be Face's boys. Because if this shit Ki was telling me was actually happening then maybe what I thought was right, that she was being set up. So I justified it to myself like that. I ain't *following her* following her. I'm following her, looking out for her.

I got to the ground floor of the block and quickly scanned the road to see where she was. I couldn't see her at first, but that was because I was looking the wrong way. She was walking in the opposite direction from the mosque I had been going to. No wonder I never saw her there whenever I went. She was going to a different mosque. Anyway my ride was parked just there on the corner so I quickly jumped in even though I knew it was risky to be taking it out on the road. But truth be told this whole thing was really getting to me and I needed to find out if the place she was going to was safe. I pulled out of the road just in time to see her getting on a bus and then I followed it.

My mind was racing even then but really and truly I weren't that surprised she was going to a different mosque, there's more than one mosque in London. But what did surprise me was that she took the bus all the way to Elephant and Castle. That seemed a long way to go for one. And for two it didn't really fit to me. Wasn't it Curt who took her to the mosque that first time? Surely he would have said if he'd taken her all the way to Elephant? I kept meaning to check this with him but didn't know how to do it without sounding like I didn't trust her – or him.

I kept the bus in view but stayed a couple of cars behind. I just needed to be close enough to see when she got off. Just after the roundabout I saw her. There she was. All in her Darth Vader kit. Once she got off the bus I knew I had to be more careful because even if no one else recognized my ride, there was no way Ki would miss it if she saw it. So I decided to park up and follow on foot. In the end it wasn't that hard to follow her because with her wearing that burkha thing she probably couldn't hardly see anything but her own feet. She turned down into a side street and I followed.

What surprised me though was that she didn't stop at no building that looked to me like any mosque. She was outside a building with nothing to see but a black door. I saw her then check her phone and then ring the bell.

I waited hidden in a doorway and watched. My heart was going for some reason I couldn't explain. A few seconds later the door opened and she walked in. I was a blank. I couldn't even guess what the hell she might be doing there. Maybe this was where the girl lived? Could it be that? Could it actually be a mosque? I know that sometimes a mosque is just a person's house that has been like converted. I waited a couple of minutes and then made up my mind to knock on the door. If she was there, this girl, then maybe I had a few questions of my own to ask her. I walked up to the door that Ki had just walked through and took a breath. I pushed at it but it was locked. I looked up at the building to see if there was anything interesting about it but I couldn't find anything that stood out. It just looked like one of those places that you could walk by without even noticing. That was the weird thing about the place. There was nothing about it told you what it was. It definitely didn't look like no mosque. And then there was the people.

There weren't any. The place was deserted. There was nobody queueing up to get behind this door.

It didn't feel right to me. So I walked past and decided to wait at the bottom of the road. Maybe it weren't such a good idea to go into a place without knowing what is inside it. I keep watching for twenty minutes or something but nobody walks in or out the whole time. Just then I see right at the end of the road, squeezed between a silver VW Golf and a black BMW X5, almost out of view, is a thing I recognize. That ice-blue Alpina. I just have time to register it when the door to the building opens again and I see Ki. She steps out, sorting out her burkha, and goes back up to the main road. She doesn't even turn back so I don't even have to hide. I ain't even sure whether I even would have hid to tell you the truth. I was so confused. This couldn't be no mosque that she'd just come out of, and that ice-blue Alpina, what was that about?

I can't work it out. It's too weird to make any sense. Anyway I am about to go and follow her when I see the door open again. I half expect another burkha to walk out. But I'm wrong about expecting that. What comes out is some white man. Six-foot-odd. Short blond hair. Grey suit. He turns the same way that Ki has gone but then stops halfway up the road and fishes for something in his pocket. The lights on the Alpina flick twice and he gets in and drives away. It must have been this fucker that had dropped her off to that other estate. But why? And who was he?

I should have realized then. But I didn't. I swear. I didn't even have a clue.

Look I know that this speech is long. It is bare long. But I feel like I need to tell you all the details of the thing so that you can feel me. And so now this Judge is telling me with his huffing and what have you and the snide looks he is giving me that I need to speed this shit up. It was the one thing my QC says to me just before I sacked him. He said keep the speech short enough to keep the jury's interests up. An average speech, he goes, should be like two hours max. But I can't do no two-hour speech for this. Even he couldn't do a two-hour speech if he was being charged with murder himself. It's like a thing you only get to know when you are in it. So I take it all on board. And I will speed it up. But it's not a kind of thing like I *want* to skip stuff out. I don't. But I don't want to lose you either.

But what I will tell you is that I did have it out with her when I got back to my yard. I looked at that Alpina pull away, and my head was full with just this one repeating thought. *What is going on? What is going on?* I walked back to where my ride was parked up and got in. I drove back to the flat in a daze. What could she even say to all this? This was not a thing she could lie her way out of. Too much needed explaining.

I went in and waited for her. She wasn't even that long behind me and when she came in she had that smile for me that she had shown me before and which had stopped me then from saying what I wanted to say. But this time, I wasn't having it. She shut the door quietly behind her and whipped her burkha off and hung it on a chair by the table.

'Hi,' she goes, 'everything alright? Any food going?' She is cool as she has ever been and I don't know how she can do it.

'What the fuck is going on Kira? I know about the other guy,' I say from behind a cup of tea I am drinking.

She freezes in the middle of rooting around in the fridge. I see her take a breath like she is considering her options. Finally she goes, 'It's not what you think.'

'How do you know what I'm thinking?' I say standing up so I can look right at her face when she turns around.

'You ain't thinking this,' she says her head still facing the fridge.

'Thinking what?' I go, trying to keep the volume out of my voice.

'I can't tell you. But you have to trust me,' she says turning to me at last. Her face is calm. Not like I expect it to be at all. There's no nervousness. She ain't acting caught out. She seems, I don't know, kind of relieved.

'How?' I shouted. 'How the fuck am I supposed to trust you after this Kira? Especially when you won't tell me what's going on?'

'Just – I promise. I will tell you everything. After. Tomorrow.'

And at the end of the day what choice did I have? She

324

was going to tell me and right then that had to be good enough. But I was an idiot. I should have made her say. I should have maybe worked it out. It was all there. All the pieces were there, I just didn't know how to make them fit inside each other.

So, now I can tell from the Judge's face it is time to get to the main point. And what you need to know about that most of all is the plan, innit. So Friday night came, the night that Face was going to be in the club, and Curt swung by early so we could go over the details of the plan again. We were all a little bit wired and the conversation was quite minimalist. He had managed to get his hands on a nine mil that wasn't too dirty. It had been used in some robberies here and there but as far as he knew there weren't any murders on it. He had brought it over in a McDonald's bag and set it down on our round kitchen table.

I opened the bag to take a look when Curt's giant hand came out of nowhere and swatted me away.

'Use the gloves man,' he says and fishes out a pair of latex gloves from his jacket pocket.

I put them on and open the bag. The gun is in there, lying fat in the bottom like a big black lump. I pick it up and feel its weight in my gloved hand.

'Loaded?'

'Five rounds. It's all I could get.'

'Guys, you ready? If anything's not clear, now's the time,' says Ki stepping into the room from the bedroom.

She is in sky-high heels and a black-and-white dress. Her hair is up and the make-up is only just there. She is beautiful.

'Yeah man,' says Curt who hardly notices her, 'let's jet.'

'You got your two-ways?'

We nod.

'Remember, keep it on that channel. There's no phone reception in the club,' says Ki and holds out a sports bag.

'Doesn't really go with the dress,' I say but she isn't in the mood.

I take the sports bag from her and slip the gun inside. I peel my latex gloves off and shove them in my jeans. Then we leave.

As we walk down the steps I hang back and let Curt head out in front. I pull Ki back a little by holding her wrist. She turns and looks at me. I want to say something, anything, just to connect with her, but I can't think of any right words to say. In the end I say nothing. She holds my eyes for a few seconds.

'I'm sorry,' she says and then stops and kisses me on the cheek.

Once we are on the street we stream off in two different directions. Ki goes one way to look for a black cab. Curt and I head for the bus stop and wait for the bus. We both have on almost identical white hoodies and white trainers. We know about the cameras on the bus. We want them to get us. It's all part of the plan that Ki has gone over and over. After a few minutes, the right bus comes and we jump on and head to the top deck and sit at the back so no one can hear us. In the end it doesn't matter that much because for the whole journey neither Curt nor me can think of anything to say.

The next fifteen minutes are slower than they should be. They stretch out until some part of me feels like we have been on this bus for an hour. Every now and then I catch myself panicking and then have to slow breathe until I am okay again. My brain is on a loop I can't get it out of. This idea of doing a murder. Not someone else pulling the trigger and taking a life. And not like in a film or on *Call of Duty* but in real life. With blood. With a person's face in front of mine and his smell in my nose. That kind of murder. I am going to do this thing that once it is done will stick to me for ever and be a part of me. When I get up in the morning there will be half a second where I know I will forget it ever happened. A half a second where I might think it was a dream or just even something we talked about but never did. And then that half-second will pass. And I will drag myself through the day until it ends. And then, the next day, it will happen all over again. Like a prison sentence but worse because there's no end time. All there is is a hope. A hope that one day it will stop feeling real and become a dream. I don't know for sure. All I got to go on is the feeling I had when Ki had been taken. That's what it felt like to me. And that is what brings me round again. Kira. I can't lose her. I can do this for her. I can do this for her even though it will mean that I am doing it every day for the rest of my life. Because without her, there isn't anything.

The club we are looking for is directly on our route and the bus makes a pass almost bang outside the front entrance.

Already the Friday night crowd is building up. A small queue has just started up and people seem to have lives that have nothing to do with shooting and gangs and raised heartbeats. It feels weird even to be out, watching people with normal lives. The bus has stopped but we don't move even though we are right outside the club. Then after a couple of moments it lurches off again leaving the club behind and taking us with it. As we pass it I look out of the back and just catch a glimpse of Ki. She is tiny against a mountain of a man she is standing next to. Ain't no bouncer going to turn her away looking like that, I am thinking, even if he didn't know her. As the club fades out of view, I catch a flash of a smile that isn't meant for me and one I haven't seen in weeks. Then she turns and slips through the double doors into the club, the bouncers following her with their eyes.

Five stops later Curt and I get off. We are half a mile away from the club but it's exactly where we need to be right now. The kiss on my cheek still tingles and I feel like it should feel like a good luck charm, but it doesn't exactly. But it does feel almost, what, holy? I nearly touch it but then stop at the last moment. I don't want to take the shine off it. It sounds stupid now but I needed it there to protect me. I still don't know why she said she was sorry but I put the thought away till later.

The main road is busy like it always is at this time of night at this time of the week. People out, needing to wash away their week or just to celebrate the end of it. Everyone just wanting to forget their lives for just a few hours. We mingle in with them as they walk by. We could even be them. Just normal people doing normal things in a normal life.

Curt nudges me as we approach the first side street we see. We walk down it and as we do I unzip the bag I am holding and take out a black hoodie as Curt takes off his white one. I hand the black one to him and he puts it on. Then I do the same. Both white hoodies go in the bag. Next, the trainers. We change our white ones for black ones that are in the bag and put the white ones in their place. It's all done so quickly and casually that we barely break our stride. We get to the end of the side road and turn left so that we are now walking parallel to the main road. My heart starts picking up pace again. My hands are sweating but I can't do anything about that. I wipe them down on my hoodie but I don't say anything to Curt. Curt strides on as if he has closed his mind to everything else. Something in his face tells me that he is going to treat the whole thing like this. One foot then the next.

In another twenty minutes or something we can see the back of the club. We pull the hoods down as we head towards it. There is a skip on one side all filled with rubble. I pull on my gloves as we near the skip, ducking under its cover, and take the gun out of the bag and put it in my waistband. I make sure nobody is looking.

I fish into the bag again and take out a smaller bag, it's a white plastic carrier bag. It has another hoodie in it and some tracksuit bottoms and trainers. I hide the sports bag with the white clothes we had been wearing in the skip under a bit of wood panelling. I do it quickly as I am walking and I know if anybody was watching they would have hardly noticed it. As we leave the skip behind, all I have in my hands now is the white carrier bag. The sports bag, the white clothes and the white trainers are all left behind now in the skip and a part of me feels like I am leaving some of my life there with it.

We keep walking towards the club in our dark clothes. I look at Curt. The dark of his clothes and the dark of the night and the darkness of his face all merge into one. He says nothing but pulls his hood down tight over his eyes. I do the same. We know there are cameras on this road but as long as we can keep our faces hidden it doesn't matter. As far as anybody who looks will be able to tell we were the two boys on the bus in white. We were never these two boys in black. The cameras. We can't avoid them whichever way we approach the club. There are cameras all over London. We can't dodge them all, so we just have to use them to our advantage. Let them tell a different story. Let them be our alibis.

In another two minutes we are at the back entrance to the club. I am starting to breathe heavy now even though I've only been walking. For some reason this isn't as easy as what we did in the trap-house, which now seems a different lifetime ago, even though it's only a couple of weeks ago. I try make my breathing normal again and then nod at Curt. I am ready.

We are at the rear doors of the club. Curt leans his weight against the door and it opens up, just like Ki had promised. We look at each other and then slip quietly inside and pull the door to. Ki was right about this too. It is dark. The lights, if there ever were any in there, have blown. I take my phone out, turn it on and use it as a torch. I don't realize at that time that even as I turn it on it is sending a signal to a phone mast that will tell the prosecution in months from now exactly where I am.

The phone gives me just enough light to see by and just as Ki had said, there is a door off to the left just before the stairs. We push it. It opens. Curt and I duck in and all around us is nothing but heavy blackness. I feel along the wall for a switch and find one. The room fills with light. I see Curt's face, his eyes screwed momentarily against the whiteness of the light and then an almost smile. We are in.

We slump down on the floor with our backs against the door so if someone pushes it we will know about them before they know about us. I put the carrier bag down next to me and both Curt and I take out our two-ways, turn them on low until they hiss and wait.

Curt's face is like a mask. You can't see what he's thinking. I reckon that if you took a picture of that moment even he wouldn't be able to tell you what he was thinking. I wonder just then whether he is thinking anything. Just the plan maybe. Only the plan.

Luncheon adjournment: 13:01

36

14:05

The plan is for Ki to wait until she spots Face. If she sees him she radios through. If she sees anything else, she radios through. If she sees trouble she radios through and we walk out. We cannot take more risks than we are already taking. Once we know Face is here in the club, we will wait until Ki sees him go to the toilets. If it looks safe, in other words if he goes in alone, then she calls it through and I head out of the room and up the small flight of stairs at the end of the corridor. The steps lead to the main club. The toilets are just there. The first door I come to on the left is the men's. I go in, I do the thing and I leave. Ki only calls it in if we can get Face otherwise we are out of there.

Curt will stay where he is. We need him to make sure that the exit is clean and if it gets dirty for him to clean it up for us and make us a way out of there. Once the hit is done, I am supposed to meet up with Curt in the room where we are now and then call it through to Ki and wait for her. She comes, she changes into the clothes I have brought for her in the plastic bag. Then we all leave.

I look around the back room and try to concentrate on

some detail of it just to calm me down. But it's impossible. The room is hot even though there is no heating in it that we can see. Curt is sweating a bit but then he's a big guy and them big guys can lose some serious water. I think he's nervous though. I know I am. We sit there saying almost nothing for half an hour, just listening to the white noise of the radios. Even though they are turned down proper low we can hear them crackling still. I am lost in my own mind and by the look of him I guess Curt is too.

Ten minutes or an hour passes and the radio is annoyingly still giving us the silent treatment. I can't stand the tension. I wish the fucker would just buzz with Ki's voice now. I don't even mind whether it comes over just so that she can call it off. I just need something to happen soon.

'Curt.'

Curt is still sitting next to me. His legs are out and he is breathing deep breaths that shift the whole of his body up and down as if he is bobbing on a wave. The heat coming from him is powerful.

'We have to do this, right?' I continue, 'I mean we got no choice innit?'

'Yeah man,' he says, wiping his face. 'Way to look at it is that it's already done. We already made the choice.'

I nod more to myself than him.

'I'll do it if you like,' he then says without looking at me. 'It makes more sense. I done this before.'

I look at him not believing I'm hearing what I am hearing. 'You done what before?'

'Don't act like you don't know.'

'Fuck man. I thought we were brothers. Blood. You couldn't tell me this before?' It feels like bricks are falling on my head.

'The fuck was I supposed to say?' he says wiping his face again with his hand. 'Anyway point is, I do it for you. Say the word.'

Then I look at him and say, 'Nah man, you done too much already.'

Just then the radios crackle loudly and Ki's voice comes travelling over to us. It sounds as if she is a world away. A call from a different planet. Like Armstrong when he calls from the moon.

'Move,' she says, her voice is sharp and cuts through all the static. 'You got to move now. Face is in the toilets now. You got to move now.'

Curt looks at me and then drags himself slowly to his feet but I know he's moving as fast as he can.

'Fuck where's the towel?' I say. Suddenly I feel my head spinning in panic. My hands start to clam and I wipe them over and over across my clothes.

'Shit it must be in the hold-all in the skip. Here use this,' he says and pulls out the other hoodie in the bag, the one meant for Kira, and hands it to me.

I take it and wrap the gun in the sweatshirt keeping one hand on the handle of the gun.

'Okay man. I'm about to do this thing,' I say and step into the corridor.

I walk quickly along the darkness. I haven't got time

to use my phone for light. It's okay though because I can see a crack of light where the top of the steps meets the bottom of the door. I head for it.

I push to open the door but it's stuck. Shit we hadn't checked. Why didn't we check while we were sitting there for all that time waiting for Ki to radio? Shit. I push against it but it seems to be locked. My mind is stumbling around and it can't think in a straight line. What the hell am I going to do, I am thinking. I pull the two-way from my pocket and talk into it.

'Curt I need you man. The door is locked or something. I can't get in.'

He doesn't answer but in seconds I see the light from his door spread into the corridor as he opens it and heads towards me. He reaches me and waves me silently out of the way. He takes one step back and then crashes straight into the door with his shoulder. The door swings open. The music comes flooding into my ears. Curt looks at me raising his eyebrows and then turns back to the room that's been spilling light into the hallway.

I take a step. It's still dark once I get through the door but it's lighter than it was in the hallway. The bass is pounding like a giant heartbeat and it feels as if it's coming from inside me. I see the matt-black toilet door with a stick drawing of a man exactly where Ki said it would be. I push it open. The gun is wet in my hand from sweat and I drop it more than once into the sweatshirt that is covering it. I regain my grip and look about. There's nobody at the urinals. The sinks are empty. He must be in one of the cubicles. I wait. I look at the floor to calm myself. It is a kind of deep green that makes me feel like it is sucking me in.

My heart is doing its thing. Bam bam bam and for a second I forget I need to breathe. The pictures aren't coming to me. What am I supposed to do? Do I kick the doors in? Do I wait for the doors to open? We have never spoken about this part of it. It seemed unnecessary at the time. Now I think it was the most necessary part. I decide to wait. I walk to one of the urinals and stand over the bowl, the damp sweatshirt still wrapped over my hand. There is a smell of shit and piss and bleach. It is so overwhelming that I feel for a second as if I am going to pass out.

I can hear the bass coming from the club in here but it's still low enough for me to hear the splashes coming from one of the cubicles. Then as the flush goes, suddenly the deep drum beats from the club rise in a wave and then pitch down once again. Like it does when someone has opened the door. Shit. Somebody has come into the toilets. I look round as casually as I can. How will I even know whether this guy is with Face or not? What do I do with him? Do I wait? Do I shoot him too? My eyes begin to focus and the person who has just walked in becomes sharp. Almost too sharp.

Fuck. It's Ki. Her legs out wide over the green floor so that she seems like the Statue of Liberty. Her face is like glass, telling me nothing.

She puts her finger to her lips signalling me to stay quiet as I am about to scream out at her. Fuck.

I point at the cubicle where the flush has just gone and she nods. I don't know why she is here. I wave one arm crazily telling her to leave right now. But instead she reaches into her handbag and pulls out a door wedge, puts it on the floor and then kicks it under the main door to the bathroom. I want to push her out but there's no time. The cubicle door begins to rattle. I turn around to face it, my gun at waist height. The gun is doing its thing again and whispering at me. *Shoot. Shoot. Shoot.* The weight of it is now making my arm ache and I feel like shooting it will make it lighter. And at that moment it is all that I want to do. Just to shoot it and lighten this weight. I see the face. Then it hits me. I don't even know what Face looks like.

The man looking at me is tall and good-looking. He has a face like a film star. He looks expensive. He looks like a man who could rule the world. He looks at me, just about registering my presence and then follows my eyes to where Ki is standing. You can see the look of confusion in his eyes before something clicks in his brain. He shouts out to the other cubicle like he's begging it to open.

'Face!'

Then it does. The other cubicle door opens.

Time freezes.

I see the other man. Face. Something about him jars. There is nothing special about this man. He's just a man.

Any man. This man that I am about to kill. In my mind he was a monster. He was the Devil even, maybe. But the man who looks back at me is scared. He has seen the gun. But more than that he has seen my face. He knows what that means.

There is a split second right then that I feel as if I have come out of my body and I am standing watching every-one including myself. I have a kind of smile on as if I'm interested, as if I'm wondering what I will do. Will I shoot him? Will I walk away? Will it be black or will it be white? Or is this one of them grey areas or is it all kind of colours? Right now it feels like everything has been turned over and upside down. I feel as if the sky is under my feet. I am in a new dimension it seems to me. Some upside-down place where the outside is inside and where the sky is green.

Just then it hits me all at once. The craziness of this life I am in that doesn't even feel like my own any more. Everything that has happened in the last few months starts playing over in my mind. It is there on a spinning reel, the images flashing faster and faster. So fast now that I am dizzy and sick. I want all of these names now to be gone. All of these names for things I never knew before. All the Guiltys, the Facemen, the JCs, the crews, the guns, the life. I want it all washed out of my head. I want to go back to that time. When I didn't even know how good life was. I don't even know how I got here any more. I don't remember choosing any of it. It just happened. It feels as if every last thing made every next thing happen and now I can't control any of it.

It was for Ki, I remind myself. Everything is for her. Jamil has told this man Face who she is and that he must kill her. I am doing this for Ki.

It's only when she screams that I come back into my body and feel the gun heavy and pointing down in my hand.

Two shots later both men are dead. They fall heavy to the ground, faces ruined by a single bullet each. Face lands face up. His eyes just staring out. I find myself looking into them. Frozen. I think I see the moment when the life leaves them and I can't turn away.

Ki's voice screams out my name and I look to see her turning towards the door and kicking the wedge, the doorstop, away. She pulls open the door but as she does another face stares straight back at her. She is quick though. Her adrenaline has kicked in and all of her movements are smooth and fast. Her brain is working at speeds now I cannot even track. She sees the man at the door and knows she has to keep him out until we are clear. The key is there in her eyes. Those silver flashing eyes that make cars stop in the road. She opens them wide at the man and they suck him in like black holes. His face changes. The world has vanished for him until there is only him and this girl with those eyes. She slips an arm around his neck and pushes him back out and follows him into noise of the club. Her other hand behind her back. I push through past them both and as I head to the door that leads to the steps going down I grab Ki by the wrist and pull her with me.

We tumble down the steps where Curt is waiting with the back-room door open so that there is light to see by. He leads us both into the room and leans against the door. I am bent over double trying to catch my breath and to fight off the pain that is now in my stomach. Ki though is a straight six. The power in her is smooth and effortless.

She quickly hitches her dress above her waist and pulls on the tracksuit bottoms that Curt hands her, kicking off her heels as she does. She looks at me. I look back at her. I don't know who looks stranger. My heart is still racing which is muddling my mind.

'Top.'

I look at her puzzled. I don't know what she is saying.

'Top,' she says again this time louder, indicating my hand.

I look down and then slowly begin to fall back into the moment. I hand her the sweatshirt after unwrapping it from the gun which is still hot in my hand.

In a few seconds the three of us are spilling into the street and are free. We get our hoods up, heads down and walk along the same route that I had taken earlier with Curt. Still nobody has said anything. We can hear a bit of commotion from the club's front entrance. I think that I can hear snatches of people shouting about police. We carry on walking though. Away from the entrance.

Each step takes us further from danger and closer to safety. Every step is a step to a new life. If we are lucky it could even be a step to our old life. The noise from the crowd fades out. A siren is in the distance but is coming closer.

I turn to look behind me. A couple of people start to make their way down the side street behind us. Young men both of them. They are half running, and we can hear them as they get closer to us. They are obviously excited by whatever they think has happened in the club but they are trying to stay casual. The usual thing. Little boys wanting to be big mans. I glance around careful to keep my face hidden to check where they are and what they are doing. They are looking back to the front of the club, for the ruckus that they do not know we caused.

We slow up a little waiting to let them pass us. It's better that we can see them than they can see us. In a few moments they have overtaken us. They are just two boys really. Skinny. Happy. Laughing. Innocent. Up ahead I see one of them nearing a car and making it bleep. Its indicators flash to life. MK3 Golf GTI, de-badged, Pico exhaust, Recaro seats, I think, even then after all that has happened I can't help it. The boy opens it and gets in. The other stays put until the car leaves and then gets out his phone.

Curt nudges me. This is bad. We do not need this boy to be stopping in the middle of the street. We need him ahead of us. Facing away from us. Not facing us. We cannot be seen. There is still stuff to do. We need to pick up the bag from the skip and we still need to dump the nine mil. We slow to almost a standstill but we cannot avoid passing the boy. He is directly in our path. There is no choice though. We have to keep moving. We get close enough that we can almost hear his conversation on the phone. Even in this light, there is no doubt but that he will be able give to a half-decent ID of us if the Feds ask him. We have to keep our faces down. We keep walking, our heads pointed to the tarmac. All we can see are our feet.

This is why it isn't till we were less than fifty feet away that I realize how bad this is.

'Fuck. Curt you see what I'm seeing?' I say when I am sure.

He raises his head a fraction and peers out from his hood. 'Shit. Jamil! What the fuck is he doing here?'

Seeing him there is a shock. Why is he there? Of course looking back it's not that much of a surprise. He must have been with Face or going to see him. He obviously doesn't know that Face is dead, though, judging by the easy way he is chatting on his phone.

But what happens next is just some bare weird shit I can't even explain.

Break: 15:05

37

It happens in a split second, before I even have time to think. Jamil is right up ahead of us and we can't even avoid him now, he is too close. I reckon if we turned around now it would have just been too obvious and he would have seen us and – maybe not then but later – put two and two together, and lined us up. Truth be told though I'm not sure that I was even thinking that at the time. All I knew is that we were walking in one direction and he was there.

We carry on walking. I remember I have got my head down still and my hood pulled low. I can see Curt, huge beside me, walking his big bear walk. Ki is right behind us just a step or two away. Jamil is getting closer. Maybe thirty feet away at most. I give Curt a nudge with my elbow to see whether he has any ideas but he says nothing. From the looks of it, his idea is to style it out and just carry on walking. This is madness though because that boy if he sees us or even if he thinks he has seen us is going to be running his mouth about having seen us there. And Ki. Shit, he's not going to miss her, is he? Even in joggers.

Then just as I am about to suggest turning back, even though that would be walking straight back to the club, Ki pushes past me and Curt. I look up and suddenly she has broken into a run. At first I think she is running away because she has seen JC and I almost call after her. Now this? I was thinking. Now she's running away? Is she stupid? That is all we need, JC to look up, clock her and that's it. And fuck, the CCTV! We don't want CCTV to see anyone running right about now. What the fuck's she playing at? I nearly call after her but that was just going to worsen it.

Then I see that I have got it all wrong. She is not just running along the road that he happens to be on. No, she is running straight at Jamil. Nothing in that picture fits. It just don't make no sense to me.

I can only watch as she flies towards him. His face changing as he realizes he knows her. He is putting it together. It almost seems as if he is going to stop her and chat to her. Then he looks behind her and sees us. His face changes. By then though, it's too late. The next thing he knows is the pavement. Ki is standing over him with a gun in her stretched arms. She has shot him. I am stunned. Curt's jaw drops open.

I don't know why she has done it. Even if he saw us, it didn't matter that much that he needed to be shot. Would it have been better that he didn't see us? For real it would have been. It would have been better that he didn't have no stories to tell anybody who was prepared to listen to his bullshit. And better that he couldn't tell no Feds anything if he wanted to be one of them kind of guys. But this? There was no need for this. This was the whole point of it. JC was nothing. I could have shut that fucker up in a second by myself if I had to. It was the Olders. It was the protection that protected him. We didn't need him wasted. I look for Ki's eyes in the darkness, as I draw up close, my heart now stopped. She looks at me. The eyes are blank. I cannot read them any more. Then she runs.

I watch her as she carries on running to the corner of the road, where a taxi pulls up, its yellow light harsh against the black sky. I look at Curt. His face says everything and nothing. He is cemented to the ground in shock as she disappears in the cab. In the end I have to physically pull him by the arm before he wakes up.

'Come on,' I say. 'We got to bounce.'

Since we have no time to think of a plan B, we follow the plan we had laid out at the beginning as best as we can now that Ki has done this. The bag is collected from the skip. The white sweatshirts come back on. The trainers too. In a few minutes we are back on the main road, waiting for a bus to take us home. We are wearing the same clothes that we left the flat in. We are all in white. The men who went into the club, if they ever try looking for them, were in black. It's still a perfect alibi.

We burned the black clothes. We found a bit of greenery that wasn't quite a park and not quite a verge and poured

a load of petrol on them and lit them. The gun we buried.
It didn't matter that much if it was picked up since there
were no prints on it and it was dirty anyway. The important thing was the DNA on the black clothes. That we
had to lose and now it's all gone into the grey sky. The
ashes go up into the sky and then start falling again like
dirty snowflakes. I look at Curt, as the ash settles on to
his hair and his face. He hasn't spoken a word since Ki
shot JC. Nothing about this night makes sense to him
any more. That much you can tell from his face even if
you can't tell a single other thing from it. It even don't
make sense to me but then Curt don't know yet what I
know.

When we reached the flat and opened the door, I had,
truth be told, expected Ki to be there. I thought she
would be sitting at the table even though I couldn't picture her expression. I needed to see her. I needed to see
her face so I could know that what had happened had
happened. I needed to know why she had done it. I
needed to know that the right thing had been done.
Only her face could tell me that.

It was Curt who saw it first.

'She's been. And gone,' he said and pointed to the
table.

There, on it, was the sweatshirt she had been wearing. I
recognized it from the Chinese writing on the back. On
top of it was a gun, Baikal. Gangster's gun of choice. The
gun I thought was missing. She had it all this time.

Curt looked at me and then shook his head. 'This is fucked up,' he said.

I started to speak but he stopped me. 'I don't want to know,' he said. 'I don't even want to know.'

'Look. This ain't on me Curt. She did this shit by herself. And I ain't even told you what went down in the toilets.'

'Well it sure the fuck ain't on me bruv. She's your girl. The fuck she at?' he says throwing his hands up in the air.

'I'm supposed to know where she's at?' I start switching at him, 'Why don't *you* tell me where she at?'

'Me?' goes Curt coming right into my face. '*Me?*'

'Yeah you. You're the one who's been giving her lifts to this mosque. You're the one she splitting all this vine with bruv. All this, "Tell Guilty to get himself some fucking body armour."'

'Fuck you bruv' he says pushing me hard with a giant paw. 'What I did, I did for you and your family man. Fuck is wrong with you? I'm supposed to tell Ki to fuck off when she asks for a lift to Elephant? Or when she tells me a bit of news?'

I look at him and then I am all out of answers. 'I don't know man. I don't know anything any more,' I say and sink to the floor.

'Nah you don't. You don't know nothing,' he says and turns and walks out of the door slamming it as he goes.

*

I waited for days for her to come back home or even to contact me but she didn't. I even went to that building that I followed her to that day where I saw the blond guy. But nothing. The doors were locked shut. It was back to being what it had been before, just an empty building that you would walk past a dozen times in a day and not even notice that it had ever been there.

I thought back to the conversation I had with Kira after I got back from having followed her there that day, the day before the shooting. Judge this is relevant now. I remember the shock in her eyes when I told her I followed her. Then how her expression changed when I told her I knew she weren't going to no mosque. And how it changed again when I mentioned the blond man.

That night. After the club. She was going to tell me then but then it all went sideways and now she had bailed. Looking back now, I should have been able to work it out for myself. I had all the clues. But I ain't got that type of mind you get me? I just couldn't put them Legos together. I think it was the fact that she was gone that was clouding my thinking. Where the fuck had she gone, man? Why wasn't she calling? I couldn't do anything without knowing where she was. It was as if I had to know before the rest of me would allow myself to go on. Till then I was just waiting.

Curt went off to Spain a few days after the whole club thing. He left the money behind and when I called him to ask him what I should do with it, he just said, 'Keep it, man. It weren't ever about the money.'

'But you need it. What about Guilty?' I say.

'He let me go. I told him I'd dealt with Face and he let me out. Even gave me a present.'

I leave the words hanging, thinking of something to say. Finally I remember there is something I want to ask him.

'How you even get tied up in that crew anyway, blood?' I say.

'I don't know, man. It's long.'

'It's okay. I got nothing but time right now,' I say.

'Glockz had Mum on the hook for some brown and when she couldn't pay one day, they told me I had to pay in some other way. So that's what it was. They made me collect a debt. Then over time, when the shit got heavy, they gave Mum more drugs and then they called me to collect. You know I weren't ever really a gang type of guy. And I still ain't. It's just they always got a way to get you on the hook.'

'Shit. Sorry bruv. I didn't know.'

'Nah. It's okay. Then last year shit got heavy one day and some dude pulled a knife at me. So I turned it back on him. Then Guilty didn't need to find ways of getting me on the hook no more. I was fucked. Glockz or Feds. That was my choices.'

I then remembered what he told me at the club about how he'd killed someone. And I wondered then how many people my best friend had ghosted.

'Maybe I come out there and see you,' I go.

'If you do, make sure you bring your sister. I got some explaining to do to her but I ain't got it in me right now.'

'Bless?' I say. 'Explain what?'

'Nah, fam. It's nothing. Just you know, say I said hi. And to your mum.'

Like with you now, I tried to tell him about Ki and what had happened in the toilets, but he didn't want to know. He was done with it all. He was tired. I think at the end of the day, his patience had just emptied out.

'You need to leave too bro,' he said to me finally.

'I can't man. Not without Ki.'

'That girl's playing you. Just bounce, man. It's time,' he says quietly.

I had booked myself a new ticket to Spain that day but even as I did it I knew that I weren't going to ever use it. Not without Ki.

'I can't.'

I waited for Ki. I believed she wouldn't leave just like that, after everything. So I just laid back and waited. It would maybe be a day or two more and she would come in through that door. The main heat was over now. For some reason the shootings in the club didn't even make the news. Two men killed and nothing. But the other one did. This one, I mean. JC's. But even that was over in a couple of days or so. The whole Brexit thing was bigger news now. So I knew she would come back. She had to. She had nowhere else to go. She was lying low. I couldn't find her but that was just because she was clever. She's lying so low that a person like me ain't ever going to find her. She was definitely coming back though, I knew that. That was for sure. I just had to wait. But I tell you, it was like losing her that first time. All over again.

So when the police came a week later and broke down the door, everything was still where it was. The Baikal, the hoodie, the money, my e-ticket to Spain, the passport, the phones. Me. After that, well you know about after that, innit. Curt was right. I should have bailed but I didn't understand what was up or down at that time.

Break: 15:35

38

15:45

Even after I was arrested for JC's murder and remanded I kept thinking, she will come back. Even if not in a straight line kind of thing, I thought at least maybe the police might pick her up. I didn't care at that point. I just needed to see her and even if I couldn't see her like face to face, if I knew she was alive, that would have been enough for me.

But she didn't come. It was just me. And that was maybe the hardest thing of the last year. It wasn't the being in prison. It wasn't even really facing a murder charge. It was Ki. Just not knowing.

The remand time I coped with. Because it's remand and not convicted status it means that I get more or less as many visits as I want. Bless and Mum come as much as they can. In fact I seen them more in the last year than I had before. At first I didn't want them to come. Being in that visitors' centre with all them other prisoners is dirty, you know what I mean? You can't even properly have time together. They should give you like a room or something so there's a place you can, like, cry. Not me, obviously, but them. But they had to hold it all in and save it up till they left. So believe me a few times I thought about not sending them a visiting order. But then it's been kind of a good thing I guess. It helps prepare a person. Gets them ready for prison. Not me. Them.

I did ask the Governor once why can't we have like private rooms and shit but he said there was too many problems with that. 'But we're working on it,' he said, 'and you're not the first person to mention it. It's a good idea.' It is a good idea. Maybe that's something you lot can write to your MP or whatever about after this.

Anyway. This next bit is, well, you could say is like a really important piece of the jigsaw as the prosecution have been saying. Like the whole thing is a jigsaw that you can't really understand what it is until the last piece goes in and then the whole thing is clear. I think that is a bullshit example, personally. I don't know nobody who didn't know what the picture was when the last piece ain't gone in yet. Everyone can already see what it is. It's just a bit annoying. So I guess this next bit ain't a jigsaw piece. It is like an engine piece. It is like a spark plug. Without this, the engine don't run. It don't even start.

So I have to take you back to the start and that thing with my brief. You lot probably still think what a stupid thing to sack my brief for the speeches. He was so good in the trial, wasn't he? Why would I sack him? I told you that it was partly because I wanted to tell the whole truth and he didn't want me to. Well, what he didn't know is what I am about to tell you.

Right before that meeting with my QC – the night before, in fact – prison staff told me I had a visitor. And instead of leading me to the visiting room he took me off to some small room in some different part of the prison. I never even been to this part of the block before, I thought it was all staff areas.

When I went in, the first thing I thought to myself was, shit, they did my suggestion. Private room. So I sat down and waited for Mum to come in or Bless. The guard locked the door and said he was just coming back with my visitor and I waited. Nothing to do but wait in this place. The walls even were boring. Just bricks painted white. Just one window, looking in not out. Just one table. Just two chairs. Just this concrete floor. Still, man, a private room, I thought, then I thought, shit, it's going to be all tears.

A few minutes go by and I am getting a bit vex because all them minutes come off your visit. Screws like to delay everything so an hour's visit becomes like twenty minutes by the time everyone's ready. Some people don't even get told of their visits. Screws can fuck with you like that. But at least I've been told about mine. And this is what I am saying to myself when the guard comes back. Keys go in the door and it opens. That's when I see her.

Kira.

*

Shit the look on your faces! Trust though, that ain't nothing to what my face must have been like. It wasn't just that I had been waiting for long to see a girl that I loved. Or a girl that I risked my whole life for and who just disappeared on me. Or even a girl I didn't even know was alive or dead. She was my life, blood. And later, when she left and I didn't know whether I would even ever see her face again, I felt like what a drug addict must feel like to be told there will never ever be no more drugs for you. And then when I saw her, there after a full year, in front of me, my life just changed again.

'Ki!' I almost shout it. I can't believe what I am seeing. It's really her. They say about a person who is beautiful that she is like a picture. Kira right then was like a picture but not in them kind of ways. Yes, she was beautiful still. Those eyes were as dazzling as ever. And even standing there in just jeans and a white cotton shirt she was stunning. But she was like a picture – like she wasn't real. Like you look at a picture and know that it's a person in there but you also know it's not a real person whose face you can touch or whose warm breath you can feel. It's just like a imagining of a person. That was what she looked like to me.

'You got twenty minutes. No more,' goes the screw and he's gone. The door's locked again but he can see through the windows.

'Hi,' she says. Just that. Her eyes are safely behind the lids.

'You come now?' I ask.

I am halfway between tears and screams. I am so angry and confused and vex and all them things that I can't even order my thoughts.

'Sorry,' she says and sits down opposite me and unfolds her hands. It's been a year since I saw that face and the reality of it sitting in front of me with them eyes staring at me feels unreal.

'I hope you got better than sorry. Where the fuck you been Ki?'

'Away.'

'Away?' I go. 'I know *away*! But where away? And how the fuck you get in here anyway? What's going on?'

For a moment I'm not sure whether she is going to get up and leave and it sends a panic to my heart. She picks up her handbag and then puts it back down again. I'm surprised they even let her have it in here.

'They arranged it,' she says looking down at her hands.

'They?' I go. My heart is beating blood to my temples and I can feel my face throbbing. I don't know if I can control myself.

'Well, James,' she says looking at the ceiling. 'James organized it.'

'Who the fuck is James?' I say.

'The guy. You know at the place with the black door,' she says looking down.

'James? You have to be fucking with me Ki, *James*?' I say and laugh but it's one of them laughs.

'That's his name,' she says and folds her arms tight across her chest.

'I don't give a shit about his name. Who the fuck is he?'

'He's the one who arranged it,' she says now looking at me. 'He watched you when you followed me to the place, in Elephant and Castle.'

'Watching me? Why?' I shout out. I am vexed at the thought of this James guy watching me following her. Badly. Like I'm some kind of child.

'Listen I am so sorry —'

'Fuck sorry, yeah. We can chat about sorry laters. For now though, what the hell is going on? Was this the shit you was going to tell me after the shooting?' I say getting up. The table is cemented into the floor and so cannot move when I go to stand and so I sit back down again and stare at her in anger.

She doesn't say anything. She looks at me and then looks down at her hands again like there's nowhere else for her eyes to go. It looks like she is wiping away a tear but right then it's the last thing that I am concerned about.

'Why did you shoot them Ki?'

'What?'

'Why did you shoot Face and that other one in the club?' I say to her looking around to make sure no one is hearing this.

'I had to,' she says. 'You weren't going to were you?'

'What you think I was there for fun? With a gun in my hand?' I say.

'You were out of it. Your eyes had glazed over. I thought you were going to pass out,' she says and then she sighs out the next words in a half-breath. 'I had to do it.'

'But I still might have,' I say but I know by then that it's a lie. She was right. I had choked. I look down at the table. There are still questions I need to ask. I don't know how to ask the next one because I don't know what the answer is going to be. I just know whatever it is it's going to change everything. But then, everything had already changed hadn't it?

'What about Jamil? Why him? You didn't need to do it. Face was out of the picture. Jamil was just a boy. He weren't no danger to nobody.'

Ki sweeps her hand across her face as if she can make it new again. Take away the pain in it or maybe the lies in it.

'James wanted him, too.'

I almost laugh out. 'What?! What has James got to do with all this shit?'

'He's an agent.'

'An agent? What you chatting about Ki?'

'MI5.'

'MI5?' And I laughed then, so hard water came out of my eyes. I knew that reading all them books was going to fuck with Ki's head one day. But M, I, fucking 5?

'You know what you even sound like?' I say, but even as I am saying the words, it hits me. It comes at me like a fist into my face. It was true.

'He wanted Face. But he said he'd take as many as we could give him.'

'Wanted them what, dead?'

'James uses a different word. Disconnected.'

Long adjournment 16:20

IN THE CENTRAL CRIMINAL COURT   T2017229

Before: HIS HONOUR JUDGE SALMON QC

Closing Speeches:

Trial: Day 38

Monday 17th July 2017

APPEARANCES

For the Prosecution: Mr C. Salfred QC

For the Defendant: In person

Transcribed from a digital audio recording by

T. J. Nazarene Limited

Official Court Reporters and Tape Transcribers

39

So you lot have had a weekend to think about what I said on Friday. And to tell you the truth, I been thinking about it too and I been thinking about you too. Trying to work out what you are thinking.

But I know what you're thinking. You're thinking that I'm making this all up. Or, if you even believe me, maybe you think she was making this all up. Believe. I have been turning this around in my head ever since she came to see me. It's been distracting me when I should be concentrating on you. But now that you know maybe you can see why some of what I was saying weren't exactly right. And why I had to do this speech on my own.

But like you probably are, I did wonder if Ki was maybe playing me. If there was something to call her out on, trust me I would have. But I know that girl. I mean I *know her* know her. Not just the grey eyes and the smiling Kira or the books and the plans Kira. I know this Kira. The dark hidden places Kira. And whether I wanted to believe it or not I knew it was true.

So for the next twenty minutes she broke it down for

me. It started with the time she had been to the prison to see Spooks. That was when they got hold of her for the first time. Spooks had been getting more and more heat from inside and was now proper panicking about what might happen to him. Lately a few close shave things had happened to him and the boy was sweating. He tried to get some people to cool out the Glockz boys but they weren't listening no more. If anything they just turned up the heat.

Eventually, when he ran out of choices, he went to the Feds to try his luck with them. He said he'd do anything if they could get him out of his mess. Anything at all, he said, just move me somewhere safe. The police weren't that interested but when he started mentioning the names he knew, suddenly they got interested. When anyone said 'Face', someone somewhere was interested.

Feds had their eyes and ears on Face for some time and they wanted his crew for all kinds of shit from murders and guns to armed robberies and drugs.

They weren't the only ones though who had their eyes on Face. Some of the high-up people had been watching too, so Ki says to me. Once they heard that Spooks knew about Glockz' beef with Face, the MI5 boys got wide-open eyes. They had picked up some shit on their vine that tied Face in to some big drugs shipment. Ki didn't really say what, but from what she did tell me, it was something to do with maybe ten tons of class A being smuggled into the UK in ships. That's what they told her anyway but it sounded like bullshit to me.

They had been planning some kind of operation for long apparently, but they just couldn't get close enough to Face. The man was like a ghost. As soon as they thought they had him, he made a move. Made it so quick they could never catch him actually at it. That weren't surprising really because Face was the kind of guy who was always one step ahead. And you got to remember that they were using shit like phone taps to pick up his chatter or intercepting emails and stuff like that. But Face ditched his sim every other day and he didn't have no email. He would blip up on their radar like one time if they were lucky and then he would go dark for weeks until they were lucky enough to link him to another number. That is why he was a ghost. And also why they needed a ghost of their own. Someone who could drift in without attracting notice.

Then one day they got lucky. Somehow they got a hard-line into his crew. An informer. This grass they had told them about the shit that was going down with Guilty. Then from there they made the short walk to Spooks.

What they needed though was someone to give them vine and someone to make the hit. They didn't have time to do what Ki tells me they call 'planting a seed' and waiting for it to grow into a tree or some shit probably. They needed someone ready-made. They didn't have time to embed someone because they were sure it was only a matter of time before their contact was dried out.

So in no time, Spooks had his own Secret Service handler. This weren't like no police handler where you tell them some shit and the police writes some of the shit down and maybe looks at some of it later. Nah these MI boys did their work and did it quick.

Once Ki had got her visiting order from Spooks, he went straight to his new handler and told him. 'My sister – she knows Glockz. Can you use her?' he had said. 'She's clever, man. You can use her. Trust me.' Fucker hadn't even told her about it. Just sold her out like he sold her out before. These guys just nodded and in a day they knew shit about her that she probably didn't even know herself.

Once the MI boys met her, they knew she was perfect. She was smart. She knew who the players were. And she could follow a plan. It made sense to them and best of all she could move quickly.

I know from your faces that you be thinking I've gone. Ping, like that, my mind's gone. Or you probably think that I'm making this shit up. But I swear down this is the truth. This was the thing that I couldn't say and my QC didn't want me saying. Coz how can I blame MI5? That's just proper mad, crazy. And no one can believe crazy. But just stop for a minute. Think about it.

It explains some shit.

All this vine she was getting on Face. The whole mosque thing always seemed pretty fucking sketchy to me. Anyway that day they dropped her off round the back of the estate was the day they broke it down for her. 'You help us and we'll get your brother out. Witness protection protocol.'

'If I don't?' she had said.

'Then we can't guarantee what's going to happen to him.'

They weren't really expecting her to do it herself. In fact they couldn't allow her to do it herself. That wasn't in like their pay grade. It was me that was supposed to pull the trigger, which hurts like a bitch. That she was setting me up to save her waste man brother, Spooks. She just had to get me there. They supplied the plan. They took care of the door staff. They got the two-way radios. All she had to do was make sure I pulled the trigger. Or Curt. Didn't even fucking matter to them who it was. When it was all done they were going to take care of her. And Spooks. Both of them together. Gone.

And JC? That idiot wasn't even supposed to be there. I still don't really know why she shot him. He saw us I guess and that kind of fucked everything up for Ki. She couldn't have no loose end going to the Feds and lining us up for the murders in the club. Putting us at the scene. Maybe she thought it was karma. Maybe she panicked. Maybe she didn't panic but saw it all laid out. Saw how it had to play out. Truth be told, if JC had been some other place, I wouldn't even be here. The club murders would disappear. Spooks would be hidden and me and Ki? Well we would have the chance just to be us again.

I don't know why she's come to see me now, after all this time. Probably got a guilty conscience.

Shit. I get it now, standing here talking to you, telling you everything. She came because I'd done my evidence bit. You see what I'm saying? She came only after I got in that witness box and said my piece. Can't stop the trial now, is it? It's too late. She knew that. It's too late to touch her. Thing I don't get though is why she came at all then. Clean her conscience or something? Maybe that's it. Maybe she felt guilty. She should. She is.

I been here in front of you all these days taking her murder on my own head for what? For what? For love? You think so? I thought so. But I also know that if I knew then what I know now that she could sell me out for her brother, for herself, I ain't sure I would have kept her name out of it. I would have told you straight. She lined me up for it to get herself out of it. Simple as.

But – she did come at least. And it weren't no easy thing either. She was in protection apparently. She weren't even supposed to exist any more. It was only because she threatened to fuck the whole thing up in the open that they allowed her to see me at all. She wasn't even Kira any more. She was some other person altogether.

But still. She came. You get me. And here we are now.

'So you can make this thing disappear? Get them to say "Not Guilty" and tell the truth?' I'd said to her when it was nearly twenty minutes up and the guard was knocking on the door.

'I can't,' she said.

'So what now?' I said looking at those eyes again. They were brimming wet but still crazy beautiful.

She stopped and looked at me for a moment and then

said softly, 'Why didn't you go away? I thought you would have gone.'

'Gone? I was waiting for you. Not even a telephone call Ki.'

'I couldn't. They wouldn't let me.'

'Oh.'

She paused and now I see the eyes are spilling out water for real. 'Why didn't you go? You could have gone.'

'I couldn't.'

'I left you the money. And the Baikal. I thought –'

'That I'd leave you?' I go.

'No. That you'd save yourself.'

'It's not that black and white though is it? Someone has to stay behind and pay the bill,' I say.

And then she was gone.

Break: 10:45

40

PROSECUTION COUNSEL:

Members of the jury, in Hertford, Herefordshire and Hampshire, hurricanes hardly ever happen. Here at the Central Criminal Court, a second prosecution closing speech hardly ever happens. It is happening now, however, at the direction of the learned Judge.

This is an unusual case.

Not because it involves the deliberate and planned murder of a teenaged boy. Not even because it involves a murder committed with a firearm. Sadly, in London, the shooting of young men by other young men with lethal weapons has become an all too familiar story. No, this case is unusual because the Defendant in this case elected to deliver his own closing speech. He has been speaking to you now for some days. That in itself is unusual.

Unfortunately, however, the Defendant in his speech has referred to facts upon which he now relies, but which he didn't mention in his evidence. Much of what he has said is completely new. You haven't heard it before. I haven't heard it before now. Which means that he hasn't been cross-examined about the things he is now telling you. That puts you, members of the jury, at a great disadvantage. For how, unless you have heard his evidence being tested in cross-examination, do you assess the quality of it? In other words how do you form a judgement about its reliability? How can you be sure if it is true?

This is why with the agreement and support of the Judge I now address you for a second time. However, to preserve the Defendant's legal right to the final word, he is also to be permitted to address you, in reply to the prosecution speech.

I'm not going to go over everything that the Defendant has said. That would be to insult your intelligence. You have just heard everything he has to say. It is not for me simply to contradict what he says. You can see for yourselves where the weaknesses lie and it is for you to make of them what you will. No. I just make a few points for you to consider. As before. Accept them if you agree with them. Ignore them if you don't.

It is important that we are absolutely clear about this from the start. We the Prosecution say that everything the Defendant has told you in his defence is a lie.

He lied in his interview with the police and he repeated those lies from the witness box when he gave evidence. Now though we have a whole new set of lies. Different lies from his evidence. Different lies from his interview. But, we say, lies nonetheless. From a Defendant who is, quite literally, making it up as he goes along.

Let us pause, if we may, to examine this recently invented story a little more thoroughly. Here are the problems you may think that the Defendant faces.

Firstly, there is no evidence at all that the gentleman, whom the Defendant is only able to name by the pseudonym, Face was shot dead, as the Defendant now claims. There is no, and I pause to emphasize this point, there is no evidence that this man even existed because the Defendant can tell us nothing else about this other, allegedly murdered, man. No evidence that drug dealers or indeed anybody was shot in a nightclub of the name identified by the Defendant, in the circumstances he relays. None. Not a shred, not a scrap. It is not simply invention, ladies and gentlemen, it is pure, uncorroborated fiction.

If two men, nay even one man, were to be shot dead in a nightclub, you can be sure, can you not, that there would be some evidence to support it? A police report perhaps? Or is it, as the Defendant would no doubt have you believe, a result of some sinister conspiracy by MI5 that the details have eluded the police? What about the press? Not a single news report or headline or column exists of a story describing the events that the Defendant has told you. Have they too been silenced by MI5?

And what about the mysterious and beguiling Kira? Where is she? Indeed who is she? Does she exist? Are we really being expected to believe that she, the Defendant's girlfriend, was some kind of assassin recruited by the Secret Services? Never, I venture to suggest, has such unadulterated rubbish been heard in a court of law. It is not simply rubbish. It is an insult. To this court. To you.

And I finish this mercifully short address by making just two final comments. We say they are decisive. If, as the Defendant has suggested, he was prepared to shoot dead two men with a nine millimetre pistol, in cold blood, what does that tell you about the lengths to which he is prepared to go to for his own ends? Does it, ultimately, even if your credulity can be stretched to the extent that the Defendant has attempted to stretch it, help him? Or does the fact that he was prepared to murder two men convict him of the murder with which he stands charged before you?

And we finish with this question. Why has not one word of this story been repeated by the one person who could corroborate this? Curt, who might have been able to help you, has conveniently vanished. What a shame for this Defendant. Kira also has vanished and now has an imagined new identity. But there is one person who has not vanished. She indeed has been in this courtroom all along. The Defendant's sister, Blessing. Why have you not heard from her? After all, it seems, at long last, she now speaks. But not to you, ladies and gentlemen. Not to you.

Luncheon adjournment: 13:05

41

14:10

DEFENDANT:

He is basically right innit. Everything he says is basically
true. I ain't got no proof of nothing. He says that Ki
don't exist. I got no proof to show you that she does
exist. And MI5 ain't dumb enough to leave any records
of her visit to the prison. If I had known that he was
going to say them things then maybe I could have
brought some evidences about her. I could have brought
you pictures but you know what, if I had brought them,
he would have said, 'How do we know that isn't just
some next girl you took a picture of?' If I brought in
her birth certificate even, he could have said, 'Yeah that
is just someone called that name. How do we know
you know her even?' This could go on and on. At the
end of the day some things though, you got to take on
trust. Some things I take on trust too.

I take on trust that the world is round. I can't see it
round with my own eyes but I take a picture's word for
it. I take on trust that Obama is a real person in Amer-
ica. I ain't never seen him for real. I ain't even ever seen

anyone who saw him for real. I seen him on some TV screen. I am being told that he was a president or whatever. I don't know for sure that he was. I don't know for sure that this man here is a QC. He tells me he is and I take that. So now I am in the same boat and I am asking you to take a seat on my boat. Take it on trust. You can take some things on trust.

Ki used to read a lot of history books and shit. Henry the this and his twelve wives and whatever. And in them books there is always a bit in it where you get told this king had this advisor and this many servants and this is what they did here and what they did there and this is what this guy had for breakfast and rah rah rah. And I always said to her, how the fuck they know that? She used to say back, they work it all out from other stuff. They find a painting here and it shows some guy. Then in a writing somewhere they have a description of an advisor and then someone says, hang on, maybe it's that guy in that painting. Then someone else goes, well he's holding a couple of dead ducks in that hand. And then he says, oh he must like shooting. And then another guy goes, well he's definitely shot two there so he must be a good shot. And then someone else goes, look at what he's looking at, he is looking at that little boy, oh he must be a paedophile or whatever. What I think is that's bullshit. What I think is that it's quite a good story of what the shit could mean but it's not proof is it?

So I kind of got a problem innit? What makes my story the real one of what shit actually went down?

375

Everything I said is just like the history books. It's just joining the dots but it might not be the real picture. I say to you that this thing happened and then the next thing happened and this is why it happened. But it don't mean that the shit actually happened. It just means that I said it happened like that. That probably don't mean shit at the end of the day. It's just a theory. So I'm kind of shafted innit?

But then, the prosecution and the way they are saying what they are saying happened is the same kind of shit innit? It's all just a theory. They can't prove that I shot Jamil because they don't have any witnesses to that shooting at the end of the day. They can't prove that my blood got there the way they say because they don't have a witness to say, 'Oh this is how he got the blood on him.' They can't say that the firearm discharge residue was because of me shooting him or someone else shooting him, like Kira, wearing that top or me wearing it when I carried Jamil out of the trap. They can't show nothing for sure. They can't even prove that what I am saying never happened and what I am saying about how it happened didn't happen in that way. They can't show you an evidence to prove that Ki did not exist or Curt or Face or Guilty.

So where we at now? Everything just becomes about maybes. Maybe this happened. Maybe that happened. But what's the good of that? It ain't no good to have maybes. Like the prosecution said, you got to be sure, not maybe sure.

There a few things you can be sure about though. First is that Jamil was shot dead. The second thing is that out of all the people in this room, only I know for sure how he was killed. Even the prosecution have to agree with that. Either I shot him or I was there when he was shot by Kira. The third thing is that there is thirty thousand quid in my flat. What the prosecution can't say is what their theory is about how I got that cash. The only theory you got is mine or some other theory you can think of. But what else could be the reason I got the money? Did I rob a bank? Did I win the lottery? It's got to have come from somewhere innit?

Then there is this next thing. Jamil got shot for a reason. People don't usually get shot for no reasons. Again the prosecution is saying that they don't need to prove motive or whatever. But what kind of sense is that? There has to be a reason and the only reason you got is the one I gave you – because just saying someone is 'waste' don't mean nothing. That ain't a reason to kill a person.

I know what I told you is the truth. Do you know what though, at the end of the day, maybe none of it matters. I'm half in the mind of just putting my hands up to this and saying I did it.

If I admitted I shot him, would that make it easier for you? Would you be able to walk away from this with a clear conscience and think to yourself, 'We did the right thing?' Okay then I did it. I shot him up. He was a waste man. He pissed me off or whatever and I killed him with my Baikal. Shot him dead. On the streets. Wearing my Chinese-writing made-in-Taiwan hoodie. I jumped in a cab. I bought a ticket to Spain and was going to go and fly off. I ain't sure where I got the thirty gees but who cares about that? And I ain't sure why I didn't go to Spain. And I ain't sure why I didn't go on the run with my thirty gees instead of waiting there for the police to come arrest me. And I ain't sure why I left the gun in the flat. But they got me banged to rights.

So now what? Are you happy now? You know I get life for this, is that a fair thing in your mind? Is just the fact that I shot him make it fair to lock me up for the rest of my life? What if it was you? But it wasn't never going to be you though was it? You was never going to be meeting him on your front door. You don't have to deal with no drug dealers on your street. You got better things to do. You got jobs and bare opportunities. What do I have?

The only thing I had was Ki and she's gone. And whether you believe in Ki or not, you can believe that she was a real person. She came into my life on a bus and changed my life. Then she left. Like that. I get what the prosecution is saying. But you can believe that she exists. Or if not, that someone like her does exist whatever her name might be. It's not impossible is it that I was in love with a girl who changed everything for me?

But it's the whole MI5 thing. You can't believe that.

But here's the thing. You can if you want to.

You do believe that MI5 does exist. You can believe

that MI5 can get up to some shady things. You know they are secret but you also know that people have to be working there. You know that there are somewhere in the world some real people who are MI5 and that MI5 does its shit and when it does the shit happens the way it has to – and it's secret. And you don't want to know the details. Fuck even I don't want to know the details. But you still want the shit to be done.

Don't let him fool you innit. He says them three little letters in a way that makes them so big. 'M' – 'I' – '5'. And the way he says it makes me wonder whether MI5 even exists at all. He makes it sound like he has just said 'The X-Men'. But you know MI5 is a real thing. So what is so wrong about them putting a bit of quiet pressure on some next girl so they can do their thing? They know her weaknesses. They know about Spooks. They can disappear him. Keep him safe. Keep her safe. Keep them unknown.

And if you stop and think about it, you know this shit happens. I mean actually happens. Just think about that Russian man, Litvinenko. He was poisoned with like a uranium or some shit at the tip of an umbrella. In broad daylight. And we know this happened. We know he was assassinated. And it sounds all James Bond and even though we know it happened and we know it happened probably lots of times before then, we don't want to believe it. It fucks with our happiness. We would rather believe that some white lady that looks like a teacher runs our country and that only ordinary boring things

379

happen here like NHS or cuts or what have you. But shit is darker than that. Even I don't want to believe it. I want someone to say that it's all conspiracy theory and our world isn't like that. But it is. And it is like that a thousand more times over because most of the shit you can believe is shit we will never know about. Shit that we will never be allowed to know about.

So here we are members of the jury. When I started off this speech I never thought I could do no five-hour speech like Palmerston. But shit, I did ten days. Maybe not as good as he would have. Maybe not with all the smooth words that can make you think of a higher cause like he did. I can't even match in days what this prosecutor said just now in ten minutes. It's like he just exploded my whole speech. That is the power of a person who can use his words. But I am glad I did my speech at the end of the day, because I worked something out while I was telling you all this. I worked out what he meant – that guy in the mosque when he said all people ain't the same but that they could be. I ain't the same as you, and you ain't the same as me, but you could be too if you tried.

So try now. Try and be me.

Up to you innit at the end of the day.

Guilty or not guilty?

JURY OUT:

IN THE CENTRAL CRIMINAL COURT   T2017229

Before: HIS HONOUR JUDGE SALMON QC

———————————

Verdict:

———————————

Trial: Day 39

Tuesday 18th July 2017

APPEARANCES

For the Prosecution: Mr C. Salfred QC

For the Defendant: In person

Transcribed from a digital audio recording by

T. J. Nazarene Limited

Official Court Reporters and Tape Transcribers

Author's Note

In the course of the last quarter of a century, I have met thousands of people from all walks of life, caught up in the criminal justice system.

One of the things that you pick up quickly as a criminal barrister is that intelligence is not necessarily synonymous with education, nor are the two things always interchangeable. So many times I encountered brilliant young men without a single qualification. Youths who could construct poetry on the spot but who called it rap. Lads who understood difficult legal concepts easily once you broke it down to them and, most surprising of all, boys who could dissect the evidence in their cases like professionals.

This point was brought home to me one day when a young man I was representing was being cross-examined about the location of his mobile telephone using cell-site technology. The case was a serious one involving an allegation of robbery and was being prosecuted by experienced Counsel. It soon became clear that the defendant had so thoroughly mastered the experts' reports that the Crown could not lay a glove on him. It was at once an impressive display and a salutary lesson.

After this, I always made sure to keep an open mind about all of my clients. I also tried to remember that behind the pink ribbon of a brief lay the freedom of a real person who deserved every ounce of effort on their behalf. One day many years ago, after I finished a closing speech on behalf of a client, a young man accused of dealing drugs, he came to me to thank me for my speech. I remember that he said he was grateful because he felt he could not have said what needed to be said in the way that I had. That stuck with me and over the years I wondered why it was that a defendant could not say what he needed to say. We have the best criminal justice system in the world in trial by jury. Trial by jury itself, being in theory a trial by one's peers. However, the reality is that young disadvantaged males from difficult social and personal backgrounds are not usually tried by people like them.

I began then to wonder what it would be like if those accused of crimes were tried by people like them. And if that were to happen, how a speech made by such a person might sound. And although I sometimes felt moved by what I was being told by defendants about their lives, and what seemed to me to be the inevitability of their situations, I was unable to express it in the way that they had done to me. My dilemma was how to move the court in the same way that a defendant had moved me.

It wasn't long, then, before the idea of a novel in which a defendant made his own closing speech was born. The real advantage was that in doing that he could be tried not just by a panel of twelve, but a panel consisting of everyone who could hear him: a panel of readers.

It was important to me in *You Don't Know Me* to deal with the real problems faced by those who end up in the criminal justice system. In my experience, a disproportionate number of young, socially disadvantaged men from BAME backgrounds find themselves caught up in the system. I know there will be those who may complain about stereotyping in the book, but gang-life is a reality for some young men in certain parts of the country.

Often young men without the social support usually provided by schools and family are drawn into gang culture from an early age. The gang provides many with a parallel system of order, power, security and status where otherwise there is often a vacuum. Once you create the conditions for the emergence of sub-cultures, but remove the possibility of advancement through education, the criminal gang in a sense becomes inevitable as a route through which aspirations can find fulfilment.

That social reality of gangs was one that I felt it important to confront. I wanted, however, to take care to avoid glorifying gangs in any way. Gang life, in my view, is already over-oxygenated in popular culture and not enough is done to tackle the deliberate targeting of young people by these socially powerful organizations. The main characters in the book are not gang members. They inhabit a space in which they can shine a light on the challenges of resisting pressure from gangs. I wanted the characters to tell us about the pull of gang culture, which I have dealt with first-hand, but I wanted to give them the strength to resist it.

The defendant in *You Don't Know Me* has been written in an attempt to explode a host of sterotypes, but in a way that is relatable and realistic. In the end we must confront honestly and critically the world that faces us. Ultimately the backgrounds of the characters are less important than the questions that they ask:

Is justice absolute or are there different kinds of justice depending on who you are?

Is morality absolute or are there grey areas? How do we identify those areas?

When must personal responsibility give ground to personal circumstances?

Is guilt absolute or, for the sake of fairness, should it be viewed through a 'circumstantial' lens?

What is truth and does its weight alter in the gravitational pull of deprivation?

Do we instinctively reject the notion of innocent till proven guilty?

How much disadvantage does a defendant face simply by virtue of the fact that he is facing a charge?

Can we ever really know anyone? And how do we set about judging those we cannot properly know?

Acknowledgements

To Mama, who told me the first stories I ever heard and who instilled in me a love of reading that remains my constant companion. Without your prayers and support, nothing good I ever did could ever have happened.

To Dad, who taught me the importance of reading. Anything. Everything. Just as long as I kept reading.

And to them both together, who made me believe, despite everything, that with hard work anything was possible and that everything could be reached.

To Sadia, my wife. My life. My first reader. My second reader. My last reader, and everything in between. I write for you. Thank you for everything. For reading endless drafts. For all your ideas. For your patience. Mostly, though, for your love and faith. I still remember the words that inspired this book, 'Just write something that isn't boring.' I hope, at least in part, I managed that. I love you, wife. No I don't. Yes I do.

To my brothers and sisters, Kash, Omer, Khurrum and Aiysha. I always find my way home just by thinking about you. Thank you for making me laugh even when I am not with you.

To the Amazing Book People.

To my heavenly agent Camilla Wray (you did say 'heavenly', right?). Without you this book was destined for nothing but the quiet and lonely disintegration of bits and bytes on an old laptop. Thank you for your belief. Thank you for taking the countless rough edges away and for your polish and your ability to make a hazy and lacklustre thing a thing that could sparkle. Thank you for all the heavy lifting. And for Emad, and for making him buy it! If Carlsberg made agents, they'd probably make you – probably the best agent in the world.

To all those others at Darley Anderson who combined their energies for this book. Thank you. And particular thanks to Marc Simonsson for all his work on the TV and film side of things. You are all top class and there was never a moment when I did not feel completely safe in your hands.

To my first editor, Emad Akhtar, my spiritual brother. Thank you for everything. I am so lucky to have had the benefit of your genius on this adventure. Without you there would be no book. I cannot thank you enough for all your hard work. The detailed eye that you cast over every line. The friendship. The laughs. That cover! The huge store of street slang you had in your locker. Who'd have known! Yaar, if my book had been a damsel, you'd have been its champion. Thank you.

To the peerless Jessica Leeke at Michael Joseph for the smooth and effortless way that you took over from Emad. You did it so well that it feels that you have always been there. Thank you for your ideas, your enthusiasm, and all the things that I know you do behind the scenes, silently and secretly, but wonderfully.

To all the brilliant young things at Michael Joseph who do such sterling and difficult but masterful work. A special thank you to my amazing publicity manager Laura Nicol and the talented and relentless Katie Bowden for all their hard work, and for scattering their magic so liberally and generously. To so many others, like Annabel Wilson, Emma Brown and Sophie Wilson, and to all those hidden people who have done so much to bring this book into being.

To Leo Nickolls who designed such a beautiful and striking cover. What genius!

To Ruth Kenley-Letts and Jenny Van der Lande at Snowed-In Productions who showed such faith in my work. Thank you!

I am grateful also for the chance to acknowledge Rian Malan whose spectacular tour de force, *My Traitor's Heart*, inspired the scene in the book with the Hammerman. I recommend it to you unreservedly. Reading it enriched my life in more ways than I can describe.

To all my early readers and friends and colleagues in Chambers and at the Bar, thank you for taking the time out of your busy lives to humour me.

To Stephan, my brother, my bluds. Thank you. For your brotherhood. Your friendship. Your support. Your joy. Your randomness. Your humour. Your surreality? Everybody should have a friend like you but very few people do. Thank you for every bit of excitement you celebrated with me along the way. U R Z 1. Curt.

And finally to Zozo, who can brighten every dark corner in my life with just one smile and with just one word. 'Biiiinng!'

Reading Group Questions

The book is written by a criminal defence barrister. How do you think this shapes the tone of the book? How does it affect its authenticity?

How did you find the story's format, which is told in the form of a monologue? Why do you think the author chose to tell his story this way and what do you think it adds to the novel?

Why do you think the author does not reveal the defendant's name?

Do you think the author wants us to question the way our justice system operates? If so, how?

Do you believe that the defendant really sacked his barrister because he wanted to tell the truth? Or might there be another reason?

Despite the protection and respect joining a gang would have offered them, why do you think both the defendant and Curt resisted in the first instance?

What does this book tell us about London gang culture? How authentically did you think the author captured the voice of the defendant?

The defendant speaks fondly and at length about the women in his life – his mother, sister and girlfriend – how does this influence our judgement of him?

As the book progresses, the defendant's story becomes increasingly implausible. Why do you think the author stretches the defendant's credibility to breaking point?

The defendant in *You Don't Know Me* is clearly telling a story that's hard to believe, but given what we know about the rest of his life and its plausibility, does that mean he's guilty of murder?

Can the moral question be so strong that it can overwhelm legal guilt? Do you believe he is guilty? By the end of the book do you think it even matters?

Imran Mahmood is a practicing barrister with almost 30 years' experience fighting cases in court. He hails from Liverpool but now lives in London with his wife and daughters. His debut novel *You Don't Know Me* was chosen by Simon Mayo as a BBC Radio 2 Book Club Choice and longlisted for Theakston Old Peculier Crime Novel of the Year and for the CWA Gold Dagger, and has now been adapted into a four part drama series for the BBC. He is also the author of *I Know What I Saw*. When not in court or writing novels he can sometimes be found on the Red Hot Chilli Writers' podcast as one of the regular contributors.

@imranmahmood777

He just wanted a decent book to read ...

Not too much to ask, is it? It was in 1935 when Allen Lane, Managing Director of Bodley Head Publishers, stood on a platform at Exeter railway station looking for something good to read on his journey back to London. His choice was limited to popular magazines and poor-quality paperbacks – the same choice faced every day by the vast majority of readers, few of whom could afford hardbacks. Lane's disappointment and subsequent anger at the range of books generally available led him to found a company – and change the world.

'We believed in the existence in this country of a vast reading public for intelligent books at a low price, and staked everything on it'
Sir Allen Lane, 1902–1970, founder of Penguin Books

The quality paperback had arrived – and not just in bookshops. Lane was adamant that his Penguins should appear in chain stores and tobacconists, and should cost no more than a packet of cigarettes.

Reading habits (and cigarette prices) have changed since 1935, but Penguin still believes in publishing the best books for everybody to enjoy. We still believe that good design costs no more than bad design, and we still believe that quality books published passionately and responsibly make the world a better place.

So wherever you see the little bird – whether it's on a piece of prize-winning literary fiction or a celebrity autobiography, political tour de force or historical masterpiece, a serial-killer thriller, reference book, world classic or a piece of pure escapism – you can bet that it represents the very best that the genre has to offer.

Whatever you like to read – trust Penguin.